LEBANON PUBLIC LIBRARY
W9-BVV-356

VIKING
Mystery
Suspense

Aunt Dimity and the Duke

Also by Nancy Atherton

Aunt Dimity's Death

Aunt Dimity and the Duke

Nancy Atherton

VIKING

VIKING
Published by the Penguin Group
Penguin Books USA Inc., 375 Hudson Street,
New York, New York 10014, U.S.A.
Penguin Books Ltd, 27 Wrights Lane,
London W8 5TZ, England
Penguin Books Australia Ltd, Ringwood,
Victoria, Australia
Penguin Books Canada Ltd, 10 Alcorn Avenue,
Toronto, Ontario, Canada M4V 3B2
Penguin Books (N.Z.) Ltd, 182–190 Wairau Road,
Auckland 10, New Zealand

Penguin Books Ltd, Registered Offices:
Harmondsworth, Middlesex, England

First published in 1994 by Viking Penguin,
a division of Penguin Books USA Inc.

10 9 8 7 6 5 4 3 2 1

PUBLISHER'S NOTE
This is a work of fiction. Names, characters, places, and incidents either are the product of the author's imagination or are used fictitiously, and any resemblance to actual persons, living or dead, events, or locales is entirely coincidental.

LIBRARY OF CONGRESS CATALOGING-IN-PUBLICATION DATA
Atherton, Nancy.
Aunt Dimity and the duke / Nancy Atherton.
p. cm.
ISBN 0-670-84964-2
1. Women detectives—England—Cornwall (County)—Fiction.
2. Americans—England—Cornwall (County)—Fiction. 3. Ghosts—England—Cornwall (County)—Fiction. I. Title.
PS3551.T426A93 1994
813'.54—dc20 94-8792
CIP

Printed in the United States of America
Set in Plantin
Designed by Virginia Norey

For
Leslie J. Turek,
Consulting Gardener

Aunt Dimity and the Duke

Prologue

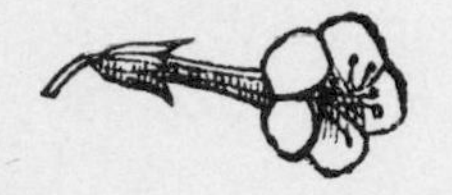

"Come back, Master Grayson!"

"Master Grayson! Stop!"

"Grayson Alexander! When I get my hands on you—"

His father's roar was swallowed by the rising wind as the boy ran down the terrace steps and sprinted for the castle ruins. Shirttails flying, he ran, heedless of the servants' cries and headlong from his father's wrath, intent only on escape. Black clouds boiled overhead and a cold wind whipped in from the sea, surging mournfully up the cliffs and snatching at his hair as he dodged through gaping doorways, past tumbledown walls, feet pounding, lungs pumping, heart breaking. Tear-blinded, tripped by a half-buried granite block, he sprawled, lay panting, then pushed himself up and ran on.

He reached the green door and flung it wide, stumbled down the stone steps into Grandmother's walled garden. A building stood there, high on the jagged cliffs above the cove, rock-steady in the wind. They called it the lady chapel, though it was sacred to no one, except perhaps to the boy. It straddled the rear wall, pointing out over the storm-lashed sea like a ship riding the crest of a wave; a small, rectangular building—rough-hewn gray granite, peaked roof, rounded door with time-blackened hinges. Moss-covered and ancient, it rose from the ground as though it had grown there, its roots buried deep in Cornwall's dark past. Reaching up to release the latch, the boy put his shoulder to the door and let himself in. Panting, he pushed the door shut behind him.

Stillness. Silence.

Light?

Uncertainty gripped him. A candle burned where no candle should be, there on the ledge beneath the stained-glass window—the jewel-hued lady window that overlooked the sea.

"Hello, Grayson." The voice was calm and soothing. "Let's see what we can do about that knee, shall we?"

A woman sat in the front row of wooden benches. As she turned her head, the candle's luster illuminated white hair, gray eyes, a softly wrinkled face, and when she smiled, he remembered: Grandmother's friend, the woman for whom Crowley reserved his deepest bows, around whom even Nanny Cole spoke gently. She was the teller of tales who brought all the servants clustering round the nursery door. Miss Westwood, at first, but later:

"Aunt Dimity?" Blinking back his tears, he made his way up the center aisle to her side.

"A rough night, I fear," she commented, removing her pearl-gray gloves. "A full-blown Cornish gale brewing. Still, we'll stay dry as tinder in here."

A capacious tapestry handbag lay at her feet. From its depths she produced a hand towel, a small bottle, a length of white gauze. "Sit down, my boy," she ordered. "This will sting a bit." With deft hands she cleansed and bandaged the knee he'd scraped stumbling in the ruins, tied the gauze neatly, returned towel and bottle to the handbag, then sat back, hands folded, waiting.

"Why didn't you come?" he asked.

"I didn't know" was the prompt reply.

Of course. Grandmother's funeral had been a shabby affair. Father would not have announced it.

"I'm so sorry, Grayson," she added. "I know how badly you must miss her."

Grayson scrubbed at his eyes with the back of a muddy fist, then stared, unseeing, at his clenched hand. Crowley, gone. Newland, Bantry, Gash. Nanny Cole would be next. She and little Kate would be sent away from Penford Hall just like the rest of the staff, and he would lose them forever.

Slowly at first, then with an urgency born of anger and despair, he told Aunt Dimity all about it. There was no one else to tell. With Grandmother dead, the village deserted, and the servants dismissed, ten-year-old Grayson was the sole witness to his father's treachery.

"No one's left at Penford Hall," he finished sadly. "And now he's . . . selling things." The low-voiced confession was spoken to the flagstone floor. "Grandmother's jewels, her paintings . . . her harp."

"Oh dear." Aunt Dimity sighed. "Charlotte's beautiful harp . . ."

"He's sold the *lantern.*" Grayson's finger stabbed accusingly at the granite shelf below the stained-glass window, where the candle now stood. "How will we hold the Fête without the lantern?" He bowed his head, ashamed of a father who knew no shame.

Frowning slightly, Aunt Dimity asked, "Are you quite certain of that?"

The boy's head swung up.

"Are you absolutely certain that the lantern has been

sold?" Aunt Dimity asked again. "I rather doubt that Charlotte would have allowed that particular item to leave the family, don't you?"

"Then where is it?" Grayson asked bluntly.

"I don't know." Aunt Dimity's gaze swept the stained-glass window and the dimly lit walls of the chapel, then she drew herself up and looked down at the boy. "But the Fête's a long way off, and we have more pressing problems to attend to. Your face, for example." Clucking her tongue, Aunt Dimity retrieved a fresh hand towel from the bag and began wiping the tear-streaked smudges from Grayson's cheeks. "I know how distressing these changes must be for you," she murmured, "and I won't tell you to be a man about it. Grown men too often forget their dreams, and some dreams are worth holding on to."

Tilting the boy's chin up, Aunt Dimity examined his face critically, then brushed his honey-blond hair back from his forehead. "You do have dreams for Penford Hall, don't you?" she coaxed. When the boy maintained a sullen silence, Aunt Dimity persisted. "You mean, there's nothing you love at Penford Hall? No one?"

All that I love is here, Grayson thought. I would do anything to save it, anything to keep Kate here and bring the others back. Aloud, he muttered, "What's the use? It'll all be gone soon and it'll never be the same again."

"Tush. Stuff and nonsense. Twaddle." Aunt Dimity sniffed disapprovingly. "My dear boy, if you expect me to pat you on the head and say, 'There, there, what a hopeless muddle,' then you've mistaken me for quite another person—someone with whom I would not care to be personally acquainted. I've no patience with such foolishness and neither would your grandmother. Your father won't always be the duke, you know. One day Penford Hall will be yours."

"It'll be empty by then."

"Then you must fill it up again."

"It'll be years before—"

"If it's worth having, it's worth waiting for."

"But—"

"And worth working for," Aunt Dimity stated firmly. "If you were not overwrought at the moment, you would see it as plainly as I do. Then again," she added, half to herself, "perhaps I'm not making myself clear." Staring thoughtfully at the lady window, Aunt Dimity put her arm around the boy, her fingers smoothing his windblown hair. "*She* would not have lost hope," Aunt Dimity said, her gray eyes fixed on the lady's brown ones. "And she faced far worse things than you're facing. Do you know the legend of the lantern?"

With a nod, Grayson dutifully recited the words he'd heard so many times before: "Once, long ago, a lady fair did love a captain bold—"

"Great heavens!" Aunt Dimity exclaimed. "Is that what Nanny Cole taught you? A lady and a captain? Dear me. Why do they fill children's heads with such piffle? She was no lady, my boy, but a hardworking village lass who served as a parlor maid at Penford Hall. And her love wasn't a captain, but the duke's son, shipped off as a common seaman. The only thing Nanny Cole got remotely right is that they loved each other." The halo of white hair nodded slowly. "Listen closely, Grayson, while I tell you the *true* story of the lantern. Perhaps then you'll understand why you must go on loving Penford Hall, come what may."

Grayson doubted that a story would save Penford Hall, or bring the servants back, but Aunt Dimity's arm was warm around his shoulders, and he had nowhere else to go. The boy nodded, then leaned against Aunt Dimity, his bandaged leg swinging listlessly.

"It is seldom wise," Aunt Dimity began, "for a poor

girl to fall in love with a duke's son. Love may be blind, but fathers most certainly are not, and the duke was not amused at the prospect of having a parlor maid as a daughter-in-law. He loved his son too well to forbid the match—I'll grant him that—but he decided to test the boy's devotion, for both his son's sake and the family's." She glanced down at the boy, saw that his leg had stopped swinging, then went on.

"The maid was sent back to the village and forbidden to set foot within sight of Penford Hall. The son was sent away for a year and a day, to sail the wide oceans as a common deckhand. The duke hoped that a taste of hard labor would cure the boy of his infatuation.

"But this was no mere infatuation. The duke's son had found his heart's desire and he vowed that his first journey would be his last. 'If you are here when I return,' he promised the girl, 'I will never leave you again.' And with that, he rowed out from Penford Harbor to meet the great four-master that awaited him in the safe waters beyond the Nether Shoals."

Grayson had turned his face to the one that hovered above them. The lady's eyes blazed suddenly as a streak of lightning split the sky, and the boy flinched at the crack of thunder that followed. Aunt Dimity's arm tightened about him protectively as she went on.

"One year passed," she told him, "and one day, and on the night of the son's return a storm blew up at sea. It was a fearful, rollicking gale, with waves as tall as Penford Hall and winds strong enough to shred the stoutest sails. Huddled safely around their hearths, the villagers knew that no ship would risk approaching the Nether Shoals that night."

"But *she* wouldn't listen?" guessed Grayson, his eyes upon the window.

"She would not," confirmed Aunt Dimity. "Though

her mother begged her to stay at home, the lass would not be swayed. 'I must be there when he returns,' she said. And with that, she took up her lantern—a plain, shuttered lantern, no more than ten inches tall, the kind used in every village house—and set out for the cliffs, where she could watch for her love's return."

The boy tensed and drew closer to Aunt Dimity, envisioning the treacherous cliffs just beyond the chapel's rear wall, and the long fall to the churning sea below.

"It was a terrible journey," Aunt Dimity continued, her voice pitched menacingly low. "She could not take the easy path, for it wound within view of the hall, and the hard path was very hard indeed. Rain pounded like hammers, wind snatched at her cloak, waves crashed before her, and dark shapes swirled on every side. A dozen times she fell, and a dozen times she pulled herself back up . . . and up . . . and up . . . until she stood upon the windlashed cliffs."

"And then?" Grayson breathed.

"Then it happened. The thing no one can explain. As she held the tiny lantern high, it began to glow with an unearthly light, softly at first, then more brightly, then blindingly, until it blazed forth like a beacon, piercing the curtain of darkness like a white-hot bolt of lightning." Aunt Dimity let the words linger, let the image of the blazing lantern fill Grayson's mind, before continuing, more quietly.

"In the first gray light of dawn she saw the ship, the great four-master bearing spices and gold and the treasure of her heart, floating in the safe waters beyond the Nether Shoals. From it came a tiny boat, gliding like an arrow across the rolling waves, straight for Penford Harbor."

"He met her on the quay," whispered Grayson, back on familiar ground.

"And he told her of the light that had guided his ship to safety. And she told him of the lantern. . . ."

"And together they told the duke. . . ."

"And the duke was filled with wonder," said Aunt Dimity. "From that moment on, he loved the lass as dearly as he loved his son. To honor her, he built this chapel, on the very spot where she'd stood, and he brought craftsmen to make the stained-glass window bearing her likeness. And in the chapel he placed the lantern, to remind his descendants of the miraculous light that had saved his son, a light that blazed forth bright as lightning, fueled by the power of a young girl's love." Aunt Dimity looked down on the tousled head at her shoulder. "And once every hundred years . . ." she prompted softly.

"And once every hundred years," the boy murmured, "the lantern shines of its own accord, and the duke of Penford must fête the villagers, in memory of the village lass, or Penford Hall will crumble and the Penford line will fade forever from the face of the earth."

"You must find the lantern, Grayson," urged Aunt Dimity. "You must save Penford Hall. Look, Grayson. Look at the lady."

Grayson stared up at the window. The lady's raven hair swirled wildly around the hood of her pale-gray cloak, but her chin was up and her shoulders were back. She thrust the lantern defiantly into the face of the storm, and her liquid brown eyes were fixed on something that remained forever out of reach. Grayson rose to his feet, pulled upward by the strength and courage in the lady's eyes.

Aunt Dimity's voice seemed to come from a long way off: "Neither mother's cry nor duke's command could stay her, neither wind nor wave could sway her, for her heart was true, her hope undying. Tell me, young Master Grayson, shall you be any less steadfast?"

Lightning flashed and thunder cracked and rain pounded down like hammers, but Grayson Alexander, who would one day be the fourteenth duke of Penford, stood unflinching.

1

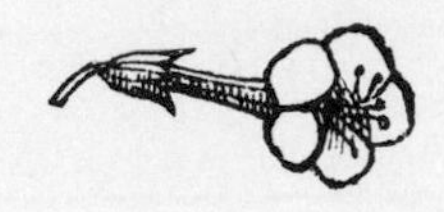

Twenty years later

"All of the good men are either married or gay," Rita declared. "And now Richard's married." She closed the file drawer with a bang.

Emma Porter touched a finger to her wire-rim glasses and cast a furtive glance at the freesias atop the file cabinet, gathered fresh from her garden that morning. The vase wobbled, but remained upright, and Emma quickly lowered her gaze to the keyboard of her computer. Bending forward, she let her long hair fall like a shield on either side of her face, determined to avoid the same, tedious conversation she'd had every day for the past six weeks.

"Not that Richard was a good man," her assistant continued, scooping up another armload of files. "I'd've scratched his eyes out if he'd run out on me like that. No eyes, no cameras, no sweet young things to drool over." *Clang!* Another drawer took the brunt of Rita's disapproval.

"Please, Rita—the freesias."

"I'm sorry, Emma." Rita's voice trembled with outrage. "But when I think of Richard dumping you like that, after fifteen years—"

"We weren't married," Emma pointed out.

"But—"

"We lived in separate houses."

"Still—"

"We were two independent adults."

"You were a *couple!*" Rita marched back to stand before Emma's desk. "For fifteen years you did everything together. You even planned your big trip together. Then he . . . he . . ." Tears welled in Rita's eyes.

Without looking away from the computer screen, Emma reached for the half-empty box of Kleenex on the windowsill behind her and handed it to Rita, silently reminding herself to buy a fresh box on her way home. It seemed as though half the women in Boston had stopped by to commiserate since the wedding and each one had ended up in tears.

"Oh, Emma," Rita managed, trying to stem the flow before it ruined her mascara, "how can you be so *brave?*"

Burying her face in a handful of tissues, Rita retreated to her own desk, just outside Emma's office. When the other women in the department began to cluster around, Emma got up and closed the door firmly. The past six weeks had taught her that a firmly closed door was the only way to keep her sympathetic underlings at bay.

Sighing, Emma reached out to the vase on the file cabinet, plucked a fragrant blossom, and held it to her nose, wishing that her co-workers would mind their own business. It wasn't as though she and Richard were facing a messy divorce. She'd had no more desire than he to be tied down by marriage vows. Theirs had been a practical relationship, separate but equal, and it had outlasted most conventional marriages. Richard had his town house in Newton; she, her Cape Cod cottage in Cambridge. He'd pursued his career in photography and she'd pursued hers in computer science. They'd been a couple for fifteen years and now they weren't. That was all there was to it.

The light on her telephone began to blink, and Emma glanced at her watch. Time for Mother's morning pep talk, she thought wryly. Returning to her desk, she tossed the freesia blossom into the wastebasket and reached for the phone.

"Hello, Mother." Emma swiveled her chair to face the windows, where the bleak Boston skyline was etched against a lowering April sky.

"Hi, Emma. Heard from that rat yet?"

Emma's gaze traveled up along the tangled strands of ivy framing the window. She reached for her pair of scissors. "No, Mother, I haven't heard from Richard, and I don't expect to." Pinching the phone between her neck and shoulder, Emma stood and began pruning the tendrils of ivy. "I'm sure Richard is much too busy with his new life—"

Her mother snorted. "His new *wife,* you mean. I told you a thousand times to marry that rat."

"And I've told you that I don't see how marrying Richard would have changed the situation," said Emma.

"It would have given you some leverage in court! As it is—"

"As it is, I own my own home, I have a very lucrative position as an executive at CompuTech, and I enjoy my freedom. I don't think I have too much to complain about, Mother, do you?"

Her mother sighed. "Honestly, Emma, I never expected a daughter of mine to just sit back and take it."

"What would you like me to do, Mother?"

"Get angry! Throw his picture against the wall! *React!* That's what normal women do. But not my daughter. I mean, Emma, honey, I know you're trying to put on a brave face, but did you really have to go to the rat's wedding?"

"That had nothing to do with bravery," Emma explained, for what seemed like the hundredth time. "It was simply a matter of facing reality."

"I'll tell you about *facing reality,*" her mother echoed scornfully. "When a thirty-nine-year-old woman gets dumped for a twenty-two-year-old ditz, she doesn't just shrug it off. You're going to have to deal with your anger, dear heart, or you're going to come apart at the seams!"

"I'm sure you're right, Mother."

There was a pause, followed by: "Okay. Have it your way. But just tell me one thing, Emma. Did you love that rat?"

Emma winced as a long strand of ivy came away in her hand. "Mother, I'm afraid I have to go now. The Danbury project is due before I leave for England, and—"

"Uh-huh. I thought so."

"Good-bye, Mother." Emma hung up the phone and put the scissors away, afraid there'd be nothing left of the ivy if she continued to prune it in her present state of mind. Trust her mother to ask the most *impossible* questions. Emma was no starry-eyed idealist. She'd known from the start that her career would leave little room for a demanding emotional life. Marriage and motherhood were out of the question, and she'd given her heart to Richard, in part, because he'd understood that. Richard hadn't been perfect—his twin passions for bad sci-fi movies and heavy-metal rock music were two reasons to be glad they'd lived apart—but he'd respected her self-sufficiency. Her mother could say what she liked; Emma had nothing—*nothing*—to complain about.

Taking a calming breath, Emma sat down, swiveled her chair to face the desk, and leaned her head on her hands.

In two weeks she'd be in England. She couldn't wait to leave.

Granted, she hadn't counted on leaving alone. Emma pulled her long hair back into a pony tail, then bent down to retrieve the file of travel brochures that filled the bottom drawer of her desk. She leafed through them until she came to the map, which she spread over the installation specs for the Danbury project. Cupping her chin in her hand, she gazed at it eagerly.

There was Cornwall, protruding like a broken branch from the southwestern tip of England, a jagged, irregular peninsula with the Atlantic Ocean to the north and the English Channel to the south. Emma had been to England many times and toured many gardens, but she'd never seen the gardens of Cornwall. She ran a finger along her intended route, pausing at the circled names: Cotehele, Glendurgan, Killerton Park, and the rest, private estates given over to the National Trust and open now to the pound-paying public.

Richard had planned to close up the studio for the summer, to lay aside fashion photography in favor of a more serious—some might say pretentious—pursuit: a black-and-white photo essay on the neolithic standing stones that dotted the Cornish landscape. Emma had been so absorbed in planning his trip as well as her own that she'd felt nothing but relief when he'd disappeared from her life for a few weeks.

She'd had no reason to worry. Theirs had been an open relationship, of course, and Richard had a long track record of short-lived flings. There'd been no reason on earth to suspect that this one would be any different.

Then the travel agent had called, informing her that Richard had canceled his airline tickets. Next, Richard had telephoned, telling her that he'd met someone special.

Finally, the wedding invitation had arrived, proof positive that Richard had disappeared from her life for good. Emma had shocked her friends and appalled her mother by attending the wedding, but she'd wanted to go. She'd needed to see the fairy princess with her own eyes.

Emma refolded the map, smiling faintly. The fairy princess—that's what Rita had dubbed Richard's bride, and Emma had to admit that it was an apt description. Graceful, slim, and twenty years Richard's junior, with hair like silken sunlight and eyes like summer skies, the fairy princess hadn't walked down the aisle, she'd floated. And Richard had been waiting for her, rotund in his cummerbund, a sheen of perspiration on his balding pate, beaming at his wife-to-be with a smile that was disturbingly paternal. Emma blushed at the memory. It had been pathetic to see her free-spirited Richard succumb to something as trite as a mid-life crisis.

Yet there it was. A fifteen-year relationship had ended with neither bang nor whimper, but with the whispery sound of an envelope slipped through a mail slot.

She'd spent a long time in her garden after the wedding, raking over the compost and wondering why she felt so . . . numb. Emma wasn't given to expressing strong emotions, but even she had been surprised by the stillness that had settled over her. Was she in shock, as her mother insisted? Or was she merely going through a natural transition that would lead, ultimately, to a mature acceptance of her new situation? Emma preferred the latter explanation. She knew that there were some things in life she couldn't change.

But there were some she could. She'd gone back into the house and spent the rest of the evening gathering up the odds and ends Richard had left behind—a worn bathrobe, a broken tripod, a stack of CDs and rock videos. As she dropped the garish video boxes in the Goodwill bin, she thought wryly that Richard's taste in music had been as juvenile as his taste in brides, and the small joke had heartened her. It seemed to prove that she was ready to face the world without Richard.

Her friends—and her mother—remained unconvinced. They thought of her as a victim and expected her to behave like one.

It was ludicrous. Why couldn't her friends be honest with her? Why couldn't they just come out and say what they were really thinking? "You're no kid anymore, Emma. You're forty, fat, and frumpy, and your chances of landing another man at this stage of the game are nil. We understand, and our hearts go out to you."

The faint smile returned as Emma put the map back in the bottom drawer. What a surprise it would be if she came home from England with a new man in tow—a six-foot-tall stunner with sapphire-blue eyes, broad shoulders, and . . .

Emma's pleasant daydream faded as common sense reasserted itself. She didn't need her mother to remind her that men—of all ages—preferred mates who were younger than themselves, girls who were graceful and slim, with hair like silken sunshine and eyes like summer skies. She knew that the doors of romance were more often than not slammed in the faces of plump, plain-looking women approaching middle age.

Emma was proud of her ability to accept the truth, and she prepared for the trip accordingly. Come May, she would be in Cornwall, where she would feast on cream teas, explore pretty fishing villages, and, best of all, enjoy the springtime spectacle of massed azaleas in full bloom. She would do everything her heart desired. Except fall in love.

"Never again," she murmured, stifling a wistful sigh. "When I come back from Cornwall, I'll buy a hammock for the garden and settle down to a life of industrious spinsterhood. But as for love—never again."

On that same day, in an Oxford suburb an ocean away, Derek Harris wiped the last trace of rain-spattered mud from the headstone on his wife's grave. He could have left the task to the sexton, but Derek had worked with his hands long enough to know that, if you wanted a job done right, you did it yourself.

He tucked the dirty rag into the back pocket of his faded jeans and rose to tower over the grave. He was a tall man, just over six feet, and his deep-blue eyes were shadowed with grief as he read the dates he'd carved into the roseate marble. It had been just over five years since pneumonia had taken her from him. The thought made his heart swell until he could scarcely breathe.

"Ah, Mary," he whispered, "I miss you."

The spiderweb tracery of budding trees stood black against a darkening sky, and a chill April wind moaned low among the gravestones. Derek shivered, and thought of going back to the house. Peter would be home from school by now, and Nell would be back from her play group, and their Aunt Beatrice would be stopping by to check up on them.

Still he lingered by the grave, unwilling to face Beatrice's barrage of questions. She'd already begun to nag him about his plans for the coming year. He wondered, not for the first time, how his sweet Mary could have had such a harridan for a sister.

Wasn't it a shame that Derek had wasted his first in history—taken at Oxford, too, more's the pity—and gone into this mucky business of restoration? You'd hardly know he was an earl's son, such an embarrassment to his family and such a keen disappointment for poor Mary. His university friends were respectable gentlemen by now—financiers and politicians, most of them—and here was Derek, at forty-five, still messing about with leaky thatched roofs, crumbling stone walls, and nasty old brasses. It had turned her hair gray to think of her only sister living in such a higgledy-piggledy household.

And now it was turning her hair white ("as the driven snow, the cold and driven snow") to think of poor Peter and Nell. Couldn't Derek see that men weren't meant to raise children? It was unnatural, unhealthy, and—"mark my words, nothing good will come of it." Surely he must see that Peter and Nell would be better off in a stable home, with an aunt and uncle who adored them and had only their best interests at heart. Surely . . .

Angrily, Derek ground a clump of mud beneath the heel of his workboot. He'd promised Mary he'd keep the family together and nothing would make him break that promise. Mrs. Higgins was a splendid housekeeper, more than capable of looking after things when Derek was away. Thanks to her, the house was immaculate, the children were well kept, and Beatrice, search as she might, could find no solid ground for complaint. He made a mental note to put a little something extra in Mrs. Higgins's pay packet before he and the children left for Cornwall.

"Thank God for Grayson," Derek murmured, blowing on his wind-reddened hands. The duke's proposal had arrived last month—a stained-glass window to restore at Penford Hall—and, with it, an invitation. *Bring Peter and Nell,* his old friend had written. *Spend the summer.* It'd mean taking Peter out of school before the end of term, but Grayson had promised a governess to see to the boy's lessons, and Beatrice, dazzled by Grayson's title, had been unable to object.

Luckily, among Beatrice's many shortcomings Derek could not, in all honesty, include a fondness for the tabloid press. Beatrice thought the scandal sheets "common" and thus remained blissfully ignorant of the dark rumors and innuendo that had surrounded the scion of Penford Hall five years ago. Fortunately for Derek, Mrs. Higgins, whose passion for the rags was second only to her devotion to the Sunday radio broadcasts of *The Archers*, was not on speaking terms with the beastly Bea.

Derek had to admit to a certain amount of curiosity about the affair, and about Grayson, as well. Theirs had been an odd friendship, blossoming briefly during the summer Derek had spent touching up the ceiling in Oxford's Christ Church Cathedral, where Grayson, still a student, had been the organist for the local Bach chorale. Grayson had expressed a keen interest in Derek's work, and they'd had a number of lively discussions over pints of ale at the Blue Boar. But at the end of the summer, when the old duke had died, the younger man had been off like a shot, never bothering to finish his degree. Derek hadn't been the least bit surprised. He remembered how Grayson's eyes had softened whenever he'd spoken of his boyhood home, how they'd blazed when he'd described his plans for its restoration.

In the ten years that had passed since then, Derek had often wondered if his young friend's grandiose plans had come to fruition. Well, soon he would find out. Come May, he'd be in Cornwall, restoring the window in the duke of Penford's lady chapel.

And after that? He balked at thinking beyond the summer. Somewhere, tucked into a far corner of his mind, was the thought that Peter and Nell should have a mother to look after them, but it was a thought he was not yet ready to contemplate.

He doubted he would ever be ready. He knew he couldn't bring himself to marry someone "for the sake of the children." The idea made his blood run cold. No, if he married again, it would be because he'd found someone to love, truly and with all his heart. And how could he do that, when his heart lay buried at his feet?

"Never again," he murmured, turning, stone-faced, for home. "Never again."

Peter Harris threw the scraps out for the cats and said aloud, to no one in particular: "The first of May. On the first of May, Dad'll take us to Cornwall and everything will be all right."

Thus reassured, Peter closed the back door, put the breakfast dishes in the sink, wiped the crumbs from the table, and swept the kitchen floor. Mrs. Higgins should've put the place to rights before retiring to her room—that's what Dad paid her for, wasn't it?—but Mrs. Higgins had spent most of the afternoon snoring on the settee in the parlor. He trembled to think what might have happened had Auntie Beatrice caught her at it.

"It'll be over soon," he murmured happily, and he believed it. Dad had shown him on the map—Penford Hall was a long way away from Auntie Beatrice.

Peter capped the milk and put it in the fridge, checked to make sure the shepherd's pie was in the cooker—Mrs. Higgins forgot sometimes—and took the box of soap flakes from the cupboard beneath the sink.

Since his mother's death, Peter had learned to clean the dishes and fold the linen and wash Nell's hair without getting soap in her eyes. He'd learned to do the shopping and sort the bills and remind Dad to pay them. He'd learned that it was best to get Nell off to sleep before beginning his schoolwork, and he'd learned—the hard way—that Auntie Beatrice *always* checked under the beds for dust. Over the course of the past few years, Peter had learned what it was to be bone-tired and burdened and constantly alert.

He'd never really learned what it was to be a little boy.

Ten-year-old Peter pushed the step stool over to the front of the sink, climbed up, and turned on the tap. He was short for his age and slight of build, with his father's deep-blue eyes and his mother's straight dark hair. He'd inherited his mother's sober manner as well, and perhaps that was why no one had noticed the changes wrought in him.

Peter himself was unaware of the change. He'd accepted his lot from the first, hoping that a reason for it would one day be made clear to him. And with the arrival of the duke's letter, the reason had appeared at last.

It was the window. The window would be the most important job Dad had ever done, the most important job imaginable, and Peter had to make sure that nothing interfered with it. Because only when it was completed would Mum be truly at rest. Then Peter could rest, too.

Peter turned off the water, then paused, distracted by a strange thumping noise in the hall. The sound was familiar, but he couldn't quite remember where he'd heard it before. Puzzled, he stepped down from the stool and crept to the hall door to peek out. The sight that met his eyes made his stomach knot with dismay.

It wasn't his usual reaction. Unlike most big brothers, Peter was fond of his five-year-old sister. Dad called Nell his changeling, because of her odd ways and fair hair, but she reminded Peter of a painting he'd seen in one of Dad's picture books, a rosy-cheeked cherub with sparkling blue eyes and a mop of curls like Dad's, only Nell's were golden instead of gray. Admittedly, none of the cherubs in the picture books had carried a small, chocolate-brown teddy bear, but Peter could no more imagine his sister without Bertie than he could picture an angel without wings. And now the sight was making his stomach hurt.

"Where did you and Bertie find those clothes, Nell?" Peter asked.

"I am Queen Eleanor," Nell announced, clutching Bertie with one hand and pinching the hem of her skirt with the other, "and this is Sir Bertram of Harris, and we do not speak with pheasants."

"That's *peasants,* Nell." Peter had known it would be a mistake for Dad to read the King Arthur stories to her, but that was not the immediate problem. The immediate problem was that Nell had dressed Bertie in Mum's favorite silk scarf and herself in Mum's pink flowery dress and white high-heeled shoes, and Dad was due home at any minute.

"You must call me Your Majesty," Nell corrected him. "And you must call Bertie Sir Ber——"

"Nell, stop playing."

"I am Queen—"

"Nell."

"Auntie Bea?" Nell spoke in her own voice, her eyes darting to the parlor door.

Peter shook his head, relieved. Nell was cooperative enough once he got her attention, but Queen Eleanor could be stubborn as a mule.

"No," Peter explained, "those clothes. It'll make Dad sad to see them."

"Will it?" Nell conferred briefly with Bertie before asking the inevitable: "Why?"

"Because they're Mum's. They'll remind Dad of her."

"And that will make him sad?"

"Yes," Peter replied patiently, "that will make him very sad." He considered telling Nell about the window, but decided against it. Queen Eleanor might turn it into a royal proclamation. "Come along, Nell. Help me pack those things up again and I'll find you and Bertie something else to play with."

"Something beautiful?"

He nodded. "Something beautiful." Peter unwound Bertie's scarf, then helped Nell step out of the high heels and slipped the dress up and over her head. He was pleased to see a kelly-green jumper and blue dungarees underneath. With Nell, he was never sure what to expect.

He followed her back to the storeroom, where she'd pried open one of the boxes in which Dad had packed Mum's things. After folding the dress and scarf, he laid them reverently on top of the other clothes, dusted the bottoms of the shoes on his pantleg, and placed them, soles up, atop the scarf. He closed the box, then turned to scan the storeroom.

"Nell," he said, as a plan began to take shape, "do you and Bertie remember the story Dad read about the Romans?"

"And the lions?" Nell asked, brightening. "And the chariots and the swords and—"

"And the noble Romans in their beautiful white gowns?"

"Yes, we remember." Nell nodded eagerly.

"Well," said Peter, plucking a clean sheet from the stack on top of the tumble-dryer, "those gowns were called *togas.* Only the richest and most beautiful Romans were allowed to wear them." Peter thought he might be stretching the truth a bit here, but never mind. He draped the sheet over Nell's left shoulder, then swept it around to her right one.

"And they wore them to see the lions," Nell said dreamily, reaching for a pillowcase with which to adorn Bertie, "and the chariots and the swords and . . ."

Peter backed out of the storeroom as Nell's eyes took on that familiar, faraway look. That should hold her until supper. He could refold the linen after she and Bertie had gone to bed.

Peter paused on his way back to the kitchen. Turning slowly, he approached the door to his father's workroom. Sometimes he needed to look in, to remind himself of the reason Dad had left so much of the work to him. Carefully, quietly, he turned the knob, opening the door just far enough to peek inside.

There were the racks of colored glass Dad planned to use in the duke's window, and the packet of photographs the duke had sent. His father had shown him the photographs of the window, explaining how he would clean it up and make it good as new. His father hadn't explained all of it, but he hadn't needed to, because Peter understood.

Peter had heard the rector explain it to some visitors, not long after Mum had died, how the soul was like a window with God's light shining through. Auntie Beatrice had got it wrong, saying that Mum's soul would spend eternity in heaven. Peter knew that it was only waiting there, waiting for Dad to make this place for it on earth, this perfect place of rainbow colors, where God's light would shine forever.

2

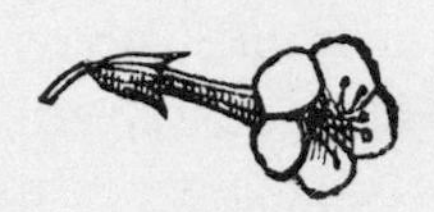

Bransley Manor was the first stop on Emma's meticulously planned itinerary. She'd learned of Bransley at a gardening seminar and toured its grounds once before, with Richard. She'd been enchanted by the avenue of monkey-puzzle trees, Richard by the hedge maze beyond the pond. Bransley Manor wasn't known for its massed azaleas, but Emma had included it on her tour nonetheless. A one-hour visit would break up the drive from London to Plymouth.

Emma parked her rental car beside an ancient black Morris Minor, the sole occupant of the manor's small parking area. Bransley was an inconspicuous British gem, well off the tour buses' beaten track, and after a whirlwind week of theater in London Emma relished the prospect of having the grounds to herself. Removing her neatly printed itinerary from her shoulder bag, she made a careful *X* beside the first entry, then took a moment to savor the scene.

The monkey puzzles were just as she remembered them, thorny and twisted and eccentrically grand. The fritillaria borders were new, though, and she wasn't sure she approved. The spiky topknots seemed too dramatic for the setting, and that particular shade of orange clashed resoundingly with the buttery tones of the stone gateposts. If she were head gardener here—

"Everything all right, ma'am?"

Emma started. A young man was standing a few yards away from her car, hunched over and peering at her, a mud-encrusted trowel dangling from one hand.

"Can I help you, ma'am?" He was wearing a tan shirt and tight jeans, and his auburn hair glinted penny-bright in the sun. He was no more than twenty, brown-eyed, freckle-faced, and well muscled, and his voice held the detached politeness that a well-brought-up young man might show to the elderly or infirm. It was the constantly reiterated "ma'am" that did it. He might as well call me "Granny," Emma thought.

"Are you lost, ma'am?" he inquired.

"No, thank you," said Emma. "I know exactly where I am."

"Good enough," the young man said. "Hope you enjoy your visit, ma'am." With a courteous smile, he walked past Emma's car and disappeared between the gateposts. Watching the sway of his narrow hips, Emma felt a wave of self-pity wash over her. Would it have been such a terrible moral compromise, she wondered dismally, to have touched up her mousy-brown hair with something livelier, blonder?

Catching sight of herself in the rearview mirror, Emma paused to take stock. Was her nose a bit too long, her jaw a touch too strong to be called beautiful? Had long hours in the garden traced fine lines across her forehead, crow's feet around her clear gray eyes? Were her wire-rim glasses dowdy and out of date? Was she?

We can't all be fairy princesses, she thought glumly. *Nor would we want to!* As self-pity veered toward anger,

Emma closed her eyes, inhaled deeply, and sought refuge in wry humor. "Well, Granny," she murmured, glancing at her watch, "better get out your cane and start cracking. Time waits for no woman."

Bransley's airy profusion of wallflowers, columbines, and tulips should have sent Emma's spirits soaring, but the longer she strolled its paths, the lower her spirits sank. By the time she reached the hedge maze, tucked away beyond the pond, it was as though a gray cloud had settled over her. She stood in the entrance to the maze, remembering Richard's shout of triumph when he'd reached the center, and knew that her return to Bransley Manor had been a mistake.

The obvious remedy was to leave at once and never come back, but as she turned to go, the young man with the trowel appeared on the far side of the pond. Emma gasped, then scurried into the maze, paying no attention to its twists and turns, thinking only that she'd rather spend the summer lost among the hornbeams than face the young man's polite smile again.

Once safely out of sight, though, Emma began to enjoy herself. She had a retentive memory and was fond of puzzles. In no time at all, she was entering the small clearing that marked the center of the maze, where she looked up in triumph, blinked, and shook her head to clear it.

She was losing her mind. First she'd let a musclebound boy send her into an emotional tailspin, and now she was seeing double. Removing her glasses, she passed a weary hand over her eyes, then ventured another look into the clearing.

They were still there: two frail, elderly women who were more alike than any two peas Emma had ever encountered in any one pod. They were dressed identically, from the tips of their white crocheted gloves to the toes of their sensible shoes. They held matching handbags—the word "reticules" flitted through Emma's mind—and wore matching straw sunhats tied with wide lavender ribbons. They were seated side by side on the stone bench beneath the chestnuts, looking at Emma with bright bird's eyes and smiling identical smiles.

"Good afternoon," said one.

"Such a lovely day," said the other.

Was it possible to *hear* double? The women's voices were as indistinguishable as their faces. "Y-yes, it is," Emma managed. "A lovely day."

"I am Ruth Pym and this is my sister . . ."

". . . Louise." Louise patted the bench encouragingly. "Won't you join us? There's room enough . . ."

". . . for three." As Emma sat between them, Ruth continued, "We're from a small village called Finch and we're here for the day . . ."

". . . with the vicar. It is a bit far for us . . ."

". . . to drive on our own. Our motorcar, you see, is somewhat . . ."

". . . antiquated."

Emma waited to be sure it was her turn to speak, then introduced herself.

"You are an American?" Ruth inquired. "And you have come all this way to see Bransley? How splendid. Are you by any chance . . ."

". . . a horticulturalist?" Louise finished.

"An amateur," Emma replied. "I have a garden at home and I love it dearly, but I pay for it by working with computers."

"But that is fascinating!" Ruth exclaimed. "You must be a very intelligent . . ."

". . . and capable young woman."

"Thanks," said Emma, vaguely comforted by the thought that, in the eyes of these two elderly maidens, she was still a young woman. "It's an interesting field, but I need something else to balance it. That's why I started gardening."

"I can well believe that," said Ruth. "Computers, we have heard, are so frightfully . . ."

". . . clean."

"A thing that cannot be said of gardens!"

The two sisters chuckled at Ruth's small joke and Emma laughed with them, relaxing as they began a steady stream of garden gossip. They asked where she'd been and where she planned to go, eagerly soliciting her opinions on pesticides, mulches, and garden designs, but offering few of their own. The Pyms were so friendly, their interest was so genuine, and their enthusiasm so contagious, that well over an hour had passed before Emma even thought to glance at her watch.

"I've really enjoyed meeting you," she said, getting reluctantly to her feet, "but I have a long drive ahead of me and I really should be going."

Ruth smiled reassuringly. "Of course you should, dear."

"And may we say what a pleasure it has been to have this little chat with you," said Louise. "Ruth and I do so enjoy coming to . . ."

". . . Bransley Manor. One meets such . . ."

". . . interesting people."

"I love Bransley, too," agreed Emma, "yet, even here—"

"Ah, you noticed." The sisters looked at her expectantly.

"The fritillaries?" Emma asked. She sat back down again. She'd been dying to get this off her chest. "It'd be hard not to notice them. *Fritillaria meleagris* might've worked in a pinch, but *imperialis?* That shade of orange—" Emma pulled herself up short, put a hand to her mouth, and blushed. "I'm sorry. That must sound pretty pretentious, coming from me. I'm sure the head gardener had a good reason for making the change."

"If he did, he was unable to explain it to us," said Louise firmly. "The *Fritillaria imperialis* was . . ."

". . . a grave error in judgment. We have spoken with the head gardener . . ."

". . . dear Monsieur Melier, and he quite sees our point."

"We hope . . ."

". . . indeed, we expect . . ."

". . . to find them replaced with something more suitable next year."

Emma would have given a lot to have eavesdropped on the Pyms' conversation with dear Monsieur Melier. She suspected that the poor man had caved in before he knew what had hit him. Gallic spleen would be no match for the Pyms' relentless British politeness.

As the sisters lapsed into a comfortable silence, Emma changed her mind about leaving. Keeping to her schedule seemed suddenly less important than sitting quietly with these two pleasant spinsters, watching the linnets dart in and out of the hornbeams while the shadows grew longer and the afternoon slipped away. Besides, she could always make up the lost time tomorrow.

"You are presently traveling to Cornwall?" Ruth inquired after a few moments had passed.

Emma nodded. "I have the whole summer ahead of me and I've never been there before and I . . . I thought some fresh horizons would do me good."

"Of course they will," said Ruth. "Cotehele is particularly lovely at this time of year."

"And Killerton Park," Louise added. "You must not miss the azaleas at Killerton Park. Great banks of them, my dear . . ."

". . . around an oriental temple."

"Most striking."

"The azaleas at Killerton Park are on my itinerary," Emma confirmed.

Another silence ensued. Again, Ruth was the first to break it.

"Might we recommend one other garden?" she asked.

"It is not well known," said Louise.

"It is not, in fact, open to the public," admitted Ruth.

"Then how would I get in to see it?" Emma asked.

"The owner is a friend of ours, my dear. Young Grayson Alexander . . ."

". . . the duke of Penford. A delightful young man. We met him quite by accident. His automobile ran off the road . . ."

". . . directly in front of our house . . ."

". . . straight through the chrysanths . . ."

". . . *and* the birdbath. So exciting." Louise sighed with pleasure. "He sent buckets of chrysanths to us afterwards, as well as a new birdbath, and . . ."

". . . kind Mr. Bantry to roll the lawn and Mr. Gash to repair the wall. We later discovered . . ."

". . . that we had a dear friend in common. Most unexpected . . ."

". . . for ours is a very small village."

"We have kept up with him ever since."

"It was unfortunate about his papa, of course."

"Poor as a church mouse . . ."

". . . and proud as a lion."

"Gone now, poor man . . ."

". . . and now Grayson has the title . . ."

". . . and the estate . . ."

". . . and the worries that come with it. You really must stop by . . ."

". . . as a favor to us. Penford Hall is on your way . . ."

". . . and you would do us a great service if you would bring him word of our . . ."

". . . continued warm regard."

"Penford Hall?" Emma asked, her eyes widening. "Isn't that where—"

"Yes, my dear," Ruth broke in, "but that was long ago and it has all been sorted out . . ."

". . . as we knew it would be. Such a thoughtful young man could not possibly be guilty . . ."

". . . of truly serious wrongdoing. Here, we'll send a note with you . . ."

". . . a little note of introduction."

Ruth opened her handbag and produced a calling card, while Louise opened hers and withdrew a fountain pen. They each wrote something on the back of the card, then handed it to Emma.

"Now, you must promise us that you will look in on our young friend."

"And you must visit us on your way back to London."

"The vicar will be able to find Finch for you on one of his maps."

"He will be able to direct you to Penford Hall as well."

"He is clever with maps. He has scores of them in his glovebox . . ."

". . . and he used every last one to bring us down from Finch today."

"Come along," said Ruth. The Pym sisters stood and Emma stood with them. "Let us find the dear man."

Emma accompanied the two ladies to the car park, where they found the vicar dozing peacefully in the back-seat of the Morris Minor. He insisted on presenting Emma with an ancient roadmap, so creased with use that she was afraid it might fall apart in her hands, upon which he marked the location of Penford Hall.

She thanked them all, promised to stop in Finch on her way back to London, and waved them off in a flurry of maps as they began their return journey. When they'd passed from view, Emma looked down at the card in her hand. On the back, the sisters had written:

This is our dear friend, Emma.
She knows gardens.

The parallel lines of curlicued script were identical.

3

"Isn't that where Lex Rex died?"

Mrs. Trevoy, the matronly widow who ran the guest house where Emma had spent the night, leaned so far over the breakfast table that the frills on her apron brushed the top of Emma's teapot. She answered Emma's question in a confidential murmur, presumably to avoid disturbing the honeymoon couple breakfasting at the far end of the small dining room. Glancing at the self-absorbed pair, Emma thought that nothing short of cannon fire would have distracted them, but she appreciated Mrs. Trevoy's sensitivity and kept her own voice down.

"Five years ago," Mrs. Trevoy hissed. "Went down just outside Penford Harbor, the whole drunken lot of them." She leaned closer to add, with obvious relish, "*Drowned like rats.*"

"Drowned?" Emma said, alarmed.

Mrs. Trevoy nodded. "Served 'em right," she went on, her ruby-red lips pursed censoriously. "Stole His Grace's yacht, didn't they? And that rubbishy noise they called music . . ." Mrs. Trevoy rolled her eyes. "Enough to make you spew. Bit of a to-do when it happened. Newsmen thick as fleas on a dog's fanny. One of the cheeky buggers wanted to stop here for the night, but I sent him on his way. My sister-in-law lives in Penford Harbor, and what Gladys don't know about human nature would fill a fly's pisspot. If she says His Grace is a nice boy, that's good enough for me." Straightening, Mrs. Trevoy plucked at the ruffles on her apron. "But that's all over now. Well, it's been five years, hasn't it? Story's as old as last week's fish, and twice as rotten. More eggs, dear?" Smiling weakly, Emma declined, and Mrs. Trevoy tiptoed from the room, casting motherly smiles on the young couple at the other table.

Emma stared out of the window. No wonder Penford Hall had sounded so familiar. Richard had been one of Lex Rex's biggest fans. And probably his oldest. Richard had plastered his studio with the rock singer's lurid photographs, watched and rewatched the videos, cranking up the sound to such ear-splitting levels that Emma had fled to her garden for respite. Richard had followed Lex's meteoric rise and been devastated by his death. He'd talked of the yachting accident for weeks, mourning the loss as though the world had been deprived of a young Mozart.

In Emma's personal opinion, the loss of Lex Rex had been a major victory in the battle against noise pollution. Still, she had to admit that she was intrigued. There was the spice of scandal surrounding the rock singer's death, and a certain shivery fascination at the prospect of seeing the actual spot where the yacht had gone down. Glancing at the honeymooners, Emma couldn't help feeling the tiniest bit smug at the thought that, but for the fairy princess, Richard could have seen it, too. Perhaps she would send the happy pair a postcard from Penford Hall, to show that there were no hard feelings.

But first she had to get there. None of her travel brochures had mentioned Penford Hall, nor could she find it in any of her guidebooks. The only proof she had of its existence was the vicar's out-of-date map, with his spidery *X* and the words "Penford Hall" written in his elegant, old-fashioned hand. Emma took the vicar's map from her shoulder bag and opened it gingerly.

There was the *X*, almost on top of the fishing village of Penford Harbor, where Mrs. Trevoy's insightful sister-in-law currently resided. A single road gave access to the coast at that point, a narrow, "unimproved" lane that turned upon itself like a wriggling snake. Very slow going. The drive there would certainly ruin her schedule and possibly rob her of the chance to see Killerton Park's azaleas in full bloom.

Emma refolded the map, finished her toast, and gulped her tea, then headed upstairs to grab her bags and pay the bill. If she left Mrs. Trevoy's guest house immediately, she'd arrive at Penford Hall in time to see the gardens gilded by the afternoon sun.

Emma passed the turnoff twice before creeping slowly by a third time. The sign for Penford Harbor was obscured by weeds, but at ten miles an hour it was visible, and she turned onto a rutted road that was every bit as narrow as she'd feared it would be.

It was not a scenic drive. Hawthorn hedges blocked her view on either side, and the situation straight ahead wasn't much better, since there was no straight ahead. Inching gingerly around one bend after another, Emma tried to skirt the deepest potholes or, when that proved impossible, to ease the car through them gently.

When the hedge on her left parted to reveal a paved and sheltered parking area, Emma pulled into it. The track continued westward, but Emma's teeth had been rattling for close to an hour and she was ready to give up on Penford Hall. No garden was worth this much trouble.

The parking area was protected by a pitched roof of corrugated metal and nearly filled by two rows of shiny new cars. Emma doubted that the owners ever used the road she'd just survived, but the sight of the cars filled her with hope. Perhaps the vicar's map would prove reliable after all.

The only available parking space was in the front row, next to a wheelless white van set up on blocks. Emma carefully nosed in beside it, released her deathgrip on the steering wheel, and leaned back against the headrest. The enveloping silence was a balm for her jangled nerves.

Settling her glasses more firmly on her nose, Emma reached for her shoulder bag, got out of the car, and edged her way past the van to the car park's southern edge. She was in a narrow, densely wooded valley. Somewhere to her right, hidden by bushes and overhanging trees, a fast-moving stream tumbled and splashed, while below her, at the foot of the valley, lay the village of Penford Harbor.

Emma murmured a heartfelt apology for ever doubting the vicar's map. The village hugged the edge of a natural harbor formed by the embracing arms of towering gray granite cliffs. A beacon flashed from the barren headland to the east, warning of treacherous waters below, while the western promontory seemed to be littered with blocks of gray stone, as though a castle or a fortress had once risen there, now tumbled into ruin.

Four fishing boats bobbed gently in the half-moon cove and fishnets were spread on the gray granite quay, where seagulls roosted in search of easy meals. The stepped and cobbled main street was lined with whitewashed houses, the doors and shutters painted with a Crayola palette of colors—lemon yellow, sky blue, tangerine. Fuchsias trailed from windowboxes, pansies filled clay pots on doorsteps, and geraniums topped old barrels along the quay.

The sounds of village life floated upward on the wind. A cloud of gulls hovered over a fishing boat just entering the harbor and Emma could hear their raucous cries as clearly as though she were standing on the deck.

Then she heard another sound, a low, tuneless whistling that seemed to be coming from somewhere in the region of her ankles. Looking down, she saw a pair of legs emerge from beneath the front bumper of the white van. The legs belonged to a chubby, white-haired man in a royal-blue jumpsuit who was lying flat on his back on a low, wheeled platform—a creeper, Emma thought it was called. The man was holding a wrench in one hand and an oily rag in the other, and when he saw Emma, he stopped whistling.

"Hello," he said. "Lost your way?"

Emma bridled slightly. The boy at Bransley Manor had made the same assumption and the question was beginning to annoy her. "No," she replied firmly. "I'm looking for Penford Hall. I believe it's very near here."

The chubby man slipped the wrench and the rag into the breast pocket of his jumpsuit, rolled off of the creeper onto all fours, then slowly got to his feet. "Not as young as I used to be," he commented, rubbing the small of his back. "Lookin' for Penford Hall, you say?"

Emma took the Pyms' calling card from her shoulder bag and presented it to him. "My name is Emma Porter. I was sent by some friends of the duke."

The man examined the card, then bent to unzip a pocket in the leg of his jumpsuit. When he stood up again, he was holding a palm-sized portable telephone. He flipped the mouthpiece down, pushed a few buttons, then held the telephone to his ear.

"Gash here," he said. "Got a visitor for His Grace. Name of Emma Porter. Sent by"—he consulted the card—"Ruth and Louise Pym. Something to do with gardens. Right. I'll wait." He covered the mouthpiece with his hand and winked at Emma. "Handy gadget, this," he whispered.

It was also extremely expensive. To see such a pricey piece of hardware emerge from the zippered pocket of a mechanic's jumpsuit was a bit unexpected.

Gash was speaking again. "Right," he said. "I'll bring her up straightaway." Gash folded the telephone and stowed it once more in his pocket, then gestured toward Emma's car. "Hop in," he said. "I'll drive."

As he maneuvered the car out of the tight parking space, Emma commented on the lamentable state of the road. "Don't get used much," Gash replied. "Not since His Grace laid in the new one. Easier on the villagers, he says. Some folks still get round by boat, o' course. Or by chopper, but that's for emergencies, mainly."

"Did you say helicopter?" Emma clarified.

"Yes, well, Dr. Singh had to have one, and since the village needed him, His Grace got him his chopper." As though suddenly remembering his manners, Gash turned to extend a pudgy hand to Emma. "I'm Gash, the mechanic up at Penford Hall."

Formalities concluded, Gash backed Emma's car out of the parking area and drove westward, beyond the point where Emma had given up. They crossed a stone bridge, then turned a corner where, mercifully, the potholed track became a ribbon of smooth asphalt climbing out of the valley. At the top, they came to another, broader road that ran along the crest of the western headland. Gash turned toward the sea.

When Emma saw the gates of Penford Hall, she very nearly changed her mind about visiting. Tall, black, and forbidding, the gates were set into imposing granite posts flanked by thick walls and topped with surveillance cameras that swept the road in steady, unrelenting arcs. She was further unnerved when a small door in the gate opened to reveal a stocky old man strikingly attired in a black beret, a khaki army sweater, camouflage trousers, and highly polished black leather boots.

"Newland," Gash murmured, by way of introduction. "Nice enough feller, but you won't get a handshake out o' him. I expect it's on account of his job."

"What *is* his job?" Emma asked, noting the wire that ran from beneath Newland's black beret to the sleek two-way radio hooked to his belt.

"Gatekeeper," Gash replied. "Newland lets the good 'uns in and keeps the bad 'uns out. Makes him a bit antisocial, if you know what I mean."

Newland squinted at them, raised a hand to his beret in a brief salute, then slipped back through the small door. A moment later, the gates swung wide and the black-topped road became a graveled drive bordered by twin banks of white azaleas, shoulder-high and exploding into full bloom.

Gash spoke again, but Emma was unaware of his words, or of the smile that had stolen across her face, or of anything except the fluttering white blossoms, fragile as butterfly wings, that seemed to beckon her onward. The walls enclosed a delicate, dark woodland carpeted with a smoky haze of bluebells and lit now and then by the hawthorn's snowy boughs and the blushing pink petals of cherry trees. Emma had scarcely drunk it in when Gash jutted his chin forward, announcing, "There's the hall."

Emma peered curiously at the gray granite edifice that had come into view on the horizon. There was no telling how old Penford Hall was or how many rooms it contained. It spilled across the headland, bristling with balconies, chimneys, and conical towers, a seemingly haphazard collection of parts that formed an eccentric and somewhat forbidding whole. Emma, who leaned toward the precise geometry of neoclassical pillars and porticoes, found the domain of the duke of Penford a bit too Gothic for her taste.

The landscape, at least, showed the touch of an orderly hand. A pair of yews flanked the broad stairway leading to the hall's main entrance, and germander hedges extended on either side to the stables, which had, by the looks of it, been converted into a single vast garage. Gash's domain, Emma thought, just as the gatehouse was Newland's.

Gash swung around the circular drive and parked at the foot of the stairs, where a pair of elderly men stood waiting. Both wore old-fashioned black suits with stiff collars and cuffs. The taller of the two was nearly bald and slender as a rake, while the shorter, round-shouldered man wore thick horn-rimmed glasses.

"The scarecrow's Crowley," Gash explained. "Crowley's head butler. The chap with the specs is Hallard, the footman. Hallard'll look after your bags."

"My bags?" Emma was about to explain that she hadn't intended to impose on the duke's hospitality, but Hallard had already removed her luggage from the trunk, and Crowley had opened the car door, saying, "Please come with me, Miss Porter."

Flustered, Emma obeyed.

4

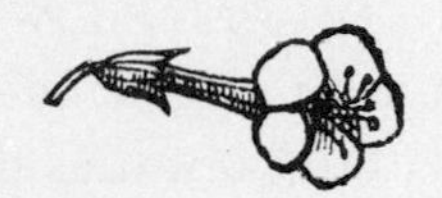

The entrance hall's plaster walls were hung with oil portraits in heavy gilt frames. The beamed ceiling had been ornamented with gold leaf, and the marble floor was a pristine cream-and-rose checkerboard. A pair of feathery tree ferns in brass pots flanked a splendid mahogany staircase that divided in two at a landing.

The landing's wall was adorned with a frieze of slender figures in diaphanous robes, painted in shades of ivory, peach, pale green, and gold. Emma blinked when one of the figures appeared to move, and it was then that she saw the woman, a flawless beauty in a gossamer gown, with hair like silken sunlight and eyes like—

Emma wrenched her gaze away. Since when had she started seeing Richard's bride in every skinny blonde that crossed her path? Besides, she thought, daring a second look, *this* skinny blonde is *famous.*

Emma might not know much about the world of fashion, but she knew enough to know that face. It had appeared on too many talk shows, shown up on too many magazine covers—and Richard had sung its praises far too often. It had been out of the limelight for some years, but, nevertheless, only a cave-dwelling hermit could have failed to recognize the model known as Ashers, the English Rose. The queen of the fairy princesses.

"What have we here?" Ashers asked, gliding weightlessly down the stairs and across the marble floor to where Emma stood.

"A guest to see His Grace," Crowley replied shortly.

Ashers looked down her delicate nose at Emma's beige corduroy skirt and loose-fitting white cotton pullover, and sniffed when she saw Emma's walking shoes. "Charming," she commented. "An outdoorswoman, I take it?" She leaned forward to peer at Emma's face. "If I were you, darling, I'd start ladling on the sunscreen."

Emma's cheeks flamed and she looked at the floor.

"Susannah!"

Emma glanced up. The cry had come from a man walking briskly across the entrance hall. He reminded Emma of the duke of Windsor: thirtyish, compact, elegant, with small, neat hands and finely chiseled features. He wore a dark tweed hunting jacket over a russet waistcoat and beige trousers; his shoes had the muted gleam of glove leather. His honey-blond hair was straight and conservatively cut, and his eyes were a deep, liquid brown.

"Welcoming my guest, Susannah?" he asked when he reached them. "How thoughtful of you. As you've no doubt discovered, this is my good friend Miss Emma . . ." He faltered.

"Porter, Your Grace," Crowley supplied, confirming Emma's guess that this was, indeed, the duke of Penford.

"Miss Emma Porter, of course. May I present my cousin, Miss Susannah Ashley-Woods?"

"So pleased to meet you," said Susannah. She favored the duke with her dazzling smile. "It's about time you balanced the table, Grayson."

"Quite," said the duke, with an uneasy grin. "Now, if

you'll excuse us, Emma and I have some business to discuss." The duke took Emma by the elbow. "Crowley, please see to Miss . . . ah . . ."

"Emma will do," Emma put in hastily.

"Just so," said the duke. "Please see to it that Emma's bags are placed in the rose suite, and have Gash return her car to the office in Plymouth."

"Very good, Your Grace."

"But, Your Grace," said Emma, "I hadn't planned to—"

"You must call me Grayson," chided the duke. "Crowley calls me Your Grace because he knows it embarrasses me. Perfectly gorgeous day, what?" The duke swept Emma across the entrance hall, around several corners, up one short flight of stairs, and down another, chattering nonstop all the while.

"I couldn't help but notice you noticing the frieze on the landing. It was done by Edward Burne-Jones. Great-Grandfather was mad for the Pre-Raphaelites, invited the chap down for a long weekend, and Eddie whipped up the painting as a thank-you. Much nicer than the usual notecard, I've always thought."

The duke led Emma into an enormous dining room and, closing the door behind them, finally came to a stop. "Sorry about the quickstep," he said, leaning against the door, "but I wanted you out of reach of Susannah's claws. I do hope you'll forgive her. She was raised by wolves, you know."

"Isn't she—"

The duke nodded gloomily. "Ashers, the English Rose. The face that's launched a thousand product lines. A somewhat distant and distaff twig of the family tree, but a twig nonetheless. The last time I saw Susannah, she was a scrawny twelve-year-old with two plaits down her back and a brace on her teeth."

"She's changed," Emma observed.

"Not enough," said the duke. "Now, Emma, my dear—"

"Grayson," Emma said quickly, "about my luggage and my car. I really hadn't intended to impose—"

"Impose?" cried the duke. "Nonsense! We've scads of rooms at Penford Hall and more cars than we know what to do with. If you need transport, give Gash a ring, and if you need anything else, call for Crowley. Now, come along, Emma, come see the garden. We've only an hour of good light left." As he spoke, the duke ushered Emma across the dining room to a pair of French doors that opened onto a balustraded terrace, where a flight of steps descended to a broad expanse of manicured lawn. The lawn ended, much to Emma's delight, at the front wall of a ruined castle.

"It *is* a castle," she murmured.

The duke had already reached the bottom of the terrace steps. At her words, he turned, smote himself on the forehead, and bounded back up to stand by Emma's side, saying ruefully, "Forgive me. I forgot that you hadn't seen the place before." He waved a hand toward the ruin. "Yes, yes—started out as a fortress, of sorts. The first duke was a bit of a blackguard, and a blackmailer as well. Got the title in exchange for a promise to stop preying on Her Majesty's shipping lanes and start protecting them."

"He was a pirate?" Emma asked with a smile.

" 'Fraid so. Must've been frightfully good at his chosen profession, to get a hereditary title as a retirement gift. Wish he'd got a bit of arable land as well, but one can't have everything. Nothing left of the original pirate's keep, of course, but . . ." The duke rattled on, telling of the castle's rise and its gradual fall as later dukes reclaimed its massive blocks to build Penford Hall—"Recycling at its finest," proclaimed the duke.

All that remained of the magnificent edifice were the four massive outer walls and a random collection of interior walls—"with the odd staircase and hearth thrown in for dramatic effect." Within the ruins, Bantry—"head gardener here, splendid chap"—had created half a dozen garden "rooms." Emma nodded her understanding, having seen something similar at Sissinghurst, in Kent, where the gardens were laid out among the ruined walls of an Elizabethan manor.

"Admittedly," the duke concluded, "the castle rather spoils the view from the dining room, but it's a marvelous windbreak, don't you think?"

Emma nodded. Like the woodland she'd just driven through with Gash, the lush green lawn could not have existed without protection from the scouring wind. East and west, the lawn had been enclosed by ten-foot walls that extended from the hall to the castle. A dozen pleached apple trees hugged the warm gray stones, basking in the sunlight.

"End of history lesson," said the duke, "and on to botany." Flashing an engaging grin, he took Emma by the elbow and guided her at a brisk pace down the terrace steps and across the lawn toward the arched entryway of the ruined castle. "I hope you won't mind if we bypass Bantry's garden rooms and head straight for the chapel garden. I'm rather eager for you to see it." He held up his hand. "Not that you'll be rushed. You must take all the time you need." The duke smiled so warmly that Emma half expected him to hug her. "Thank heavens Aunt Dimity heard my prayers and sent the Pyms to find you."

Emma was on the verge of protesting that she'd never met the duke's aunt, but they'd passed under the arch and into the cool shadows of the castle's interior, a bewitching collection of fragmented walls and roofless arcades, gaping doorways and stairways leading to open sky.

Glancing through an opening on her left, Emma saw the first of Bantry's garden rooms, a grassy courtyard surrounded by a deep perennial border. Madonna lilies, delphiniums, and bellflowers beckoned and Emma turned toward them, but stopped when the duke held up a cautioning hand, pointing to a cluster of white wicker lawn furniture at the far end of the courtyard.

"Afternoon, Hallard," called the duke.

Hallard, the bespectacled footman who'd taken charge of Emma's luggage, was seated on a cushioned armchair, tapping steadily at the keys of a laptop computer. At the duke's salutation, he slowly raised his head, blinking at them from behind his thick glasses. "Hmmm?" he murmured. "Your Grace requires my assistance?"

"Not at all, old man," the duke replied cheerfully. "Just passing through. Carry on."

"Very good, Your Grace." Hallard nodded vaguely, then focused once more on the computer screen. The sound of tapping keys resumed.

"What's he working on?" Emma ventured.

"Chapter six, one hopes, but it wouldn't do to ask. Come along, Emma, right this way."

Chapter six? thought Emma, but before she could frame an appropriate question, the duke had swept her into a grassy corridor that seemed to pass through the center of the ruins. On either side of the corridor a series of gaping doorways revealed ancient, roofless chambers that had been transformed into flourishing gardens, but the duke passed them by without comment, hustling Emma down the grassy corridor until they came to what must have once been the banquet hall.

It was now a vegetable garden. Rows of cabbages, carrots, and turnips were interplanted with marigolds, poppies, and nasturtiums, and staked tomato vines grew along the walls. The layout reminded Emma of her garden at home, with one extremely large exception.

At the center of the hall, rising high above the walls, was a domed treillage arbor, a soaring, oversized birdcage of fanciful wrought iron covered over by a healthy crop of runner beans. It was the most extravagant trellis Emma had ever seen.

The duke chuckled at the expression on her face. "Grandmother gave parties here in the old days," he told her. "Long-necked ladies in beaded dresses, gents in white tie and tails, a gramophone playing in the moonlight. Bantry made it into a kitchen garden, and very useful it is, too."

"It's impressive," Emma agreed.

"Bantry's magical with plants. Veggies and flowers will sit up and sing for him, but he lacks . . . imagination. That's why he hasn't tackled the chapel garden. Can't find Grandmother's planting records, and without them he's lost." Humming a few bars of "Anything Goes," the duke strolled along a graveled path past the birdcage arbor to the opposite side of the banquet hall. As he lengthened his stride, Emma was forced to scurry to keep up.

It was a frustrating chase. Emma caught tantalizing flashes of pink and blue and yellow and red, glimpses of clematis clambering up walls and violets peeping from the shadows, but the duke gave her no chance to savor anything. She was working up the courage to call a halt when they came to the southernmost reach of the castle, the part nearest the sea.

They were facing a tall, green-painted wooden door, the first door Emma had seen since entering the ruins. The green door was set into a sturdy, level wall that stretched east and west for a hundred feet or so. The drabness of the gray stone had been relieved by a series of niches set into the wall at irregular intervals and planted with primroses.

Gazing upward, the duke explained, "Grandmother had this wall built from leftover bits of the castle. It's twelve feet tall and three feet thick, to protect that which she held most dear." He reached for the latch. "No one's looked after it for years," he added. "Bantry's had so much else to do. . . ." He glanced beseechingly at Emma. "What I mean to say is, I'm sorry it's such a cock-up, but it'd mean a great deal to me if you could see your way clear to . . ." He gripped the latch firmly and took a deep breath. "You see, this place meant everything to my grandmother, and she meant everything to me."

The duke smiled a wistful, fleeting smile, then lifted the latch. As the door swung inward, Emma stepped past him and down ten uneven stone steps. At the foot of the stairs she stopped.

"I'll leave you alone for a while, shall I?" murmured the duke.

Emma didn't notice his departure. For a moment she forgot even to breathe, and when she remembered, it was a slowly drawn breath exhaled in a heartbroken moan.

5

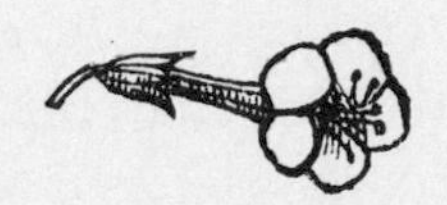

Emma stared at the ghost of a garden. The shriveled stalks that shivered in the breeze held no bright petals or sweet scents, and the withered vines that stretched like cobwebs across the walls would never blossom again. The chapel garden was a tangle of decay and desiccation, yet it held within it the sweet sadness of a place once loved and long forgotten.

Two tiers of raised flowerbeds, deep terraces set one above the other, encircled a rectangular lawn. In each corner rounded ledges rose, like steps, almost to the top of the wall. To her right lay the dried bed of what had been a small reflecting pool, and a wooden bench rested beside it, bleached silver by the sun. The garden had been beautiful once, but now the ledges were crowded with cracked and crumbling clay pots, the raised beds dotted with dried flowerheads, the rectangular lawn matted with bindweed and bristling with thistles.

A curious building straddled the center of the long rear wall, one end facing out to sea, the other planted firmly in the garden. Stubby, oblong, built of the same charcoal-gray granite as the castle, it had no belltower, no arches, nothing to entice the mind or enchant the eye. Its only decoration was a thick mat of moss on its steeply pitched slate roof, and a golden dapple of lichen above the low, rounded door. A flagstone path led from the door to the stairs, neatly bisecting the lawn.

On impulse, Emma dropped to her knees in the damp grass, parted the weeds, and dug her hand deep into the soil. She grabbed up a fistful of moist earth, sniffed at it, rubbed it between her palms, and let it fall through her fingers. "Anything will grow in this," she marveled, and felt a flicker of hope. With work and perseverance, the ghosts could be banished from this place, and the flowers that belonged here could be restored in all their glory.

When she had risen, Emma walked slowly to the door of the stubby building. She put her shoulder to the darkened wood and shoved, then caught her breath as she beheld the chapel's sole adornment.

It was like stepping into a jewel. The stained-glass window flooded the chapel with color and light, drenching the rough stone walls, the flagstone floor, and the beams overhead with rich and vibrant hues. Five feet in height, perhaps, and three feet wide, the window rendered all other decoration superfluous.

A border of red roses framed the figure of a woman. She stood against a swirling background of scudding clouds and storm-tossed trees, one hand clasping the collar of her billowing black cloak, the other hand thrust defiantly skyward, gripping a lantern that glowed with an unearthly radiance. Wind-whipped tendrils of raven hair flew wildly from the black cloak's hood, but the woman's face was as still as the surface of a cavern pool. Emma gazed up into her fierce brown eyes, then stumbled back across the threshold and through the rounded door. She leaned there for a moment, blinking dazedly in the sunlight, and when she looked up again, the garden had come to life around her.

She smelled the scent of lavender that framed the chapel door, saw the bed of irises, the splash of poppies, the glowing cluster of pink peonies backlit by the sun. Old Bourbon roses cascaded down the gray stone walls, coral bells rose from a cloud of baby's breath, and still water sparkled in the small reflecting pool.

Emma knew that she was dreaming in broad daylight, but she didn't want the dream to end. The images came to her as vividly as a memory of home and, sighing, she felt as though she'd returned to a place she'd left years ago and longed for ever since. She leaned against the chapel and watched the seasons change, until a sound caught her attention. The garden faded, the pool went dry, and she straightened, embarrassed to be found daydreaming by the duke.

But it was not the duke.

It was another man entirely. This man was tall and lean, with broad shoulders and a long, weathered face. His jeans were faded, his navy-blue pullover stained in places, his workboots scuffed and comfortably broken in. The leather tool belt slung around his hips held a hammer, some chisels, and several pairs of oddly shaped pliers. An unruly mop of salt-and-pepper curls tumbled over his high forehead, and his eyes were the color of sapphires.

"Sorry," said the man. "Didn't mean to disturb you. I was looking for Grayson."

"Grayson?" Emma said faintly.

"The duke," the man replied.

"The duke?" Emma echoed.

"I was told he'd be out here," the man elaborated. "Have you seen him?"

Emma tried to swallow, but her mouth had gone dry. "Yes," she managed, "but he's not here now."

"Ah." The man nodded. A few moments passed before he asked, "Will he be coming back?"

"I think so," Emma replied, adding helpfully, "In a while."

"I'll wait for him, then." The man walked with unhurried ease down the uneven stone steps and over to Emma's side, where he pulled the chapel door shut, then stood, looking at the decay that surrounded him. "A restful place," he commented.

Emma mumbled something, then wiped the back of her hand across her forehead, which had suddenly become damp.

"Pardon me," said the man. He pulled a handkerchief from his back pocket and offered it to Emma. "You've . . . um . . ." He gestured toward his own forehead. ". . . left some dirt behind."

"Have I?" Mortified, Emma took the handkerchief and scrubbed at her forehead. "Is it gone?" she asked anxiously.

"Not quite. Please, allow me." The man eased the cloth from her hand and with gentle fingers tilted her head back until she was looking straight up into those eyes. "There's just a tiny smudge—"

"What have we here?" asked a voice. "Frolics in the garden?"

The man swung around, flushing crimson when he saw Susannah Ashley-Woods observing them from the top of the stone stairs. Fashionably shod in three-inch stiletto heels, the duke's cousin carefully negotiated the uneven steps and came to stand beside the tall man.

"Imagine my chagrin," Susannah drawled. "I've been after Derek all week to show me his beastly window and now I've teetered out here all on my own, risking life and a pair of heavily insured limbs, only to find another woman in his arms."

"There was dirt on my face," Emma tried to explain.

"A bit further down as well," Susannah noted, gazing pointedly at Emma's skirt.

With a sinking feeling, Emma looked down to see two large stains on her beige skirt, where her knees had met the damp grass.

"I'm sure there's no permanent harm done," Susannah cooed. "Corduroy is such a *durable* fabric." Running a long-fingered hand through her silky hair, she looked from the man's face to Emma's. "What? Cats have your tongues? Don't tell me—my cousin has been remiss in his introductions. Allow me. Emma Porter, meet Derek Harris."

Derek offered his hand and Emma reached out to take it, saw that her own was smeared with mud, and snatched it back.

"Glad to meet you," she muttered, her eyes on Derek's tool belt.

"Uh, yes," said Derek, his hand stranded in midair. He smiled slightly, then raised his hand to rub his chin. "Pleasure's mine."

"Derek's here to work on the window," Susannah went on. "What about you, Emma?" She leaned forward and asked, with a mischievous smile, "Come for a peek at Penford Hall's claim to fame?"

Emma stared at Susannah blankly.

"Lex Rex?" Susannah prompted. "The pop star? Don't tell me you've never heard of him."

"Of course I have," Emma mumbled defensively. To prove it, she added the first song title that popped into her head. " 'Kiss My Tongue.' "

Emma blushed to her roots while Derek stared stolidly into the middle distance and Susannah smirked.

"Yes," Susannah confirmed, "that was one of Lex's more memorable videos. If you climb up those corner ledges you can see where he sank Grayson's lovely yacht. Surely, that's why you're—" She broke off as the garden door opened again and the front end of a wheelbarrow rolled slowly into view. "Ah," said Susannah, "Bantry has arrived."

The barrow was wielded by a short, stocky man with a wrinkled, nut-brown face and a tussock of white hair blown helter-skelter on the top of his head. Even on this fine day, he wore heavy wool trousers, a tattered argyle sweatervest, an oiled green cotton jacket, and a mud-stained pair of black wellington boots.

Derek strode over to offer a steadying hand as the old wheelbarrow, tightly covered with a patched oilcloth, clanked loudly down the steps. The thick wooden handle of a grub hoe and the bent handle of a scythe protruded from beneath the cloth.

When the two men had guided the barrow to a safe landing at the bottom of the stairs, Bantry pushed it a few feet to one side, then stood back to survey the group.

"Much obliged, Mr. Derek, sir," he said. His gaze traveled quickly past Susannah and came to rest on Emma. Grinning broadly, he crossed over to her and, before she could stop him, seized her muddy hand and pumped it vigorously.

"Bantry, head gardener, at your service," he said. "Very pleased to meet you, Miss Emma. His Grace told me you'd arrived." He indicated the tool-filled barrow with a jerk of his head. "Thought I'd make a start. Won't turn a clod without your say-so, o' course. Ah, you've been at it already, I see." He looked down at the damp soil that had been transferred from Emma's palm to his own. "Wonderful stuff Her Grace laid in here. Don't know what she did to make it so rich. She never told

Father or Grandfather and she never told me." He touched the muddy tip of his little finger to his tongue, looked thoughtfully skyward, then turned his head and spat, missing Susannah's toes by inches. "Gull shit, I think."

"Oh, my Lord," Susannah said faintly. "How very rustic." She glanced up at the garden door and said, more loudly, "Grayson, darling, did you know that Bantry's acquired a taste for guano?"

"I should think it would be an acquired taste," Grayson replied. He ran nimbly down the stairs to join the little group. "Everyone's met everyone, I trust? Good. Now, if you'll all be lambs and give me five minutes alone with Emma, I'll be forever in your debt."

Bantry climbed the stairs and left the garden without demur, and when Susannah began to protest, Derek quickly cut her off.

"Come with me, Susannah. You'll be much more comfortable in the drawing room with a tall drink."

"As long as it's accompanied by a tall man, I won't complain." Susannah took Derek's arm and Emma watched, unaccountably hurt, as another skinny blonde walked off with the man of her dreams.

It took the duke several tries to regain her attention. "I realized how off-putting my cousin can be," he said, with an understanding smile. "But you mustn't let Susannah drive you away."

"Drive me away? Oh, no." Emma stared at the green door, her face hardening as she thought, *Not this time.*

"Wonderful!" exclaimed the duke. "Now, about the chapel garden," he went on. "You needn't tell me your plans—"

"Plans?" Emma turned to the duke, feeling as though she'd missed a vital part of the conversation.

"Your plans for the chapel garden, my dear. I simply

want you to know that it's yours to do with as you like. Every resource shall be made available to you. If you need a backhoe or a teaspoon, you need only say the word. And you're to consider Penford Hall your home for as long as you wish."

"But, really, Grayson, I-I don't—" Emma stammered.

"I know what you're thinking," the duke broke in. "You're thinking there must be a catch somewhere, and you're absolutely right. You see, my dear, the chapel garden must be in some sort of shape by the first of August." Emma's jaw dropped, but the duke waved her to silence. "It doesn't have to be perfect. All I ask is that you make a start in restoring this place to the way it was while my grandmother was alive."

"But, Grayson, I—"

"*Don't worry,*" he insisted. "You were selected by two infallible judges—Aunt Dimity couldn't have chosen better—and Bantry will be here to lend a hand." The duke seemed to take no notice when Crowley, the elderly head butler, appeared at the top of the stairs.

"Supper's at nine," he went on. "Drinks in the library, eight-thirty-ish." His eyes never leaving Emma's face, he added, "Please escort this gracious lady to her room, Crowley, and see to it that she has everything she requires. I don't wish to lose her, now that I've finally found her."

6

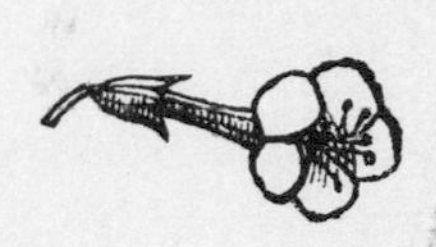

The rose suite was located somewhere between the second and third floors of Penford Hall. Crowley had explained, in a deferential murmur, that the hall was basically three stories in height, but that, owing to various quirks and fancies of former dukes and duchesses, a few half-stories crept in now and again. There were the cellars and attics, of course, but one didn't really include them, and the towers, which threw one's calculations off completely, but basically, Penford Hall had three floors. Emma had listened carefully, but by the time they'd arrived at the rose suite, she wasn't at all sure how she'd reach the library at the appointed hour.

The view was lovely, at any rate. From her balcony Emma could look out over the great lawn and the castle ruins. She wasn't quite high enough to look down into the ruins, but a few fortuitous gaps in the walls revealed the wrought-iron finial of the birdcage arbor. The dome-shaped finial was almost as elaborate as the arbor itself. It looked like a smaller birdcage set atop a much larger one, and it, too, was liberally embellished with decorative ironwork. She could see the roof of the chapel as well, pointing like the prow of a ship over the vast sweep of the Channel, where a bank of dark clouds was blowing in from the west, filling the air with the scent of rain.

Emma leaned on the balustrade and sighed. She didn't know what to make of Penford Hall. The chapel, the castle, the wonderful arbor, even the odd, stiff collar worn by the storklike head butler, all hailed from an earlier era. Yet every time she turned around she saw evidence that the twentieth century was alive and well at Penford Hall—Hallard's laptop computer, Newland's hip-slung radio, Gash's pocket telephone. Emma felt as though she stood with a foot in two worlds, and knew that she didn't belong in either.

She certainly didn't belong in such a lovely room. The rose suite was aptly named. The nightstand, the four-poster, and the writing desk, adorned with a discreet burgundy telephone and a jeweled enameled clock, were made of rosewood. The creamy walls were hung with framed botanical illustrations, hand-colored woodcuts depicting roses from bud to blossom. The quilted satin coverlet on the four-poster was embroidered with a sprinkle of crimson rosebuds, and the pair of plump chairs before the tiled fireplace were upholstered in a pattern of blowsy grandifloras.

A dressing room and bathroom adjoined the bedroom. Emma's skirts had been hung in the wardrobe; her sweaters placed in the cedar-lined drawers of the dresser. Her plastic comb and brush had been carefully arranged beside a silver-backed brush and a tortoiseshell comb on the skirted dressing table. Her travel bottles of shampoo and hair conditioner had been set within reach of a deep tub boxed round with mahogany.

Closing the balcony door against the freshening breeze, Emma looked at the beautiful bedroom, and groaned. Clearly, an error—a whole string of errors—had been made. The duke had misread the Pyms' message, misunderstood the reason for her visit, and mistaken her for someone else. If he hadn't hurried her so, she'd have explained that she hadn't been sent by his aunt to restore the chapel garden.

Not that she didn't want to. The pleasure of touring a garden couldn't compare with the joys of creating one. It was an impossible task, of course. Even a professional gardener would need more than three months to bring the chapel garden back to life again, regardless of the high-tech gardening gadgetry the duke might see fit to supply. Still, she thought wistfully, it would have been an unforgettable three months.

Her reflections were interrupted by a knock at the door, followed closely by the entrance of a petite blond teenager who was, unmistakably, the maid. Her starched white apron, dove-gray uniform, and white cap, with its ribbons and lace, looked as though they'd been borrowed from the BBC's costume department, and her curtsy was equally anachronistic. Emma's thoughts swerved from space-age gadgets to Edwardian manners, and once more she had the jangled sensation of coming slightly unstuck in time.

"I'm Mattie, miss, Crowley's granddaughter," the maid announced shyly. Mattie showed Emma a luxuriant blue terry-cloth robe in the wardrobe, then went soberly about her tasks, drawing a bath, closing the drapes, and laying a fire, while Emma changed out of her soiled skirt.

Mattie came to life only once, when Emma asked for her advice on what to wear for supper. After surveying Emma's limited wardrobe gravely, she selected the one nice dress Emma had packed, a calf-length jersey in teal, with long sleeves and a cowl neck. As she laid it out on the bed, Mattie turned the hem up to examine the stitching.

"Quality fabric, this," she murmured, and Emma, hoping to put the girl at ease, asked if she was interested in clothing.

"I love designing things," Mattie replied. "When I found out I was coming here to work with Nanny Cole, I made this." With quiet pride, she raised a hand to the ribbons of her extraordinary cap.

"It's very becoming," Emma said diplomatically. "It must be exciting for you to have Ashers staying at Penford Hall."

Mattie's face lit up. "Oh, yes, miss. Have you seen her? Isn't she lovely?" Her pretty smile dimmed for a moment as she added confidentially, "Mind you, Granddad and the others don't care for her. Well, she's always going on about that old business—"

"What old business is that?" Emma asked, walking over to warm her hands at the fire.

Mattie's eyes shifted to the hall door. "That awful singer and his band," she replied shortly. "No one wants to hear about him anymore, not after all the trouble he caused." The girl gathered up Emma's corduroy skirt and moved to the door, where she paused, with one hand on the porcelain knob. "I don't mind so much. Ashers isn't like you and me, miss. She's got what you'd call an artistic temperament. Besides, she's promised to have a look at my sketches." Mattie's radiant smile returned. "Can you imagine, miss? It's a dream come—" Mattie jumped guiltily as a knock sounded at the door.

"Mattie? Is that you?" called a woman's voice. "Be a dear and open up, will you? My hands are full."

After smoothing her apron and straightening her cap, Mattie opened the door to a dark-haired woman whose arms were wrapped awkwardly around what appeared to be a portable drafting table. A T square and a clear plastic box filled with drawing supplies were propped precariously under her chin.

"Give us a hand, Mattie," the raven-haired woman managed. She was in her late twenties, fine-boned and fair-skinned, wearing a hand-knit crewneck sweater over a well-cut pair of pleated wool trousers. When she and Mattie had finished setting up the table, she sent Mattie on her way, then turned to regard Emma with a pleasant, level-headed gaze. "The drafting table's just for midnight insights," she explained. "For the real work, you'll have the library and whichever drawing room suits you." She paused before adding carefully, "I do hope Mattie hasn't been boring you about our visiting celebrity. Did I hear something about an artistic temperament?"

"A word or two," Emma admitted.

"Well, Susannah does have a temperament, but I'm not sure I'd describe it as artistic. And then there's Syd."

"Syd?" Emma asked.

"Syd Bishop, Susannah's manager. You'll meet him at supper. He's an American, too, from Brooklyn, and he's . . . unique. At least, one hopes he is." Extending her hand, the woman crossed over to Emma. "Hello. I'm Kate Cole, Grayson's housekeeper. Sorry I couldn't come down to greet you earlier, but Mattie and I were up here, getting your room ready. Is it all right?"

"It's great, but . . ." Emma glanced at the drafting table, then plunged ahead, eager to unburden herself. "But I'm not sure I should be in it." She gestured toward the armchairs. "Can we talk for a minute, Kate? I'm afraid there's been some sort of a mix-up."

Kate sighed. "There usually is, when Grayson gets one of his brilliant ideas." As they settled into the overstuffed chairs, she went on sympathetically, "I imagine Grayson's rushed you off your feet without bothering to mention silly things like salaries and contracts and—"

"It's not that," Emma said hastily. "I'd work on the chapel garden for free, if I thought I could do the job, but, frankly, I don't think I can. I'm not a landscape designer, Kate. I'm just an ordinary backyard gardener."

Kate's brow furrowed. "But the Pyms sent you, didn't they?"

Emma explained patiently that she hardly knew the Pyms. "I only met them the day before yesterday. We spent the afternoon at Bransley Manor, gossiping about gardens."

"Ah," said Kate, relaxing. "That would explain it. They've known for months that Grayson's been searching for someone to work on Grandmother's garden. As for your qualifications . . ." Tilting her head to one side, she asked, "Did you talk for a long time with Ruth and Louise? Did they ask you a lot of questions?"

Emma pursed her lips thoughtfully. Even at the time, she'd thought her conversation with the Pyms curiously one-sided. Replaying it in her mind, she realized that it had been a fairly thorough interrogation. She raised a hand to her glasses and asked doubtfully, "Are you telling me that my conversation with the Pyms was a . . . a *job interview?*"

Kate grinned. "I know how odd it must sound, but it's exactly the sort of thing they'd do: select an out-of-the-way place like Bransley—the kind of place only a certain type of gardening enthusiast would visit—where they could lie in wait for a likely candidate, then run her through her paces."

Emma's sidelong glance still expressed doubt, so Kate tried another tack. "What line of work are you in?" she asked.

"I'm a project manager at CompuTech Corporation, in Boston," Emma replied. "I work with computers."

"All right, then, who's the most brilliant computer scientist in Boston?"

"Professor Layton, at MIT," Emma replied without hesitation. "He taught me everything I know, at any rate."

Kate gave her a quizzical look. "If Professor Layton at MIT recommended someone for a job at your company, you'd hire that person, wouldn't you?" Smiling reassuringly, she went on. "Ruth and Louise may not be professionals, like your Professor Layton, but they've been gardening since before you and I were born. I think we can trust their judgment."

Emma took a deep breath, then let it out slowly before speaking. She was accustomed to thinking in straight lines. If you needed a gardener, you looked in the phone book. You didn't sit in the middle of a hedge maze, waiting for the right one to come along. And you certainly didn't hire someone selected by such a random process. Did you?

Perhaps you did, at Penford Hall, where no one seemed to think in straight lines. The gatekeeper thought he was Che Guevara, the footman thought he was Dickens, the maid thought she was the next Chanel, and the duke seemed to think he was Father Christmas, showering the villagers with new roads and flying doctors, his servants with laptops and cellular phones. Emma's own way of thinking was beginning to bend under the influence. For a moment there in the garden, she'd thought she was Marilyn Monroe, ready to do battle with the delectable Ashers for the blue-eyed Derek of her dreams. She might as well pretend to be Gertrude Jekyll for the summer. Who would notice?

I would, thought Emma, sheepishly. I'm no more a femme fatale than I am a long-dead gardening genius, and

I can't work in the chapel garden as an impostor. If I stay on at Penford Hall, she decided, it won't be under false pretenses. She vowed silently to tell the duke the truth about herself at the earliest opportunity.

"Oh, and one other thing," Kate added, as Emma walked her to the door. "Mattie's only been here for a few months and, unlike her grandfather, she can be a bit overdramatic about Penford Hall's . . . colorful past. I wouldn't pay too much attention to what she says about that pop singer, if I were you."

Emma's understanding smile faded as soon as Kate had left the room. Great, she thought. Here I am, without a car, in a Gothic heap full of loonies, being warned off the subject of Lex Rex. What have the Pyms gotten me into?

Thanks to Crowley, who'd knocked on her door at precisely eight-twenty, Emma arrived in the library as the case clock in the corner chimed the half hour. She was relieved to see that she was neither the first nor the last to arrive. The duke was nowhere in sight, but Susannah had Derek pinned in a bay window beside a tall and quite beautiful harp, where she was lecturing him on—God help us, thought Emma—spirituality and good nutrition.

Derek had exchanged his worn jeans and blue pullover for an open-necked shirt and corduroys, and replaced his workboots with a pair of tired loafers. He seemed unable to tear his gaze from Susannah, who was wearing something black, strapless, and ankle-length that clung like paint to the places where most women had curves. Her makeup was flawless, her sleek blond hair pulled into a chignon at the nape of her spindly neck, and diamond studs glittered from her delicate earlobes. Neither she nor Derek seemed to notice Emma's arrival.

Her entrance didn't go entirely unremarked, however. Crowley had barely ushered Emma into the room when a shout rang out. "Hey! You the gal with the green thumb we been hearin' so much about? Syd Bishop's the name. Suzie's manager. What're you drinkin'?"

Syd Bishop was a paunchy American in his mid-sixties, with faded red hair plastered in long strands across his freckled scalp. His accent reeked of Brooklyn, and his voice was so loud that it almost drowned out the rumble of thunder as the first rush of rain spattered the windows. Syd's tuxedo was black—Emma gave him credit for that much good sense—but the crimson trim on the wide lapels didn't quite match the vermillion bow tie and cummerbund, or the pink-edged ruffles on the front of his white shirt.

Syd sat next to Kate Cole on a burgundy brocade couch. Kate's wine-colored velvet gown had a tight-fitting bodice and a flowing skirt, a high collar and long sleeves. Syd Bishop looked as out of place beside her as a plastic gnome in the Chelsea Flower Show.

"I'll have a sherry, thank you," Emma replied.

Syd snapped his fingers at the bespectacled footman, who stood to one side, near the drinks cabinet. "Hallard, my man, a sherry for the lady."

Emma crossed the room to sit in one of a cluster of leather armchairs facing the sofa. She tried not to gawk at Syd, but she must have failed, because, the moment she sat down, he let loose a loud guffaw.

"I know," he said, with a self-deprecating grin. "Hey, a big-time operator like me, I should know what's what in fashion, right? Wrong. Me, I'm a nice boy from Brooklyn. What I know is business. So I leave the glamour to Suzie and she leaves the bottom line to me. It works. You met Kate Cole yet?" He winked at Kate. "She's the duke's generalissimo. Great gal. If she had six inches more leg, she coulda been a contender."

Midway through Syd's speech, Hallard had come to

stand beside Emma's chair, carrying a glass of sherry on a silver tray. He remained there, staring myopically at Syd, long after Syd had fallen silent.

"Hallard," Kate Cole said softly.

"Mmmm?" Hallard replied in a faraway voice.

"I believe Miss Porter would like her drink now."

"Ah." Hallard looked down at the tray, as though surprised to find it in his possession, then bent to offer the sherry to Emma. He retreated to his place at the drinks cabinet, blinking slowly and murmuring to himself, ". . . coulda been a contendah, coulda been a contendah . . ."

"What that guy needs is a long vacation," Syd muttered.

"Kate," Emma said, "I meant to ask you earlier—Mattie mentioned that she was working with a Nanny Cole. Are you related?"

There was a snort from across the room as Susannah glanced in Kate's direction. Kate colored, but replied calmly, "Nanny Cole is my mother. She's been at Penford Hall most of her life. I suppose you could say that Grayson and I grew up together."

Again, Susannah interrupted her monologue with Derek. "Weren't you and your dear mother sent into exile, darling?"

Kate's lips tightened. "We lived in Bournemouth for a short time," she acknowledged.

"Ten years seems on the long side to me," Susannah commented, and this time Kate bridled.

Emma spoke up quickly, hoping to defuse a potential argument. "Penford Hall must have been a wonderful place to grow up in."

"You said a mouthful, little lady," said Syd. "I was just tellin' Kate, a classy joint like this'ud make a helluva set for a shoot. Whaddya think?"

Emma let her gaze travel slowly around the dark-paneled, high-ceilinged library. A thick Persian carpet covered the floor, and a pair of Chinese vases flanked the marble fireplace, where a fire blazed. Above the mantelpiece hung a portrait of an imperious, white-haired woman in a floor-length silver gown. Adorned with square-cut emeralds, she was seated beside a harp very like the one in the corner.

A mahogany staircase led to a broad gallery that ran the length of one wall. Arched floor-to-ceiling windows pierced the gallery's walls, and the glass-enclosed shelves on both levels held thousands of volumes. Here and there, a book's title, inscribed in gold leaf on a dark leather binding, gleamed in the firelight.

"So? Whaddya think? Am I right or am I right?"

Before Emma could answer, the hall door flew open and the duke rushed in. "Sorry, all," he said breezily. "Beastly rude of me to totter in so late, do forgive me. Will you listen to that downpour? Makes one glad to be indoors, what? Syd, how kind of you to dress for dinner." The duke, Emma noted, was wearing a tasteful but decidedly informal pair of flannel trousers and a fawn-colored cashmere turtleneck. "Emma, you are a vision in blue, and your hair! Your hair is like a soft mist rolling in off the sea." Gesturing toward the portrait over the mantelpiece, he added, "My grandmother. As you can see, her interests were musical as well as horticultural. She played the harp beautifully."

Syd's voice rang out. "Those are some emeralds your grandma's got on."

"Her wedding jewels," the duke explained. "My grandfather had a great fondness for emeralds." He turned to the bay windows. "Susannah, you look ravishing. And treating Derek to a talk about—which diet deity is it this week? Never mind, I'm sure it's a jolly fascinating one. Dreadfully sorry to interrupt the fun, but a higher power has informed me that our presence is required in the dining room."

"Hey, Duke," Syd said, rising to his feet, "I was just tellin' Emma how you could make a bucket rentin' this joint to the right people."

"How enterprising you are, Syd," the duke said easily.

"I got a card—"

"I believe we've accumulated quite a collection of your cards, Syd," the duke broke in. "So generous . . . Not one member of the staff has been overlooked. Emma, my dear, would you allow me the honor?"

With a shy smile, Emma placed her sherry glass on the table at her knee and crossed the room to take the duke's arm. Syd offered his to Kate, Susannah latched on to Derek's, and the three couples made their way up the hall to the dining room, Syd's voice booming, Susannah murmuring, and Emma raising a hand to rub her temple. It was shaping up to be an exceptionally long evening.

7

A candle-filled chandelier lit the dining room, and the silver-and-green velvet drapes had been drawn to reveal the rainswept façade of the ruined castle, dramatically lit by concealed floodlights. "It's better on a clear night," the duke murmured, as he took his place at the head of the table.

Emma sat on the duke's right, Susannah on his left; Kate was at the foot of the table. Syd sat between Kate and Emma, tucking his napkin into his shirt collar and beckoning to Crowley to fill his wineglass. Derek, who had yet to acknowledge Emma's presence, sat across the table from Syd, beside Susannah.

Shadows danced across the molded ceiling, and the table was a fairyland of twinkling crystal and gleaming silver. Quite a lot of silver, Emma noted. Aware of Susannah's coolly amused gaze on her worried face, Emma resolved to follow the duke's lead and hope for the best.

"Speaking of higher powers, Susannah," the duke was saying, "I'm almost willing to believe in one, now that Emma's here. She's an answer to my prayers, sent by a pair of angels in human form, who— Ah, Madama, what culinary magic have you worked for us tonight?"

A door had opened in the wall behind Emma, admitting a tiny old woman in a plain black dress, followed by Crowley, bearing a silver soup tureen, and Hallard, carrying a ladle. The old woman led the two manservants to the sideboard, where she carefully filled a soup bowl, then stood back. Hallard placed the bowl on a silver tray, and Crowley presented it to the duke. "Wild mushroom, Your Grace, with a touch of port wine."

The duke tasted the soup, then bowed his head. "Perfection," he declared.

The old woman's wrinkled face was instantly wreathed in smiles, and she departed the room in triumph, leaving Hallard and Crowley to serve the duke's guests.

"She does it every night," Susannah commented to Emma. "I find it positively medieval." She turned her gaze to the foot of the table. "But, then, so much about Penford Hall has a feudal air. It must be a special treat for you to dine with your betters, Kate."

Emma flinched, but Kate Cole merely nodded complacently.

"It is," Kate agreed. "I feel quite privileged whenever the Reverend and Mrs. Shuttleworth invite me to dine with them at the rectory in Penford Harbor. Mrs. Shuttleworth sets a shining example for us all."

Outmaneuvered, Susannah subsided.

"Now, where was I?" said the duke. "Ah, yes, my guardian angels. You would adore them, Derek. They live in a tiny Cotswolds village called Finch and they're the most incredibly identical—"

"You don't mean Ruth and Louise Pym by any chance, do you?" Derek interrupted.

"Derek, you astound me," said the duke. "Don't tell me you know them."

"I do, as a matter of fact. Worked on the church in Finch last winter, uncovering some whitewashed frescoes. Twelfth-century. Interesting." Favoring Emma with a brief glance, he asked politely, "How are the ladies?"

Candlelight glittered in sapphire eyes, and Emma's soup spoon slipped from her fingers, clattering loudly on the leg of her chair as it made its way to the carpet. She started to retrieve it, but the duke put out a restraining hand to keep her from knocking heads with Hallard, who was already bending to remove the offending utensil, while Crowley replaced it with a clean one, which Emma promptly swept from the table with her elbow.

Hallard and Crowley went into action again, Susannah tittered, and Emma blushed a shade of pink that made her grateful for the dim lighting. The duke came to her rescue, signaling Crowley to serve the next course, and continuing as if there'd been no interruption.

"But how else would they be, dear boy? There are few things in this world one can rely upon absolutely, and the Pym sisters—and I say this advisedly—are one of them."

"Tell them how you met," said Kate.

The duke obliged. "Front right tire went pop directly in front of their cottage. The road turned and I didn't. Came to a rest atop their birdbath, if memory serves. They were perfectly charming, of course. Took me in, fed me soup, gave me a kitten to play with—like being back in the nursery with Nanny Cole. Been thick as thieves ever since. Never go to London without looking in on them."

"And you, Miss Porter?" Derek asked.

"A m-maze," Emma stammered, still shaken by her mishap with the spoon.

"Know what you mean," agreed the duke, helping himself to the marbled salmon and sole Hallard offered from a silver serving dish. "But who wouldn't be? The first time I saw them, side by side, peering through my windscreen,

I thought I'd bunged my head on the steering column."

"I don't suppose you'd care to tell me who you're talking about," Susannah put in, looking peevishly at the duke.

"Ruth and Louise Pym, my dear Susannah, are antique, inestimable, and identical twin sisters."

"I knew a pair of twins once," said Syd. The duke waited for him to go on, but Syd simply stared into the middle distance, a reminiscent smile playing on his lips.

"Identical twins?" Susannah grimaced. "How ghastly. I would dread having a twin."

"The thought is an unsettling one," the duke agreed smoothly. "I would venture to say—"

"*In* a maze," Emma said abruptly. The dinner party froze as all heads, including Crowley's, turned in her direction.

"I beg your pardon?" said the duke. "I didn't quite catch—"

"I met them *in* a maze. The Pyms. A hedge maze. At Mansley Bran——" Emma cleared her throat. "At *Bran*sley *Man*or."

"Ah, Bransley Manor." The duke nodded. "Kate and I visited there as children, with my grandmother, when the Saint Johns were still in residence. That was many years ago, of course. It is a National Trust property now, I believe?" With infinite patience, the duke guided Emma through a description of the gardens at Bransley Manor, then gracefully changed the subject, giving her a chance to recover her composure. His solicitude reminded Emma that she had a confession to make, and as Crowley served the noisettes of lamb, she turned to the duke.

"Grayson?" she said softly. "I'm afraid there's been a slight misunderstanding."

"I knew it!" the duke exclaimed. "I knew the rose suite wouldn't do. Crowley, would you please—"

"Oh, no," Emma broke in. "It's not the rose suite. It's me." She riveted her eyes on the rim of his wineglass as the words came spilling out. "I'm not who you think I am. I'm just a tourist, and I met the Pyms by accident, and I came to Penford Hall to *look* at the gardens, not *work* on them."

There was a moment of heavy silence as the duke stared at her, uncomprehending. "Do you mean to say that you have to get back to your proper job by next week or something? If that's the problem, I'm sure Kate can arrange—"

"No," Emma said quickly. "It's not that."

"What is it, then? I'm sorry if I seem obtuse, but—"

"I'm not qualified to do the kind of work you have in mind," Emma explained. "I'm *not* a professional gardener."

"I see." The duke nodded thoughtfully, then rubbed the tip of his nose with his thumb. "Good heavens, Emma, how you unnerved me," he said gently. "For one earth-shattering moment, I thought the Pyms had made a mistake. My dear . . ." Susannah began a lecture on the evils of meat-eating, but the duke focused solely on Emma, leaning toward her, speaking softly, his warm brown eyes alight with understanding. "Kate tells me you work with computers, and I must believe her, but that, I think, is merely what you do for pay. Gardening, though—digging and planting, hoeing and weeding, watching the seasons change and feeling you're a part of the cycle—that's something altogether different, is it not?"

Emma nodded slowly, and the duke nodded with her.

"The thing that we love most is the thing that we do best," he murmured. "And you, my dear, love nothing quite so well as a garden. The Pyms discovered that, surely, and I saw it in your face this afternoon, just as clearly as I see it now. You could no more turn your back on the chapel garden than I could walk away from Penford Hall. Give me your hands."

Emma's hands seemed to float across the snowy linen to rest in the duke's outstretched palms. He gazed down at them in silence, then raised his eyes to Emma's once again.

"Just as I thought," he said. "Callused, strong, and exquisitely capable. All the qualifications I require. I've no doubt whatsoever that these two hands"—he enclosed Emma's in his own—"will bring the chapel garden back to life."

"Wow," said Syd, through a mouthful of lamb. "You gotta real way with words, Duke."

"Treacle," sneered Susannah, tossing back her glass of wine.

The duke took no notice of them, and Emma was aware of no one but the duke. Warmed by his touch, mesmerized by the light in his brown eyes, she felt her self-doubt melt away. At that moment, she would have followed Grayson to the ends of the earth.

"Well," she began, a bit breathlessly, "if you're sure . . ."

"I'm sure," said the duke, raising her hands to his lips, then releasing them with a radiant smile.

With a fluttering heart, Emma folded her hands in her lap. She felt as though she'd been seduced in public, but, oddly enough, she didn't seem to care. Plans began to take shape in her mind, and they kept her in a pleasantly preoccupied haze until the warm cappuccino soufflé was served, when the words "Lex Rex" pulled her sharply back to earth.

"Never replaced the yacht, have you, Grayson?" Susannah was saying. "Surprising, really, now that you can so easily afford one." Draining yet another glass of wine, she swayed toward Emma. "Wasn't always such a showplace, Penford Hall. Bit of a shambles when my mother and I came calling."

"The hall has seen its share of troubled times," Grayson acknowledged.

"Not anymore," said Susannah, waving her wineglass at the chandelier. "So why haven't you replaced the yacht? You were so fond of sailing, so good at it, too. Not like poor old Lex."

Syd looked up from his plate. "Give it a rest, huh, Suzie?"

"It's all right, Syd," said the duke. "It's true that I was once very fond of sailing. But I somehow lost my taste for it after Lex and the others died."

"Spoilt the day for you, did it?" Susannah drawled. "Spend a night or two crying in your pillow for poor old Lex?"

"Really, Susannah," said Kate, her eyes flashing.

"Lex's death spoilt quite a few days for me, actually," the duke replied tightly. "It may interest you to know, dear cousin, that drowning isn't the easy death it's made out to be. It is, in fact, nightmarish. Try, if you can, to imagine someone you care for sinking beneath the waves, helpless, struggling, gasping for breath—"

Derek stood abruptly. His face was pale and a fine line of perspiration beaded his brow. "Sorry," he said gruffly, staring down at the table. "Seems a bit close in here. Think I'll head upstairs."

Emma had no idea what had provoked Derek's reaction, but the pain in his eyes lanced through her like a knife. Almost without thinking, she, too, rose to her feet, then stood in awkward silence, not knowing what to say, embarrassed to have drawn attention to herself yet again.

Once more, the duke rescued her. Tossing his linen napkin on the table, he pushed back his own chair and stood. "I've just had the most splendid idea," he announced. His voice was light, but the look he gave Susannah was nothing short of murderous. "It's Emma's first night at Penford Hall. Why not have a little celebration? Crowley, Dom Pérignon to the music room, if you please, and open the piano. Nothing like a spot of Mozart and a tot of bubbly to brighten a rainy night." Without missing a beat, he added, "You'll join us, of course, Derek."

Derek slowly raised his head to look, slightly puzzled, at Emma. He lowered his eyes, then shrugged. "Perhaps one glass," he agreed.

8

One glass of champagne led to another, and when Emma awoke shortly after dawn the next day, she still felt a bit tipsy.

The evening had turned out well enough, in the end. The duke had proved to be a gifted pianist, and Susannah, deprived of the spotlight, had retired early, taking Syd and a good deal of tension with her. In her absence, the duke had played with renewed vigor, interspersing the promised Mozart with jaunty selections from *H.M.S. Pinafore.*

Still, Derek had never really shaken off the morose mood that had seized him at supper. He'd sipped his champagne and listened attentively to the music, but he'd said very little and smiled even less.

What had set him off, Emma wondered. Had he, too, known Lex Rex? Had the discussion of the rock singer's death reopened an old wound? Perhaps Kate had warned her off of the topic in order to avoid just such a scene. Clearly, the duke placed a high premium on his guests' well-being. Why, last night he'd made Emma feel . . .

. . . like a moonstruck teenager, she thought wryly, just

as Derek had done in the chapel garden. This would never do. She had a job of work ahead of her at Penford Hall, and lying in bed, blushing like a schoolgirl, wouldn't get it done.

Throwing off the covers, Emma reached for her glasses, then pulled on the blue robe and made her way out onto the balcony. The rain had fallen steadily throughout the night, but the storm had finally blown itself out, leaving a handful of fleecy clouds in its wake. Shreds of gray mist drifted across the great lawn and swirled among the castle ruins, like graceful ghosts from one of Grandmother's moonlit parties. The mist would be gone by midmorning, Emma thought. It promised to be a beautiful day.

After a quick bath, Emma dressed in a denim skirt, a short-sleeved cotton blouse, and her trusty walking shoes. She'd have to stock up on work clothes, but this morning she wanted nothing more than to have the chapel garden all to herself for an hour or two. Emma pulled her long hair into a pony tail, then boldly decided to find a back door to Penford Hall on her own.

Twenty minutes later, she was forced to admit defeat. It was galling, but she would have to retrace her steps and wait impatiently in her room until Mattie or Crowley or some other native guide materialized. She turned to go back the way she'd come, then jumped as a woman's voice exploded in her ear. *"What the HELL do you think you're doing here!"*

Emma was halfway through a terrified apology before she realized that the question had not been directed at her. The bellow had come from behind a closed door a few steps down the hall, and she could now make out the sound of a softer voice answering. Cautiously, Emma approached the door and bent her head to listen.

"No, you may bloody well *not* tidy up my blasted room, and if I catch you dusting under the beds in the nursery one more time, I'll tear your arm off and beat you with the bloody stump! *Have* I made myself clear?"

Emma flattened herself against the wall as the door flew open and a dark-haired, frail-looking little boy scooted out. He was pursued by a woman who was at least as old as Crowley, a head taller than Emma, and built like a Sherman tank. Her short white hair was tightly curled and trailing multicolored bits of thread. Snippets of bright-red yarn were scattered over her tweed skirt and twin set, a pincushion bristled on her wrist, and a tape measure dangled around her neck. The woman pointed a pair of pinking shears at the boy and bellowed, "Scat!"

The boy stood his ground. He was as neat as a pin, in navy-blue shorts and knee socks, a white polo shirt, and running shoes, and he regarded his formidable adversary with a look of nervous defiance.

"What about our lessons?" the boy demanded.

The hand pointing the pinking shears dropped to the woman's side. "Lessons?" She scratched her head, sending a shower of thread to the floor. "You had some yesterday, didn't you?"

"We're supposed to have them every day, Nanny Cole," the boy said doggedly.

"*Every day?* How in God's name am I supposed to finish Lady Nell's ball gown if I have to see to your dratted lessons every day? I want you outside, right now, quickstep march, and none of your cheek. Fresh air and sunshine are your lessons for the day, Peter-my-lad. Now, march!"

Scowling, the boy turned to go, but paused as he caught sight of Emma. His dark eyes narrowed for a moment; then he tucked his chin to his chest and stalked off down the hall without a backward glance. Emma cowered against the wall as Nanny Cole's belligerent gaze came to rest on her.

"Who the hell are you?" Nanny Cole barked. She thrust her face toward Emma's. "Not lurking, are you? Not snooping, like that underbred sack of bones?"

"No," Emma said hastily. "I'm Emma Porter and I was—"

"Ah." Nanny Cole straightened, put a finger to her lips, and nodded. "The garden lady from the States. Should've guessed. You have that look about you. Solid. Close to the earth." Rocking back on her heels, Nanny Cole bellowed, "Turn round, turn round, let's have a look at you. Haven't got all day."

Bewildered, but not daring to disobey, Emma turned a slow circle in the hall while Nanny Cole whipped a gold pen out of her pocket and began jotting something on the inside of her wrist.

"Mmm," muttered Nanny Cole. "Full figure, strong chin, fine head of hair. Eyes . . . gray? Yes. All right. That'll do. You can go now."

"Er—" Emma began.

"Good Lord, woman, get a grip. I can't spend all bloody morning standing in doorways."

"I was trying to get to the chapel garden and—"

"The chapel garden? What would the chapel garden be doing up here?"

"It's all right, Nanny Cole. I'll take her."

A little girl stepped out from behind Nanny Cole. She wore a short, fluttery pleated skirt and a white middy blouse trimmed in pale blue. In one arm she cradled a small chocolate-brown teddy bear in its own sailor suit, complete with bell-bottom trousers and a round, be-ribboned cap. In her free hand she held a plump, juicy strawberry.

"Good girl, Lady Nell," said Nanny Cole. "But mind how you go in that outfit. Took me all night to finish those

dratted pleats. What a bloody way to start the day . . ."
Still grumbling, Nanny Cole slammed the door.

As Lady Nell raised the strawberry to her lips, Emma wondered why the duke hadn't mentioned having a daughter. She was a pretty child, with pink cheeks, a cupid's-bow mouth, and a halo of loose golden ringlets. She might have been insipid had she been less self-possessed, but she carried herself with the dignity of a prima ballerina, and her limpid blue eyes gave Emma the uncanny sensation that a far older and wiser woman was looking out of them, taking her measure.

"We've been waiting for you," Nell declared.

"Have you?" Emma responded, surprised.

"Aunt Dimity said you'd come, but we didn't expect to wait such a long time. I'll be six in September, and Peter's *very tired*," Nell stated firmly.

"I'm sorry, Lady Nell." Emma wondered if she should curtsy. "I'm afraid I don't know your aunt, and Grayson—that is, your father—must have forgotten to tell me."

"Aunt Dimity's not my aunt, my name's not Lady Nell, and Grayson's not my father," Nell informed her calmly. "My aunt's name is Beatrice, Papa's name is Derek, and I'm Nell Harris. The boy who was here before is my brother, Peter." Nell looked down at her bear. "This is Bertie. There's four of us—Auntie Bea doesn't count. But don't worry. Mummy's dead." Nell took another bite out of her strawberry.

Mummy's dead? Emma blinked at the impact of Nell's announcement. *Derek is a widower with two children?* By the time the rest of Nell's words had registered, the child was walking away. Emma scrambled to catch up.

"Nell?" she asked. "I'm very sorry to hear about your mother. . . ."

"She died a long time ago," said Nell. "I was just a baby. Now, turn left at the dog, then straight on to the big fat cow."

Emma looked up in alarm, then realized that Nell was referring to the paintings that covered the corridor's walls. From Nell's point of view, the scruffy-looking mongrel peering out from under the table was no doubt the most memorable feature of a hugely complicated family scene, almost certainly seventeenth-century and Dutch. The "big fat cow" was some eighteenth-century landowner's prize breeder, done in the unmistakable wooden style of George Stubbs. It was such a simple means of navigation that Emma kicked herself for not having thought of it sooner. She began to pay attention to the paintings they passed, and by the time they reached the staircase leading down to the entrance hall, she felt as though she could find her way back to Nanny Cole's room unaided. Not that she had any intention of doing so in the near future.

Halfway down the main staircase, Emma tried again. "Nell, what did you mean when you told me not to worry?"

Nell's only response was a reproachful, sidelong glance that seemed to say, "You know very well what I meant." Cowed by the truth, Emma decided to ask no more questions.

Nell led the way through the labyrinth of first-floor corridors to an airy storeroom piled high with linen, where she opened a door and stepped out onto the great lawn. Emma paused to thank Nell for her help, but the little girl kept walking, picking her way delicately through the wet grass, still nibbling on her strawberry.

Emma watched with dismay as Nell headed for the castle ruins. She hadn't planned to spend her first, precious morning sharing the garden with anyone, much less babysitting. When they reached the arched entrance in the castle wall, she stopped. "Thank you," she said, kindly but firmly. "I think I can find my way from here."

Nell turned on her a look of weary tolerance. "Emma," she said, "Bertie and I don't talk a lot and we don't need looking after by anyone but Peter."

"But I didn't say . . . That is, I'm sure your brother is . . ." Much too young to be in charge of a nearly-six-year-old like you, Emma thought, but she bit back the words. She wasn't at all sure she could win an argument with Nell. "I guess I don't know many children like you," she said defensively.

"We know," said Nell, "but we can fix that." She turned to call a greeting to Hallard, the nearsighted footman, who was back in his wicker armchair, tapping at his keyboard, then proceeded down the grassy corridor toward the banquet hall, with Emma trailing slowly in her wake.

The banquet hall was deserted. Some of the vines on the birdcage arbor had been knocked loose by last night's rain and Emma paused to tie them up again, looking over her shoulder to see if Bantry was around. She felt ill-equipped to deal with Nell's unnerving pronouncements on her own.

By the time Emma finished retying the vines, Nell had left the banquet hall. Emma hoped that the little girl had decided to go somewhere other than the chapel garden, but her hopes were dashed when she rounded a corner and saw Nell lifting the latch on the green door. Emma was still several yards away when the door swung wide.

Nell made no move to enter the garden. She stood in the doorway, clinging tightly to her bear, and Bertie's black eyes peered imploringly over her shoulder, as though pleading with Emma to hurry up.

"Nell?" Emma called, hastening to the child's side. "What is it? What's—" Emma froze as she saw Susannah

Ashley-Woods sprawled facedown in the grass at the bottom of the uneven stone steps, very near the old wheelbarrow. Her blond hair lay like a silken fan around her head, a gleaming black heel dangled from one shoe, and a thin trickle of blood trailed from her shell-like ear.

Kneeling in the doorway, Emma turned Nell to face her. "There's been an accident," Emma said, amazed by the steadiness of her voice. "Susannah's shoe broke and she fell down the stairs. You understand?"

Curls bobbing, the child nodded.

"I want you and Bertie to run back to the hall as fast as you can. Tell the first grown-up you see to call for a doctor. Can you do that for me?"

Nell gave another emphatic nod, then darted back up the corridor, with Bertie flopping limply, clutched in a dimpled fist.

Emma rushed down the steps to kneel at Susannah's side. She breathed a sigh of relief when she pressed a hand to Susannah's neck and detected a pulse. Bending lower, she saw that Susannah's eyes were closed and her left cheek was pillowed in a blood-soaked clump of grass.

"Warm. I have to keep her warm," Emma muttered. She grabbed blindly for the oilcloth on the old wheelbarrow, but it was no longer there. Frantically scanning the ground, she saw it lying a few steps away on the flagstone path. She scrambled to retrieve it, then spread it over Susannah's prone form and waited.

"My God . . ." Grayson stood at the top of the stairs, his face ashen. "Is she dead?" he whispered hoarsely.

Emma shook her head. "Have you called for an ambulance?"

Before the duke could answer, Kate Cole appeared beside him, carrying a heavy wool blanket. She hurried down the stairs, spread the blanket on top of the oilcloth, knelt, and with a practiced hand lifted Susannah's eyelid.

She nodded, then took hold of the woman's wrist. "She's still with us," Kate confirmed, "but Dr. Singh had better get here quickly."

"Should we take her into the hall?" Emma asked.

"Best not," said Kate, gently placing Susannah's limp arm beneath the coverings. "There's not much blood, but there's a nasty bruise on her temple, and no telling what the fall might've done to her neck." She rose to her feet and regarded Susannah grimly.

Her gaze fixed on the bloodstained grass, Emma backed away until she bumped into the chapel door. There she stood, clasping and unclasping her hands, watching Kate direct the action as more people crowded into the grassy space at the foot of the stairs.

Crowley arrived with another blanket, and Hallard was next, carrying a first-aid kit. The distant sound of a helicopter reached Emma's ears just before Bantry stepped past the duke. The head gardener paused when he saw Susannah, then hurried down the stairs to confer quietly with Kate. Crowley joined them, and Emma caught something about "the men from the village" and "alerting Newland at the gate" before Crowley nodded and left.

"Dr. Singh'll be here straightaway," Bantry announced.

Still at the top of the stairs, the duke pointed downward. "It's those damned shoes," he said. Susannah's broken high heel protruded from the edge of the oilcloth. "If she hadn't insisted on wearing such absurd footwear, this never would've happened."

After checking Susannah's pulse once more, Kate went up the stairs to take hold of Grayson's hands. "We'll have to prepare a statement," she said.

"Of course," said the duke, and, "*Damn.*" Turning to Bantry, he asked, "Is Lady Nell all right?"

Bantry nodded. "Mattie's lookin' after Lady Nell, and

Mr. Harris is out lookin' for young Master Peter. Seems the boy's disappeared."

Emma wanted to tell them all that Nanny Cole had ordered the boy outside to play, but her teeth were chattering so badly that the most she could manage was a strangled squeak.

"Here, now, Miss Emma." The head gardener stripped off his oiled green jacket and walked over to where she stood. "You've had quite a shock. You come with me to the kitchen and we'll have Madama make you a nice cup of tea. There's a good girl, now, come along." As he spoke, Bantry draped his jacket around Emma's shoulders. It was still warm and smelled comfortingly of compost and pipe tobacco. The head gardener put a wiry arm around her shoulders as well, guiding her up the stairs and past the green door. Emma turned in the doorway to look once more at the nightmarish scene, and saw Grayson fire a questioning look at Kate, whose only reply was a minute shrug.

9

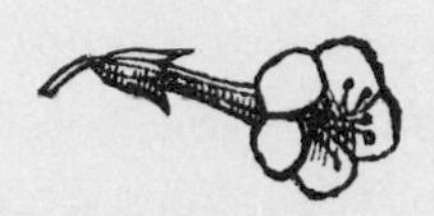

In the kitchen, bacon sizzled on a griddle, an outsized teakettle sent a plume of steam toward the vaulted ceiling, and Madama stood at the massive stove, using a wooden spoon to stir a row of bubbling stockpots and to direct the activities of a trio of white-aproned girls who scurried back and forth from the stove to the long oak table in the center of the cavernous room.

The girls were busily replenishing the breakfast plates of a dozen men in workboots and thick sweaters who sat at the table, talking in a low rumble among themselves while they ate. Like Newland, the gatekeeper, each wore a radio unit on his hip and an earphone in one ear.

Nell sat at the far end of the table, calmly devouring a large bowl of plump strawberries and heavy cream. Beside her, Mattie stared down at her teacup. Nell merely nodded when Emma and Bantry came into the room, but Mattie half rose from her chair. "Is she—?"

The girl's breathless question silenced the room, and every face turned to look expectantly at the new arrivals. Emma pulled Bantry's jacket around her self-consciously and looked across the sea of unfamiliar faces to Mattie.

"Susannah was still unconscious when we left her," she said, "but she was alive."

"Dr. Singh's flyin' her into Plymouth," Bantry added.

"Thank the Lord." Mattie leaned forward on her hands for a moment, then pushed back her chair and stood upright. "I should pack a bag for Miss Ashers," she said. "Mr. Bishop can bring it to her. She'll be wanting her own things when she wakes up."

"Run along, then," said Bantry. "I'll see to Lady Nell."

Mattie hurried from the room and Bantry exchanged sober greetings with the men as he and Emma made their way down the length of the table to sit on either side of Nell. Two of the serving girls peered curiously at Emma, and she overheard one of them murmur "the garden lady" before Madama rapped the stove sharply with her spoon and sent them back to work. The rumble of voices and the clatter of crockery resumed, and a moment later one of the girls placed a cup of strong, sweet tea before Emma, followed quickly by a plateful of fried eggs, sausages, bacon, and grease-drenched toast. Emma glanced at the plate, shuddered slightly, and reached for the tea.

"You can have strawberries, if you like," Nell suggested helpfully.

"I'll just have tea for now, thank you," Emma murmured.

The noise subsided once more as Derek came into the kitchen, his arm around Peter's shoulders. Derek looked haggard, but the boy's cheeks were flushed, his eyes bright, and he walked with a bounce in his step.

"You're sure you heard nothing?" Derek was asking.

"I told you, Dad. I was out on the cliff path, reading. I didn't even know she was there until everyone started to shout."

"All right, son, all right." Derek pulled the boy to him

in a rough, sideways hug, then let him run to Nell's side.

"She's not dead," Nell informed her brother bluntly.

"I know," Peter replied, "but she's gone." The boy glanced over at the stove. "Madama, may I have strawberries, too, please?"

"Miss Porter? If I might have a word?" Derek gestured to the fireplace, where a tall settle offered a degree of privacy. Emma slipped out of Bantry's jacket and returned it to him with a murmur of thanks, then joined Derek on the high-backed wooden bench.

"Miss Porter," he began. "Emma. Want to thank you for looking after my daughter. Traumatic experience for such a young child. Not sure—" Derek stiffened as a thin, high-pitched scream sounded in the distance, then was abruptly cut off.

Knives and forks clattered to the tiled floor as the men at the table sprang to their feet and streamed through the kitchen door. Derek rose, too, and stood looking distractedly from the door to his children until Bantry waved him on.

"Go, man, go," Bantry urged. "I'll keep an eye on the young 'uns."

Pausing only to drop a kiss on the top of Nell's head, Derek raced from the room, with Emma hot on his heels, following the thud of retreating workboots to the entrance hall.

Emma felt as though she'd stumbled into a war zone. The chubby mechanic, Gash, was holding the front door open and the roar of an idling helicopter thundered through it on the wind. Newland, with his black beret tilted at a rakish angle, was barking orders to the group from the kitchen. Two men in windbreakers were wheeling Susannah toward the open door on a collapsible stretcher, her neck strapped in a padded brace, her head swathed in bloodstained bandages, and Syd Bishop trotted alongside, carrying the overnight case Mattie had packed.

Mattie lay at the foot of the main staircase, her head cradled in Kate Cole's lap. Beside them knelt a bearded man in a white turban and caftan, brown socks and sandals, and a black leather bomber jacket. Crowley hovered nearby, white-faced, while the duke patted his shoulder, and Hallard stood to one side, observing the scene with intense concentration.

"What's happened?" Derek asked.

"She's fainted," replied the bearded man. "Some people do, at the sight of blood." Standing, he reached over to touch Crowley's arm. "Not to worry. Get her to bed and keep her warm. She'll be up and running again after a few hours' rest."

"Very good, Dr. Singh," Crowley replied.

Syd had followed the stretcher-bearers out to the waiting helicopter, and Dr. Singh ran to catch up with them. The men from the kitchen had dispersed, and Newland and Gash, after conferring briefly in the doorway, had headed out after the men, closing the door behind them.

The duke knelt beside Mattie. "Poor child," he murmured. "Hallard, please fetch the brandy and bring it up to Mattie's room. Ask Madama to send up a pot of tea, as well." As Hallard sped off in the direction of the kitchen, the duke lifted Mattie's slight form in his arms and carried her up the main staircase, with Crowley close behind.

Kate Cole hung back. Looking worriedly from Derek to Emma, she said, "I'm afraid that Grayson and I must leave for Plymouth shortly, to prepare for a news conference there this afternoon. We'll want to keep the press away from the hall, you understand, so we may have to stay on a few days, until things settle down."

"Using Grayson as a decoy?" Derek asked.

"More like a lamb to the slaughter," Kate confirmed. "You've no idea what we went through when Lex died. Photographers behind every bush. So we may be away for some time. I hate to leave you short-handed, but with Crowley looking after Mattie—"

"We'll be fine," Derek assured her. Kate nodded gratefully, handed Derek a card with a phone number where she could be reached in Plymouth, and turned to run up the stairs. Dr. Singh's helicopter roared briefly overhead, then faded in the distance.

The entrance hall was suddenly silent. Derek looked down at Emma. "Library?" he suggested hesitantly. "Drink?"

"Maybe two," she replied.

Emma rested her elbow on the arm of the brocade couch in the library and ran a finger around the rim of her glass. It was almost ten A.M., and she wished she'd eaten breakfast. The first sip of the duke's single-malt whiskey had steadied her nerves, and the second had cleared her head, but a third, taken on an empty stomach, would probably put her under the table.

She glanced over at Derek. He sat at the other end of the couch, legs crossed and arms folded, frowning silently at the empty hearth. He hadn't moved since Bantry had stopped by to ask if Master Peter and Lady Nell might go with him to Madama's kitchen garden. Even then he'd only nodded.

He wasn't worrying about Susannah, Emma knew. He'd responded to Emma's words of consolation with a blank stare, followed by a shrug and an automatic "Bad show," as though he'd momentarily forgotten who had been injured.

Was he still brooding over his children? Emma honestly

didn't think he had much to worry about on that score. Nell seemed to be handling the situation very calmly, and Peter appeared unfazed. Emma suspected that the children were more resilient than their father gave them credit for.

Emma, too, had recovered quickly, not only from the morning's shocking events, but from her brief infatuation with Derek. She was no longer tongue-tied and clumsy in his presence, at any rate, and she thought she knew why: Whether widowed or divorced, a single man raising a family was invariably looking for someone to mother his children. And since motherhood, even by proxy, had never been one of Emma's career goals, Derek was indisputably out of bounds. The realization came as a relief; Emma was tired of making a fool of herself over a pair of handsome blue eyes.

"Derek," she said, putting her glass on the end table, "I think I'll step outside. I need a breath of fresh air."

Derek surprised her by immediately unfolding his long limbs and rising from the couch. "I'll come with you," he said. And then, as they were strolling slowly across the great lawn, he surprised her again by saying that it was his first visit to Penford Hall.

"I thought you and Grayson were old friends," Emma said.

Derek pursed his lips. "We met in Oxford ten years ago," he said. "I was touching up some plasterwork in the cathedral and he was practicing a Bach cantata on the organ." Derek stopped walking and swung around to face the hall. "Haven't really been in touch since then." Raising a hand to shield his eyes from the sun, he tilted his head back and let his gaze travel slowly along the irregular roofline. "A hodgepodge," he muttered, "but a structurally sound one." He looked over his shoulder at Emma. "You wouldn't call Penford Hall a ruin, would you?"

Pointing at the fragmented façade of the castle, Emma replied, "*That's* a ruin."

"But he was talking about *that.*" Derek gestured to the hall. "Natural enough, given my line of work."

"Which is . . . ?" Emma prompted.

"Hmmm?" Derek looked at her vaguely, then nodded. "Ah, yes. I'm, um . . ." He patted the unbuttoned breast pocket of his shirt, then began to search through the pockets of his jeans. He extracted a penknife, a keychain, a few coins, a tape measure, miscellaneous rubber bands and bits of string, and what looked like the remains of a roll of duct tape before coming up with a crumpled and lint-covered business card, which he handed to Emma. "Don't use the cards much," he muttered. "I work out of my home and, well, it's a word-of-mouth sort of trade."

"*Harris Restoration,*" Emma read aloud, smoothing the card as best she could. She noted the Oxford address and phone number, then tucked the card into the pocket of her denim skirt. "You do restoration work?"

"Right. Rotted timbers, damaged frescoes—"

"Stained glass?" Emma put in.

Derek gave her a sharp glance, then lowered his eyes and resumed walking. "Only natural that Grayson would tell me about his plans to refurbish the hall. Roof leaked like a sieve, he said, and damp had buckled the floorboards. Fact is, he left me with the distinct impression that the place was a bit of a shambles."

"But that's what Susannah said last night," Emma exclaimed. "You remember—at supper?"

"Yes. She also said he was a sailor." Derek rubbed his jaw, then turned to look down at Emma. "Busy tomorrow?"

"I-I don't know," Emma stammered. "It depends on—"

"Good." Derek pointed to the balustraded terrace. "Meet me there, say, eleven-ish? Got something I'd like to show you. Need to know—" He broke off, and the worried frown returned to his face. "No. Wait till tomorrow." And without saying another word, he swung around and strode swiftly back into the hall.

Emma turned to look up at Penford Hall. As far as she could tell, the octagonal slates on the roof were all present and correct, the forest of chimneys stood strong and tall, and the leaded glass sparkled in the many and variously shaped windows, not a pane cracked or missing. People sometimes spoke disparagingly of their own homes, especially when they were stuck with a place that didn't suit their taste or their style of living, and Susannah might ridicule her cousin's home out of sheer spite. But Grayson seemed to love the rambling, Gothic sprawl. If he'd called Penford Hall a ruin, Emma suspected that he hadn't been speaking figuratively.

"You there! Miss Porter!"

Emma looked up and saw Nanny Cole leaning out of a second-floor window some twenty feet to her left. In one massive arm Nanny Cole held a brown-paper parcel; with the other she beckoned to Emma. Obediently, Emma strode over to stand beneath the open window.

"Where the hell is everyone?" Nanny Cole bellowed. "And what was the quack doing here?"

"The duke's cousin fell and hurt herself in the chapel garden," Emma called back. "The doctor came to take her to the hospital in Plymouth and—"

"Never mind," barked Nanny Cole. "I can guess the rest. Brats all right?"

"Fine," said Emma.

"Loving every minute of it, I'll wager, the bloodthirsty little beasts. Where's Mattie?"

"In her room," said Emma. "She fainted—"

"Yes, yes," Nanny Cole broke in impatiently. "Dratted child. That's what comes of hero worship. Well, I can't spend all day running a blasted delivery service. This is for you. Catch!"

The parcel was bulky but soft, and Emma caught it easily. When she looked up again, the window was shut. Curious, Emma carried the parcel over to the terrace steps, where she sat and opened it. It contained two pairs of generously cut denim trousers, with elastic waistbands and padded knees, and two violet-patterned gardening smocks with deep pockets and hammer loops. Emma stared in puzzlement at the smocks for a moment, then shrugged, gathered up the discarded wrapping paper, and headed into the hall to change, murmuring wryly, "If ever there was a sign from heaven . . ."

10

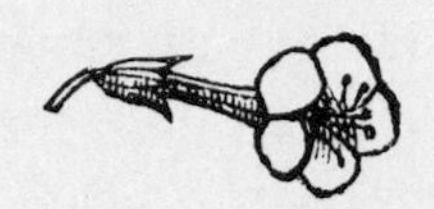

All I need now are work gloves, Emma thought as she stepped into Madama's kitchen garden. It was late morning, the mist had cleared, and the sun was shining brightly overhead. Squinting skyward, Emma reminded herself that a sunhat might not be a bad idea, either. She was about to add a pair of wellies to her mental shopping list when she stopped midway down the rows of radishes, to gape at Bantry.

The old man had lurched out of a shadowy doorway a few yards away, brandishing a stalk of celery and growling ferociously. A bit of rag bound a pair of carrots to his head, like horns, with the greens trailing behind in a verdant, ragged mane. Emma took one look at Penford Hall's head gardener and burst out laughing.

Bantry's growling ceased as he stood up. Grinning good-naturedly, he untied his makeshift headband, put one carrot in the bib pocket of his canvas apron, and offered the other to Emma, who accepted it gratefully.

"Just havin' a bit o' fun with the kiddies," he said. "Tryin' to, anyway. Not really their cup o' tea, I don't think."

"Don't they like vegetable monsters?" Emma asked.

"Oh, I dunno." Bantry glanced over his shoulder. "Master Peter tries, but it shouldn't be so much of an effort, now, should it? And Lady Nell, she's just gone half the time." He touched the side of his head. "Up there. Talkin' half to that bear o' hers and half to herself. Never know what she's goin' to say next, that one." Bantry eyed Emma's new attire shrewdly. "So you're startin' in today, are you? Well, and why not? Constable Trevoy's been up from the village to take his snaps. He says it's clear enough what happened, and it's not as though the young lady's passed on." He turned as the sound of whispering came through the veil of vines on the birdcage arbor. "All right, you two," he called, "come on out. Miss Emma needs our help in the chapel garden."

Emma touched the old man's arm and shook her head. "I don't think Derek would approve of the children going in there so soon after the accident," she said.

"May be you're right," Bantry acknowledged equably, "but you could fill a barn with what Mr. Derek don't know about young 'uns." He bit into his celery stalk and chewed for a moment before adding decisively, "Won't do 'em a bit o' harm to go in there. Best for 'em to face it fair and square, or the bogeyman'll move in and they won't want to face it at all."

Peter and Nell were waiting expectantly on the steps of the wrought-iron arbor. Nell and Bertie had exchanged sailor outfits for matching cherry-red sweaters and scaled-down bib overalls. Peter still wore his white polo shirt, but had traded his short pants for a pair of neatly creased khaki trousers. Bantry beckoned to them to follow as he and Emma crossed the banquet hall, and the four of them entered the grassy corridor together.

An unanticipated flutter of dread ran through Emma as they drew closer to the green door, and the children, who'd been talking quietly as they walked, fell silent. Bantry must have sensed their rising unease because, when they reached the door, he turned to address the children. Bending down, his hands braced upon his knees, he said, "You both know about Miss Susannah bumping her head this morning, right? Well, now, I'm not goin' to lie to you. There might very well be a splash o' blood or two where she fell, but there's no need—"

"Like when the lions tore the Christians limb from limb," Nell put in with a knowing nod. "Or when Lancelot stabbed the Black Knight to the heart."

"Or when Professor Moriarty smashed on the rocks at the Reichenbach Falls," Peter added thoughtfully, but Nell objected that the water had probably washed *that* blood away, so it didn't really count.

"What about when Duncan Robards knocked his tooth out at football?" Peter proposed. "He was bleeding all over the place."

Bantry gave Emma a sidelong look and stood upright, muttering, "Don't know why I bother. . . ."

Bantry pulled the green door open, and for a moment they stood together, peering down at the grassy space at the bottom of the stairs. The oilcloth had been removed and a pair of stout planks had been placed on the stairs—a ramp for the wheeled stretcher, Emma thought. But the main focus of her attention, the damp grass near the tool-filled wheelbarrow, where Susannah's battered head had lain, had been obliterated by the passage of many feet.

Nell turned a reproachful eye on Bantry. "No blood," she said, somewhat testily.

"Wait," said Peter. He leaned forward slightly, then ran down the planks to point triumphantly at a dark stain on the handle of the grub hoe.

"Let me see." Nell shouldered her way between Bantry and Emma and joined Peter beside the wheelbarrow.

Brother and sister bent low over the stain, discussing it with an almost clinical detachment.

"She must've whacked her head on the hoe when she fell," Peter reasoned, and Nell nodded.

"That's as may be," Bantry said, walking briskly down the planks, "but *we'll* be whackin' weeds with it." He picked up the grub hoe and the scythe and carried them over to the chapel.

"What are you doing, Mr. Bantry?" asked Peter.

"Movin' the tools into the chapel," Bantry explained. "Remember the rain we had last night? Might come back again tonight, and as we'll be needin' the barrow, and as I don't want my tools to get rusty, I'm goin' to put 'em inside where it's dry."

"But Dad won't want the chapel cluttered up," Peter objected.

Bantry shifted the load in his arms and looked curiously at Peter's worried face. "Don't your father look after his tools?" he asked. "That's all I'm doin', son. Your father won't begrudge us a bit o' roof. Now, you come over here and see that it's all stacked tidy."

"It's all right, Peter," said Nell. "Bertie says that Papa won't mind."

Peter glanced at his sister and seemed to relax a bit as he strode over to lend Bantry a hand. When the barrow was empty, Bantry looked up at Emma and asked, "Where do you want us to begin?"

The rest of the morning passed quickly. Bantry and Peter stripped dead vines from the walls, Emma turned the soil in the raised beds, and Nell trotted to and fro, carrying armloads of debris to the wheelbarrow, while Bertie sat on an upturned bucket, supervising.

Bantry and Emma took turns wheeling the barrow up the ramp and tipping its contents in a windswept, rocky meadow outside the east wall of the castle. A broad path cut through the meadow, a bright-green ribbon of moss running through the gorse bushes and clumps of tamarisk, and beyond the path the land fell away abruptly, dropping nearly two hundred feet to the foaming waves below.

"The cliff path," Emma said. She turned to Bantry. "Isn't that where Peter was this morning?"

"Aye," said Bantry, "but Master Peter knows not to go beyond the path. And Lady Nell's not allowed outside the castle walls on her own."

Emma nodded absently, listening as Peter called to Nell to bring him the pruning shears. Only fifty yards separated the cliff path from the east wall of the chapel garden. If Susannah had cried out, Peter almost certainly would have heard her. She must have fallen silently, Emma thought with a shudder, and quickly thrust the matter from her mind.

It was nearing one o'clock when a heavyset man with a bristly red mustache appeared in the doorway of the chapel garden. Emma recognized him as one of the men she'd seen eating breakfast in the kitchen. Like the others, he had a radio clipped to his belt, but at the moment he was also burdened with a large wicker hamper.

"Mr. Bantry, sir," he called respectfully, coming down the stairs, "Madama thought you might be wanting a bite to eat."

"Madama was right, Tom," said Bantry. He stepped down from the low retaining wall and walked over to take charge of the hamper. "Everything peaceful?"

"So far," the man said. He nodded pleasantly to Emma and the children before leaving.

Emma stuck her pitchfork in the ground, Peter tossed a last handful of dead vines in the wheelbarrow, and Nell went to fetch Bertie before joining them on the stairs. Once Bantry had handed plates and glasses around, he set out a jug of cider, a bunch of grapes, a round of cheese, a long loaf of crusty bread, a covered bowl filled with rosemary chicken, and a dozen strawberry tarts topped with shredded coconut.

"God bless Madama," Bantry said reverently, and Emma murmured a heartfelt "Amen," smiling when Nell's hand darted toward the tarts. Bantry clucked his tongue and the hand hesitated, then picked up the bunch of grapes instead.

"Who was that man?" Emma asked, opening the cider. "The man who brought the hamper."

"Tom Trevoy," Peter informed her. "He's the chief constable in Penford Harbor."

"He's the *only* constable in Penford Harbor," Nell added.

"Trevoy?" said Emma. "I think I met a relative of his. She runs a guest house where I stayed, near Exeter."

"That'll be Tom's Aunt Mavis," Bantry confirmed.

"Why's Tom wearing that thing in his ear?" Nell asked.

"That's a radio," Peter explained. "It's so he can talk with the other men. Isn't that right, Mr. Bantry?"

"Aye," Bantry said shortly. "Now, who wants a nice bit o' cheese?"

Emma finished pouring the cider, then put the jug down and leaned back to survey the results of the morning's work. Clearing away the dead growth had given her a better idea of the chapel garden's basic shape and structure. There were more weeds to pull, more vines to remove, but her next step would be to the drafting table, to make some preliminary sketches. When the meal drew to a close, she declared a half-holiday.

"You've earned it," she said, plucking twigs from Nell's curls. "You're hard workers and I want you both to know that I really appreciate all your help."

"No one works harder than Peter," Nell informed her. "At home, when Papa's away, Peter—"

"Would you like me and Nell to take the hamper back, Mr. Bantry?" Peter interrupted, getting to his feet.

"Miss Emma and I'll see to that," Bantry said. "Run along and play, now, the both of you."

"But I wanted to tell Emma—" Nell began.

"Here, Nell, have the last tart," said Peter, thrusting it toward her as he hustled her up the steps. "You heard Mr. Bantry. We're supposed to *play* now."

Bantry waited until the children were out of earshot, then shook his head. " 'We're supposed to *play,* now,' " he mimicked gruffly. "Lad acts like it were an order." Piling dishes into the hamper, he went on. "Has a bee in his bonnet about keepin' busy, that one. Left him alone in my pottin' shed for five minutes last week, and when I came back, he'd swept the floor."

Emma nodded. "Nanny Cole seems to be having the same problem," she said. "She was reading the riot act to him about it this morning."

"Somethin's frettin' at him." Bantry looked thoughtfully at the closed door and rubbed the back of his neck. "Don't know what it is, but somethin's got him all wound up. Here, pass me that glass, will you?"

Emma shook the last drops of cider from her glass. "Maybe he's not used to having men patrol the house he's living in," she suggested. She caught Bantry's eye as she passed the empty glass to him. "That's what Newland and Chief Constable Trevoy and those other men are doing, isn't it?"

Bantry didn't answer until the hamper had been repacked and the lid closed. Then he leaned back on his elbows, his eyes on the chapel door. "I expect Tom's auntie told you what happened here a few years ago."

Emma nodded. "She said there'd been some trouble with the press after that rock singer drowned. Kate Cole seems to think it might happen again. Do you?"

"Miss Susannah's what they call a celebrity, isn't she?" Bantry retorted. "And what with that old business and all, I reckon the vultures'll take an interest, right enough." His kindly gray eyes turned to slate. "We're not about to go through that again."

"How can you stop it?"

"Our Kate'll stop it, all right," Bantry said grimly. "Pride of Penford Harbor, is our Kate. She's a solicitor, you know."

Emma looked away, to conceal her surprise. House-keeper, lawyer—Kate seemed to be yet another multitalented member of the Penford Hall staff. From what she'd said about managing the press conference in Plymouth, she seemed to be Grayson's public-relations officer as well. "How bad was it when Lex died?"

"Bad enough." Bantry leaned forward, his shoulders hunched, his elbows on his knees, toying with a decapitated dandelion. "Don't want you to get the wrong idea," he said slowly. "We're decent folk. We believe in a free press, same as other decent folk, but those fellers printed nothin' but lies. Village had just got back on its feet again, but them vultures tried to turn it inside out." He shook his head. "Caught 'em in the schoolyard, worryin' the children, for goodness' sake."

"But why were they so persistent?" Emma asked. "What were they after?"

"Proof," Bantry said, tossing the dandelion into the wheelbarrow. "The bastards were looking for proof that His Grace murdered that bloke."

"Nothin' like a good murder for sellin' papers."

Bantry's words returned to Emma as she sat at the

drafting table. Several hours had passed since she'd returned to her room, but the bitterness in Bantry's voice remained fresh in her mind. Clearly, it had been a galling experience for him to see his fair-haired boy mauled by a sensation-seeking press. Emma thought she could understand the old man's outrage, and she felt sorry for Grayson as well—it couldn't be easy, having celebrities keel over on your doorstep once every five years. Yet she, too, was curious to know what had led Lex Rex to his watery grave.

Richard would have been able to quote chapter and verse to her from the press coverage in the States, but Emma doubted that Richard's new bride would appreciate the phone call. Emma couldn't bring herself to press Bantry for details, either.

Leaning back from the drafting table, Emma examined her sketches, feeling a rush of pleasure when she saw how well they'd turned out. More often than not, her preliminary scribbles consisted of ragged lines, symbolic circles, rows of *X*'s, and lots of small arrows. These were finished drawings. There was the lavender hedge, on either side of the chapel door, and there were the irises and poppies, the old Bourbon roses and the clouds of baby's breath, exactly as she'd envisioned them the day before. It had come so easily, too, as though another hand had been guiding hers. Emma smiled at the notion, put her pencil down, and stretched. Once she added a touch of color to the drawings, she'd present them to Bantry for inspection.

She'd show them to Peter and Nell, as well. She was surprised to realize how much she'd enjoyed the time she'd spent with Derek's children. There'd been that odd moment of near-mutiny when Peter had objected to Bantry's stowing the tools in the chapel, but after that he'd been fine. Bantry might teasingly label him a workaholic, but Emma had never considered industriousness to be a fault.

In his own way, though, the boy was as disconcerting as his sister. If Nell was too direct, Peter was too wary. When he looked up at Emma with those huge dark eyes —so like his father's—there seemed to be things going on behind them he'd never let her see. And there'd been that unsettling bounce in his step as he'd come into the kitchen, after learning of Susannah's accident. . . .

Emma bent to tidy up the drafting table, since it was time to dress for supper. Children must be subject to mood swings, the same as adults, she thought. Maybe Peter hadn't liked Susannah. She might have hurt his feelings—she seemed adept at that—in which case her accident would have been good news as far as he was concerned. Emma just wished she knew for sure that he'd been on the cliff path that morning, as he'd claimed. She'd have to remember to ask Derek about it tomorrow.

Emma smiled as she glanced at the crumpled business card propped crookedly against the jeweled clock on the rosewood desk. Mattie had rescued it from the pocket of her denim skirt when she'd shown up a half hour earlier to hang the freshly laundered corduroy skirt in the wardrobe. Looking pale but composed, the girl had apologized briefly for "making a scene," then whisked Emma out of her gardening clothes and into the blue robe. She'd also delivered a hand-knit cardigan made of a heathery gray-blue angora wool—another present from Nanny Cole, whom Mattie described as a champion knitter.

Emma wondered briefly if Nanny Cole was under orders to supply all of the duke's guests with complete new wardrobes, then dismissed the thought with a laugh. She doubted that the blustery old woman took orders from anyone, including His Grace. If Nanny Cole had given up nannying for knitting and sewing, it had undoubtedly been her own decision. Emma had no idea why Nanny Cole would bestow such a gift on her, but she knew just what to do with the sweater. It would look very well with her charcoal-gray trousers tomorrow, when she kept her appointment with Derek.

11

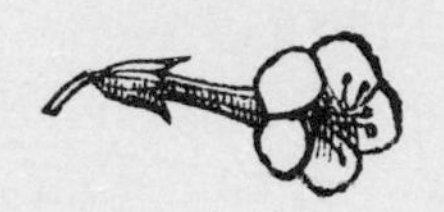

Emma stepped onto the terrace the next day to find Derek standing motionless, staring at the castle ruins, his hands thrust in the pockets of his faded jeans. He acknowledged her arrival with an absent nod. "Good news about Susannah," he announced. "Kate called from Plymouth."

"I heard: unconscious but stable." Emma turned from closing the French doors to see that Derek was already halfway across the lawn, head down and striding at top speed toward the arched entryway in the castle ruins.

A day ago Emma would have tripped over her own feet, trying to catch up. Now she watched with quiet amusement as Derek came to an abrupt halt, looked around in confusion, then turned back to her, bewildered.

"Good morning, Derek." Emma descended from the terrace one deliberate step at a time. "Did you sleep well? Isn't it a beautiful morning? And, by the way, do you think you could slow down, so I won't have to run to keep up with you?"

Derek took the rebuke gracefully. "Sorry. Hear the same complaint from Nell all the time." He swept an arm toward the arched entryway. "Please, you set the pace."

Mollified, Emma crossed the lawn, and they entered the castle ruins together. "What was it you wanted to show me?" she asked.

"This and that." Derek cast a glance over his shoulder. "Chapel first, then the library. Hope you don't mind." He smiled nervously when he saw Hallard seated on the wicker chair, tapping the keyboard of his laptop computer. "A pity Susannah hasn't regained consciousness, but at least she hasn't gone downhill."

Emma nodded. Mattie had come to share the news with her first thing that morning. Derek had nothing new to add to Mattie's report, and they walked down the grassy corridor in silence. Emma watched with increasing perplexity as Derek's eyes darted from doorway to staircase, scanned the way ahead, and turned to look back the way they'd come, and when she realized that she was doing the same thing, she stopped and turned to peer at him. "Are you looking for something?"

Derek blinked down at her for a moment before replying, "Suppose I am, actually. That's why I wanted to speak with you. Need another outsider, someone who's not familiar with Penford Hall, to bounce some ideas off of. Thing is"—he glanced over his shoulder—"just as soon we weren't overheard."

Emma looked around uneasily. Lowering her voice, she asked, "Does this have anything to do with Susannah?"

Derek was silent for a moment. Then he shrugged. "It might."

Emma nodded and they walked on, neither speaking again until they were in the chapel, with the door closed. Emma stood quite still, transfixed by the window's radiant beauty, but Derek went right up to it, frowning.

"Fair warning," he said, stalking back to Emma's side. "Going to sound a bit daft, but bear with me. If you still think I'm off my nut by the time I've finished, we'll forget the whole thing." He looked down at her anxiously. "What d'you say?"

"Go ahead," said Emma. "I'm listening."

Derek turned and pointed at the window. "Exhibit number one. What do you make of her?"

"She's glorious," said Emma. "Is she a local saint?"

"Semimythic heroine would be more precise. Legend has it that she used that lantern to guide one of Grayson's ancestors past the Nether Shoals one stormy night. Stood on this very spot. Chapel was built in her honor, window created to record her brave deed."

Emma walked halfway down the center aisle, noticing things she'd overlooked during her first, brief visit. Bantry's gardening tools were there, arrayed neatly along the back wall. Six rows of plain wooden benches sat on either side of the chapel's main aisle. A few feet to the left of the window was a back door even lower than the one they'd just come through. Centered beneath the window was a small granite shelf—for posies, Emma thought, though the shelf was empty now. But there were no tools, no scaffolding, nothing to indicate that any work was taking place.

"Isn't this the window you're restoring?" Emma asked.

"It was supposed to be," Derek replied, "but it's wrong, it's all wrong."

"How do you mean?" Emma turned to look at the window as Derek walked past her to stand before it.

"Her cloak, for one thing. What color would you say it is?"

"Black," Emma replied. "A sort of translucent, smoky black. Why?"

"According to the legend, the lady should be clad in purest white. Grayson claims that when he was a child the cloak was gray. His staff back him up. They all claim that the cloak, and only the cloak, has gradually changed from white to black. Now, I'm the first to admit that glass can change color, that it can cloud up or weather or get dirty." He looked at Emma expectantly.

"I'm with you," she said.

"None of those things have happened here. So, unless a chemical reaction has occurred that is entirely without precedent in the history of glass-making, I've no way to account for the darkening—no proof, in fact, that it's even taken place. Do you follow?"

"Just talk, Derek," Emma said impatiently.

Derek flushed. "Sorry. Being pedantic. Trouble is, I've tried to explain it to Peter and he's refused to understand. Boy's taken a liking to the lady. Been after me to 'fix her cloak.' That's what Grayson wanted me to do, of course. He'd hoped I could change the color with a chemical treatment, which I can't, or simply replace the glass, which I'm extremely reluctant to do, now that I've had a chance to examine it firsthand."

"Why not?"

"I'm very good at my job, Emma, but whoever created that window was a master. Wouldn't dream of interfering with his work. Grayson's disappointed, naturally, but he sees my point and quite agrees."

"But Peter doesn't?"

"No. Don't know why. He's usually quite reasonable." Derek ducked his head. "Don't know why I'm going on about my son at the moment, either, when I've so much else to tell you. Shall we continue on to my second exhibit?" Derek strode up the center aisle to open the back door, and Emma followed him out. Sunlight blinded her for a moment and she blinked rapidly, then gasped, pressing herself back against the chapel wall, panic-stricken.

She was standing on the edge of a cliff. Like the lady in the window, Emma could look straight down two hundred feet to the monstrous waves crashing on the rocks far below.

"I say . . ." Derek peered at her worriedly. "You don't suffer from vertigo, do you?"

For the first time, Emma became acutely aware of the thundering surf, a sound that had hitherto gone as unnoticed as the beating of her own heart. "It's a little late to be asking that question, isn't it?" she managed.

Derek seemed perplexed, a little hurt. "Wouldn't have let you stumble," he said. "That's why I came out first."

Emma tore her gaze from the crashing waves to glare at him, but he'd already turned away.

"Exhibit number two," he said, opening his arms to indicate the panorama of sea and sky. "What strikes you immediately about this setting?"

Now that she'd caught her breath, Emma had to admit that she wasn't actually teetering on the edge of the cliff. It was the openness of the spot that had startled her. No stunted trees or tangle of bushes blocked the sweeping view, and no rail or retaining wall warned of the two-hundred-foot drop to the sea. All that stood between her and the precipice were a few yards of tussocky ground.

She released her hold on the chapel and took a cautious half-step forward. Ahead of her, the English Channel stretched blue to the horizon. To her left, the beacon flashed from its rocky promontory, and to her right, beyond the chapel, the cliffs curved abruptly inward. She suppressed a shudder as a gust of wind snatched at her hair.

"It's unprotected," she said, in answer to Derek's question. "No shelter from the wind. I wouldn't want to be out here during a storm."

"But Grayson claims that this window's been out here, in all kinds of weather, for hundreds of years. Now, look." Derek reached up to run his hand across the irregular surface of the window. "You see? No pits, no scratches—no sign of weathering whatsoever. Even the solder is intact."

Emma frowned and leaned back against the wall. "So Grayson's supposedly ancient window shows no signs of age?"

"Strange, isn't it?"

"As strange as calling Penford Hall a ruin."

Derek's face lit up. "Nell's right. You do catch on quickly. Can't wait to show you the house plans. Here, let's go to the library."

Putting a protective hand on Emma's arm, Derek walked with her around the outside of the chapel garden to the rocky meadow where the cliff path began. The scent of gorse blossom was heavy and sweet and the air was clear. Emma could see the nests of gulls and black-faced oyster-catchers on the opposite cliffs and hear their constant cries echoing off the scarred rockface. Once they were on the path, Derek dropped his hand and they strolled side by side.

"According to Grayson," Derek said, "the original lantern, the actual, tin-shuttered candle lamp used by the lady in the legend, is supposed to be kept on display in the chapel. Legend has it that the ruddy thing lights itself once every hundred years. When it does, the duke of Penford is required to throw a sort of elaborate bean-feast. Supposed to take place this year, in fact. It's called the Fête, and it carries all sorts of historical weight with the villagers."

Emma recalled both the duke's request that she have the chapel garden ready by the first of August and the empty shelf below the lady window. "The Fête's coming up in August," she guessed, "but the lantern's missing, and Grayson can't hold one without the other."

Derek looked impressed. "Exactly right. Keep it to yourself, though, won't you? The staff know the lantern's gone, but the villagers don't and they'd be very upset."

Emma agreed, though she didn't really understand what all the fuss was about. "Why doesn't Grayson have a copy made?"

"I can tell you Grayson's reason. He spoke with such conviction that I can recall his words precisely." Derek turned to look intently at Emma. "Grayson said, 'I don't think you understand, old son. I believe in the legend. When the day of the Fête arrives, I fully expect the lantern to shine.' "

Emma's eyebrows rose.

"Quite," said Derek. "He asked me here not only to restore a perfectly sound window, but, because of my expertise in rummaging around old buildings, to search Penford Hall for an antique, self-lighting lantern."

As they approached the hall, Emma wondered how to pose her next question. Grayson appeared to be disturbingly willing to believe in anything related to the family legend—an ancient window that seemed untouched by time, a cloak that had mysteriously changed color, a lantern that lit of its own accord. Emma had heard of eccentric Englishmen before, but . . . "So, you're worried about the duke's . . . um . . . sanity?" she asked hesitantly.

"Worse than that, I'm afraid," said Derek, but he would say nothing more until they'd made their way through a door in the east wing and down a series of deserted corridors to the dark-paneled library. It, too, was deserted, and Derek's voice seemed startlingly loud as he crossed the room to take a large black morocco portfolio from a bookstand near the gallery stairs. "Grayson gave me a detailed set of house plans," he explained, "so I could search the place from top to bottom."

"Has anything turned up?" Emma asked.

Derek laid the portfolio flat on the long marquetry table behind the couch, then gestured to the portrait over the mantelpiece. "The dowager duchess's emeralds," he answered. "But Nell and Bertie stumbled over those."

"Nell and Bertie found Grandmother's wedding jewels?" Emma asked doubtfully.

"Stumbled over them. They were underneath a floorboard in the nursery. Must've thought it was the one place the old duke wouldn't look."

"*Who* must've thought?" Emma asked, thoroughly confused, but Derek's long strides had already taken him into a shadowy recess in the corner, where he bent low to retrieve a second portfolio. Its faded black leather was crumbling, one corner was cracked and peeling, and the covers were held together by frayed ribbons.

"Misplaced two sheets from the plans Grayson gave me," Derek said, laying the second portfolio beside the first. "Embarrassing gaffe, for a supposed expert in old houses. Came down to see if I could root out another set on my own. Found this." He placed a hand on the second portfolio. "It's the kind of survey that's done when a chap's thinking of putting his place on the market."

Derek gently teased the ribbons apart and opened the second portfolio. Emma glanced at the date on the topmost sheet. These house plans had been made fifteen years ago, only ten years before the most recent set.

"Like you to compare the two," said Derek. "They're a bit technical, I'm afraid, but, well, do your best."

Emma smiled tolerantly as she paged through the detailed drawings. She'd installed her share of mainframe computer systems over the years, laid cable in air-conditioning ducts, and rewired entire offices. She doubted that Derek could teach her much about reading house plans.

"You see . . ." Derek's fingers began to trace lightly across a page, then stopped as he cocked an ear toward the ceiling. Slowly, he raised his eyes to the gallery. "Nell," he said, sounding mildly affronted, and Emma looked up to see a curly blond head and a fuzzy brown one peering through the gallery's wooden railing.

"What are you doing up there?" Derek demanded. "Where's Peter?"

"Bertie said Peter needs time to himself," Nell explained. "And we found a little door up here, so—"

"Please inform Bertie that Emma and I would like some time to *our*selves, as well," said Derek. "Go ask Peter to read you a story."

"But Bertie said—"

"One moment, please, Emma." Taking the stairs three at a time, Derek ran up to the gallery, where he bent to confer with his daughter.

Emma turned back to the house plans and paged through them slowly, stopped, then started again. "New wiring," she murmured. "New plumbing . . ." Twenty years ago the rose suite hadn't even had a sink, let alone its own bathroom, and there'd been no fancy stove in the kitchen. She looked up as Derek returned, a bemused expression on his face.

"Nell gone?" she asked.

"Yes, but . . ." Derek rubbed the back of his neck. "My daughter informs me that it's nearly lunchtime." He reached down to toy with one of the frayed ribbons. "Have you any plans?"

Emma shrugged. "I'd intended to go down to the village to buy a few things this afternoon."

"All right." Derek took a deep breath, then jammed his hands into his pockets. "We'll go down together, then. They do a slap-up lunch at the Bright Lady—the village pub." He hesitated before adding apologetically, "Seems I've also agreed to have supper with my children in the nursery this evening. Don't know quite how it happened, but . . . well, rather awkward. Means you'll be dining alone."

"That's okay," said Emma. "I'm used to it."

"Shouldn't be," Derek snapped. He flushed, then jutted his chin toward the gallery. "That is to say, my daughter, Nell, wondered if you might join us for supper." A look of concern crossed his face. "You *are* eating, aren't you?"

Pulling in her stomach, Emma replied stiffly, "I'm not dieting, if that's what you mean."

"Thank God. After a week of Susannah and her food-fads, I'm ready to set light to every diet book on the market. Nothing wrong with a healthy appetite. Why, Mary could put away—" He faltered, then went on, haltingly. "My late wife enjoyed food. Don't know where she put it. She was small, like Peter. Same dark hair, too." He glanced at Emma, then quickly looked away. "She died just after Nell was born. Pneumonia."

Was that it? Emma wondered. Was that why he'd been so upset by the duke's graphic description of drowning? Emma knew there was no set timetable for grief, but five years seemed a long time for a mere anecdote to elicit such a strong reaction. Yet, looking at him now, hearing the pain in his voice, she knew it must be so. She felt a brief stab of envy—what must it be like to be missed so desperately?—but recoiled from it. If Derek's wife had loved him, she would not have wanted him to mourn like this. "I'm very sorry," she said.

"Me, too." Derek busied himself with closing the portfolios. "Look, why don't we head down to the village now? I can explain the house plans to you on the way. Don't mind walking, do you? Nell said it wouldn't bother you."

"Did she?" Emma smiled. Clearly, she'd made more of

an impression on Nell than she'd realized. "I suppose Bertie expressed an opinion of me, too?"

Some of the strain seemed to leave Derek's face as he gave Emma a sidelong look. "He did, in fact. Thinks you're quite splendid."

Emma had never received praise from a stuffed bear before, but as she watched Derek return the portfolios to their respective shelves, she felt irrationally pleased.

12

The cliff path wound around the east wing of Penford Hall and skirted the edge of the walled woodland before beginning a gradual descent into the valley that held the village of Penford Harbor. The prickly gorse soon gave way to bracken; the windswept rocky meadow to the still, sun-dappled shelter of the trees.

Derek had pulled off his sweater and tied its sleeves around his waist. He wore a wrinkled blue chambray workshirt underneath, and as he rolled up his shirtsleeves, Emma noticed his sinewy forearms. She wondered fleetingly how such strong hands could perform such delicate tasks—uncovering a whitewashed fresco, repairing fragile stained glass—then realized that Derek's eyes were on her, and redirected her gaze.

"Don't suppose you were able to make heads or tails out of the house plans," Derek said.

"I managed to pick out a thing or two," Emma admitted, amused but slightly nettled by Derek's condescending tone. "The plumbing and wiring have been completely revamped. New access panels, stack vents, feeder cables, supply lines, a whole new distribution board. If the cutaways are any indication, some floors have been raised and leveled, and a new roof's been put on." She glanced slyly at Derek. "Have I left anything out?"

"Er," said Derek.

"If I really struggled, I'll bet I could even figure out why you showed the plans to me," Emma continued, enjoying his discomfiture. "Let's see, now. The older plans suggest that the hall was in pretty bad shape fifteen years ago. If the old duke had them made up in order to sell the place, the family's finances must have been shaky, too. Your aside about the duchess's emeralds seems a little ominous. Why would she hide them in the nursery unless she was afraid that her son might try to sell them? And if Grayson's father was down to selling his own mother's wedding jewels—" She stopped walking and turned to face Derek, who was staring at her in amazement. "How am I doing?"

"Um." Derek blinked. "You work with computers, don't you?"

Emma nodded. "Sometimes my firm installs them. In great big buildings. With reams of technical drawings."

"Ah." Derek scuffed at the ground with the toe of his workboot. "Didn't mean to sound patronizing. Most women—"

"You'd be surprised at what most women know," Emma said lightly. "At any rate, I *do* see what you're getting at. Penford Hall underwent a major renovation five years ago. It must have cost a fortune."

"Repairs on the roof alone would run upwards of a hundred thousand pounds," Derek confirmed.

"A hundred thousand . . ." Emma gulped. "Just for the roof? Where did Grayson get money like that?"

"Susannah asked me the same question," said Derek. "Seemed to think I'd know."

"You were friends," Emma reminded him.

"Haven't seen him for ten years," Derek retorted. "And I never visited the hall. When I managed to make that clear to Susannah, she began asking me about Lex Rex. Went on about it until I was ready to chuck her over the nearest wall." Derek frowned suddenly, as though a new thought had occurred to him. "She must've been looking for me yesterday morning, when she . . ." His voice trailed off.

"Fell?" Emma suggested.

"That's the problem, you see." Coming to a halt, he turned to regard Emma worriedly. "A wealthy rock star drowns nearby, and Grayson's suddenly wealthy enough to refurbish the hall. Susannah claims to see a connection . . . and suddenly she's not around to ask uncomfortable questions anymore."

"No." Emma shook her head. "Grayson couldn't . . . He wouldn't . . ." She bit her lip, then tried again. "What I mean is, Grayson's so . . ."

"Charming? Gracious? I quite agree. But he's also a bit of a madman, wouldn't you say? And he knows how to sail, Emma. He's grown up hearing tales of shipwrecks and piracy, and he told me he'd do anything to make sure the bloody lantern lit on schedule. And in order for that to happen, the duke of Penford must be in possession of Penford Hall."

Emma opened her mouth to protest, then closed it again. After all, Mattie had told her outright that Susannah had been an unpopular figure at Penford Hall. Mild-mannered Bantry had come close to spitting on the duke's cousin, Nanny Cole had complained of her snooping, and, however well Kate had tried to hide it, she'd been annoyed by Susannah's needling. And Grayson . . . What had he said about his cousin? *She was raised by wolves, you know.*

She gazed at Derek, shaken. "Do you know what you're suggesting?"

Sighing, Derek ran a hand through his curls. "I know, and I hope it turns out to be a load of rubbish. But what if it's not? What if Grayson was involved in Lex's death? What if he got his hands on Lex's money? What if Susannah's found a way to prove it?"

Emma felt a sudden chill. When Kate had called this morning, she'd mentioned bringing Susannah back to Penford Hall as soon as she was well enough to travel. If Derek was right, if Susannah had discovered something connecting Grayson to Lex Rex's death, the hall might not be the safest place for her to recuperate. "Tell me more about Lex Rex," she said.

They walked slowly. Derek conscientiously moderated his long stride, and Emma was in no hurry. The path would eventually take them to the car park, and from there they would enter the village by the main—indeed the only—street. Until then, Emma had a lot of catching up to do. She listened closely while Derek told her what he knew of Charles Alexander King, more commonly known to his legion of fans as Lex Rex.

"They met in Oxford," Derek began. "Grayson was attending lectures and Lex was holed up in a garage somewhere, working on that first, dreadful video."

Emma searched her memory. "The black-and-white one with all the scratches?"

Derek nodded. "*Eat Your Greens.* In seven ear-splitting minutes, Lex managed to offend environmentalists, vegetarians, pacifists, and right-thinking people everywhere. Everyone else thought he was fantastic. Grayson must've thought so, too, though I'm hard-pressed to say what they had in common."

"It wasn't the music," Emma objected, recalling the fine precision of the duke's playing. "Perhaps he enjoyed the shock value. The old duke couldn't have approved of Lex."

Derek shrugged. "Whatever the case, the friendship didn't last. The old duke died and Grayson came back to Penford Hall, while Lex went on to fame and fortune. Five years later, I was reading about them in the papers."

"Wait," Emma broke in. "Didn't you meet Grayson at about the same time?"

"If you're wondering whether I met Lex as well, the answer is no. I should think it would be self-evident. I was a grown man, with a . . ." He faltered, recovered quickly, and went on. "With a wife and an infant son to look after. Hadn't any time to waste hanging about garages with the likes of Lex Rex."

A breeze rustled the leaves overhead, and a chaffinch streaked across the path. Emma watched Derek from the corner of her eye, saw his jaw muscles knot, his hands clench behind his back.

"Now, where was I?" he asked gruffly.

"Lex had gone on to fame and fortune."

"Right." Derek cleared his throat. "According to the newspaper accounts, Lex decided to pay his old friend a surprise visit. Treacherous things, country houses. Never know who's going to turn up."

"Sounds like the voice of experience," Emma said wryly. "Do you have a country house?"

"Family does. In Wiltshire. Comes to me when the old man pegs out."

"You don't seem pleased by the idea," Emma observed. "Don't you want the family mansion?"

"Too many strings attached." Derek's mouth quirked in an ironic smile. "My father disapproves of my profession. I'm the son of an earl with the soul of a bricklayer. The lord of the manor is not supposed to get his hands dirty."

"And a woman's place is in the home. I've been hearing that since I was old enough to wear an apron. Ridiculous, isn't it?" Emma picked up a stick and knocked the head off of a stray dandelion. "Your father should meet my mother. The world seems to be full of disappointed parents."

"A good many disappointed children, as well, I'll wager." Derek's smile softened.

"Please," Emma said, "go on with the story. I'll try not to interrupt."

"Interrupt all you like," said Derek, with a sidelong glance. "I don't mind." His curls tossed in the breeze and the sunshine made his blue eyes sparkle. Emma fumbled with the stick, then tossed it hastily away.

"Lex decided to surprise Grayson . . ." she prompted.

Derek gazed at her a moment longer, then ducked his head and continued. "Surprise was on Lex, as it turned out, because Grayson wasn't at home. Papers made a lot of fuss about this particular point, until it came out that Grayson had been in France, negotiating the repurchase of paintings his father had sold some years before. Grayson was understandably reluctant to advertise his father's penury."

"But if Grayson wasn't home . . ."

"His staff is awfully fond of him, don't you think? Terribly eager to please?"

"I suppose, but . . ." But it makes sense, Emma thought. It could have been a plot, with Grayson as the mastermind and the staff as co-conspirators. She thought back to her first evening at Penford Hall, to Grayson's soothing, seductive words at the dinner table. She'd joined his cause without a second thought. If he inspired such devotion in a total stranger, what kind of fierce loyalty might he inspire in his staff? "Go on," she said.

"Lex arrived, with his band in tow, and no Grayson to

surprise. Fools got into his brandy, then decided to hoof it down to the Bright Lady."

"That's the pub in Penford Harbor?"

"Where we're heading now. The band downed a few pints, jumped aboard Grayson's yacht, and took it out into one of the worst gales Cornwall's seen in fifty years. None of them were sailors, and the yacht was in poor repair. Miracle they got the ruddy thing going at all. But no one tangles with the Nether Shoals and lives to tell about it."

"The ship was wrecked?" Emma asked.

"Smashed to matchsticks. The band . . ." Derek's lips tightened. "They searched, of course. Grayson came tearing back from his trip to mount his own search, as well. But the currents around the Nether Shoals are notoriously unpredictable, even in fair weather. In that storm . . ." Derek shook his head. "Could be as far away as Spain by now."

Emma drew her sweater more closely around her. "And the press gave Grayson a pretty hard time?"

"Had a field day," Derek said. "Cro-Magnon musician perishes on aristocrat's leaky yacht—it was tabloid fodder. Yet another scandal at Buck House took the pressure off, but not before some enterprising journalist discovered that Lex had been virtually penniless. There was no estate left, after all the bills had been paid."

Emma wasn't surprised. The scenario was a familiar one—too many rock musicians lived life at high speed, spending their money faster than they earned it. Emma frowned suddenly and came to an abrupt halt.

"Penniless?" she repeated. She batted at a fly that buzzed in her face. "Then what are we worrying about? If Lex was broke, why would Grayson . . ." She hesitated, then finished lamely, ". . . do what you think he might have done?"

"This is the tricky bit." Derek peered cautiously into the woods on either side of the path, before saying, very quietly, "Lex's books—his financial records—were a bit of a mess. That's what gave rise to speculation in the first place. No one was quite sure what had become of his money, you understand?"

Emma nodded.

"The tabloids lost interest, and so did I. But Susannah didn't." Derek glanced around again, then leaned closer to Emma. His voice sank to a whisper. "Apparently, she befriended a chap, a banker. Happens I know him. Very precise sort of fellow. Collects butterflies. Susannah asked him to look into things, and he came away saying that there was something odd about the way Lex's accounts were set up. Nothing he could point a finger at. Just gave him a queer feeling that things weren't quite pukka."

"But how could Grayson—"

"Fiddle the books? No idea. Curious, though."

Emma agreed. As they resumed walking, she murmured, "It's a lucky thing Susannah's friend never talked to the press."

"Winslow?" Derek snorted. "Safe as houses. We were at school together. Hasn't changed a bit. If it hasn't got wings and antennae, he can't be bothered with it."

"I suppose that's why she approached him. If Susannah had blackmail on her mind, she wouldn't want to broadcast what she'd learned," Emma mused. Question after question cartwheeled through her mind. Had Grayson lured Lex down to Penford Hall? Had the shipwreck been planned? Had the staff been involved? Emma knew enough about computer security at banks to know that no electronic records were completely safe from prying eyes. It wouldn't be easy to break into private financial files, but it could be done. All you'd need was a fairly sophisticated . . . "*Hallard,*" she breathed.

"Where?" Derek asked in alarm.

Emma shook her head. "No, Derek, I didn't mean that. I just thought of a way for Grayson to syphon off Lex's funds. What do you suppose Hallard's doing with that laptop computer?"

"Hallard?" Derek said doubtfully. "Seems a bit dotty to me."

"Hackers frequently are," Emma replied dryly.

"Hackers?"

"Creative computer programmers," Emma explained. "Sometimes called computer nerds. They've been known to break into systems just for the fun of it."

"Fascinating."

Emma nodded, but her mind was already on other things. "Were there any witnesses to the shipwreck?"

"Only a few," Derek replied. "That's another thing that has me puzzled. Five years ago, the village of Penford Harbor was virtually abandoned."

The abandoned village is thriving, Emma thought, looking around the pub.

The Bright Lady was a low, whitewashed stone building on the harborfront, tucked between a half-timbered inn and the narrow, two-story harbormaster's house, which now served as Dr. Singh's infirmary. The pub was warm and cozy, dimly lit by the sunlight falling through the bull's-eye windows in the front. Pewter tankards and lengths of fishing net hung from the raftered ceiling, a back corner was devoted to a well-used dartboard, and a time-worn but lovingly polished bar jutted out into the center of the room, dividing it in two. On one side of the bar, an aged spaniel slept before a crackling fire, and the red-haired chief constable, Tom Trevoy, sat at a bare wooden table, writing doggedly on a pad of yellow paper and nursing a pint of the local ale.

Emma was sitting on the other side of the bar, at one of a half-dozen tables draped with linen and set with silver. Her table was in the front, near the windows, and she had a clear view of the harbor. Derek was speaking with three elderly women at a table in the back, answering the question Emma had heard many times as she and Derek had strolled down from the car park to the harbor.

Would Susannah's "mishap" delay the Fête? Everyone they'd met—from Mrs. Shuttleworth, quietly tending the marigolds in front of her husband's church, to the irascible Jonah Pengully, at whose ramshackle general store Emma had purchased work gloves, a sunhat, and a pair of wellington boots—had asked Derek the same thing. Faces had fallen when he'd declined to give a definite answer, but the villagers remained hopeful that word would come down from Penford Hall before nightfall.

Emma sipped her cider and watched out the window as three fishermen guided their boat into the harbor. She knew without looking that the boat would be in perfect condition, not a speck of paint chipped off of its sky-blue prow. She knew it because everything she'd seen so far in Penford Harbor had been perfect.

The church, with its ancient carvings and shining brasses; the tiny schoolhouse, with its computer terminals; the bakery, the butcher's shop, the boathouse—nothing was rundown or weatherbeaten. The whitewashed cottages, roofed in blue slate or wheat-colored thatch, looked as though they'd been painted fresh that morning.

The air of well-being was more than skin-deep. According to Derek, the small fishing fleet provided the village and the hall with a great variety of seafood, and Mr. Carroway, the greengrocer, grew vegetables all year round in a solar-heated greenhouse behind his shop. An inland town supplied Mr. Minion, the butcher, with mutton and beef—it was his van that Gash had been repairing—but

Herbert Munting, a middle-aged widower with a passion for poultry, provided him with chickens, geese, and other feathered delicacies from his multilevel henhouse. Mr. and Mrs. Tharby, the proud owners of the Bright Lady, made their own ale, pressed their own cider, and experimented with flavored liquors, but claimed that Crowley was the local authority on wine-making.

Penford Harbor's air of cheerful self-sufficiency should have been appealing, but Emma found it almost eerie. It was too polished, too pristine. Old Jonah Pengully, with his cluttered shop, moth-eaten gray pullover, and curmudgeonly manner, had come as a refreshing change of pace.

Emma turned away from the window as Derek took his seat, and nodded when the matronly Mrs. Tharby stopped at their table to assure them that their lunch would be right out. When she'd left, Emma murmured uncertainly, "Did we place an order?"

Derek smiled. "One doesn't order at the Bright Lady. One eats whatever Ernestine Potts decides to serve. She trained under Madama, so there's no need to worry. Matter of fact, I've promised to bring Nell a pot of Ernestine's jam."

"Strawberry jam?" Emma asked.

"Why, yes. How did you guess?"

Emma studied Derek closely, wondering how he could possibly be unaware of his daughter's fondness for strawberries. "She seems to eat a lot of them," she replied carefully.

"Is that unhealthy?" Derek asked, faintly alarmed. Emma reassured him as Mrs. Tharby returned with their food.

"Supreme of Cornish turbot," Mrs. Tharby informed them as she unloaded her tray. "Filled with a light scallop-and-grainy-mustard mousseline, and served on broad beans cooked French-style with a Chablis sauce. Ernestine's having fun today. Enjoy." She'd just turned away when the front door swung open.

"Hello, boys!" Mrs. Tharby called. "Your missus is expecting you for lunch, Ted."

Three fishermen had come into the pub, their rubber boots trailing water, their hands and faces reddened from the wind and sun. Emma recognized them as the three she'd seen sailing into the harbor moments before. The youngest appeared to be in his late twenties, the oldest somewhere in his thirties. Emma thought she detected a family resemblance in their upturned noses and dark, wavy hair, and a moment later, Derek confirmed it, introducing her to the Tregallis brothers: Ted, Jack, and James.

"Told Debbie I'd stop by here to drop off the papers," Ted replied to Mrs. Tharby as she headed for the kitchen. "How're things up at the hall, Tom?"

"Peaceful, so far," said the red-haired chief constable.

Ted placed a bundle of newspapers before Chief Constable Trevoy while Jack and James came over to shake hands with Derek. Their heavy wool sweaters reeked of sweat, diesel oil, and fish.

"Press conference went well," Ted called from the chief constable's table. "Seen the rags yet?"

Derek shook his head. "How bad is it?"

"See for yourself." Ted brought several of the papers over to Derek. The first contained a black-and-white photograph of a scantily clad Susannah cavorting beside the words:

ASHERS SMASHERS!

"Blast," Derek muttered. "Must've got the snap from Syd."

"Bastards probably nicked it off him," said Jack, wincing as Ted jabbed an elbow into his side and told him to mind his language.

"The other one's not so bad," said Chief Constable Trevoy, holding up a second newspaper. Its front page featured an unflattering photograph of Grayson surrounded by white-coated doctors, paired with a gorgeous shot of Susannah in a semitransparent gown, stretched full-length on her back on a rocky beach. The headline screamed:

FALLEN BEAUTY!

"Doubt Debbie'll let me keep 'em in the house," said Ted ruefully. "Not with Teddy around. My ten-year-old," he explained to Emma.

"We could keep 'em on the boat," Jack suggested, and was rewarded with a swift clout in the head from James, who asked, "This won't affect the Fête, will it, sir?"

With admirable patience, Derek confessed yet again that he really didn't know, and the Tregallis brothers trooped off to Ted and Debbie's house for their midday meal, while Chief Constable Trevoy scanned through the rest of the papers. Mrs. Tharby returned to the table shortly, with a fresh round of drinks. Before leaving them to enjoy their lunch, she put a hand on Emma's arm. "I just wanted to say what a pleasure it is to meet the garden lady. God bless you, dear. I've heard so much about you." The Penford Hall grapevine, it seemed, was linked directly to the village.

13

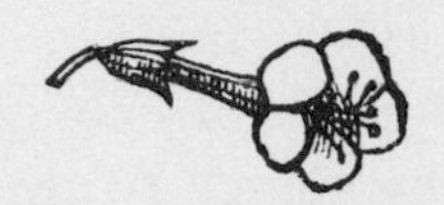

Emma leaned over the retaining wall of the gray granite quay to look down at the lapping waves, while Derek stood beside her, facing the village. In the harbor, a gull plummeted headfirst into a wave, then rose back into the air, wings straining, a sliver of silver in its beak. A cool breeze caressed Emma's face as she followed the gull's flight upward and along the edge of the enclosing cliffs.

It was like standing at the bottom of a canyon. The curving walls were neither as steep nor as barren as they'd appeared from above. The rockface was cross-hatched with cracks, and a scattering of twisted cedars, buckthorn bushes, and tufts of purple rock samphire clung to narrow ledges.

The beacon and the chapel stood like sentinels on either side of the narrow opening in the canyon wall, where the sea swept in. Emma could easily imagine Grayson's pirate ancestor hiding out in this sheltered cove, though he would have had to be a good seaman to maneuver his ship past the shoals. Emma's gaze came to rest on a spot just beyond the mouth of the cove, where the water swirled and eddied, and ruffling waves seemed to break on an unseen shore.

"The Nether Shoals," she murmured. She and Derek had retraced Lex's steps from the door of the Bright Lady to the very spot where the duke's yacht had once been docked. The cleats were still there, set firmly in the stone walkway, even though, as Susannah had taken pains to point out, the yacht had never been replaced.

But nearly everything else in Penford Harbor had been. Derek observed that the village had almost certainly undergone a renovation as extensive as the one that had taken place at Penford Hall. "I know how long it takes for rafters to settle, new thatch to turn from yellow to dusty brown," he'd told her. "It's not an exact science, but I'm willing to swear that most of these buildings were decaying ruins in the not-too-distant past. Someone's done a great deal to lure people back here and make them want to stay."

Derek turned to her now, his shoulder brushing hers as he leaned beside her on the wall. "Another odd thing about the Penford family legend," he murmured. "In order for Grayson to bring it to fruition, there must also be a village."

Emma shivered. "Let's go back to the hall," she said, glancing upward. The sky was clouding over and the waves were kicking up. "I need to think, and it looks like another storm is moving in."

Derek telephoned from the Bright Lady, and Gash came to meet them at the car park, then drove them the rest of the way up. The azaleas fluttered by, but Emma scarcely noticed them, and when the hall came into view, she smiled ruefully. She was ashamed to admit it, but the past two days had, without doubt, been the most interesting two days in her whole life. And a part of her didn't want them to end.

Lady Nell, Master Peter, and Sir Bertram of Harris request the pleasure of your company at supper tonight in the nursery.
At seven o'clock.
Dad's coming, too.

The last two lines had been added as a postscript, crowded in below the tempera-paint scrolls and flowery flourishes that framed the rest of the hand-printed text. Emma stood on the balcony and reread the invitation. It had been lying on the floor just inside her room when she'd returned from Penford Harbor, as though someone had slipped it under the door. She hadn't yet sent her reply.

Derek had given her so much to think about. She would have liked to spend some time in the garden—she always thought more clearly with a trowel in her hand—but the clouds had moved in and the air was heavy with ozone. Suddenly, there was a patter of rain, then a downpour, brief and powerful, followed by a steady, ground-soaking shower.

It's a good thing Bantry stored the gardening tools in the chapel, Emma thought, turning to go inside. Otherwise, they'd be—

Emma froze in the doorway, then turned slowly back to watch the falling rain. It had rained the other night, as well, the night before she and Nell had found Susannah. There'd been a heavy mist that morning, too. Bantry had tied an oilcloth over the wheelbarrow to protect his tools from just such weather, as any good gardener would.

But the oilcloth had not been on the wheelbarrow that morning. When Emma had reached for it, she'd found it on the flagstone path. Yet the tools had been bone-dry when Bantry had taken them from the barrow that afternoon. Emma touched a hand to her glasses, then folded her arms, perplexed. Someone had removed the oilcloth from the wheelbarrow sometime after the rain had stopped and the mist had burned off. Someone had been in the garden on the morning of Susannah's accident.

But who? Emma couldn't imagine Susannah soiling her hands on the old oilcloth, and if Bantry had untied it he wouldn't have left it lying on the path.

Peter, perhaps? He'd spent the morning on the cliff path, very near the chapel garden. He might have slipped inside to take a peek at the tools. It was only natural for a little boy to be curious about such things.

Should she ask him about it tonight? Emma glanced down at the neatly printed invitation, and shook her head. No need to spoil the children's grand occasion. She would ask Bantry about the oilcloth in the morning.

A hail of raindrops gusted onto the balcony and Emma ducked into the bedroom. Wiping the rain from her face, she crossed to the rosewood desk to compose an acceptance, then rang for Mattie to deliver it.

The invitation suggested that supper in the nursery would be a formal affair, and Emma went to the wardrobe, wishing she'd brought something other than her trusty teal, only to find another dress hanging in its place. Emma's hand slid slowly down the door of the wardrobe, then rose to adjust her glasses. She could scarcely believe her eyes.

Silver-gray satin gleamed like liquid moonbeams in the lamplight. The dress was simply cut, with three-quarter-length sleeves, a close-fitting bodice, a modest décolletage, and a full skirt that would fall just below her knees. Emma reached out a tentative hand to touch the skirt and sighed as the lustrous fabric rustled beneath her fingertips.

"Excuse me, miss."

Emma jerked her hand back and turned to face Mattie, who was standing in the doorway of the dressing room.

"I wouldn't handle it, miss, not until you've had your bath." When Emma made no reply, the girl added uncertainly, "I did knock, miss, but you didn't seem to hear."

"That's all right," said Emma, coming out of her daze. "But this dress, Mattie. Did Nanny Cole . . . ?"

"Lady Nell and I thought you might be needing a few extra frocks, seeing as you'd brought so few of your own, and Nanny Cole agreed. I hope you don't mind."

"Mind?" Emma looked back at the dress and smiled dreamily. "No. I don't mind."

The nursery occupied several large rooms on the top floor of Penford Hall. Peter was waiting for Emma at the door to the central room, which he referred to as the day nursery. He escorted her to an armchair, brought her a glass of fizzy lemonade, then stood nervously adjusting his tie and tugging at his blazer.

"You look very distinguished tonight," said Emma. She leaned forward for a closer look at his tie. "Are you at Harrow this year?"

"No," Peter replied. "This is Grayson's old tie and his blazer, too. He lent them to me for the evening. Nanny Cole had to take up the sleeves." He pulled at a cuff. "Papa wanted me to go to Harrow. That's where he went. I wanted to go, too, but—" Peter bit his lip.

"But what?" Emma coaxed.

Peter lowered his eyes, then murmured confidentially, "It's a boarding school."

"I see," said Emma, though she did not see at all.

"Grayson's been teaching me cricket," Peter continued conversationally. He frowned and pursed his lips. "I think I'm beginning to see the point of it."

Emma sipped her lemonade, uncertain what to say. She wasn't used to children pondering the meaning of schoolyard games. She wondered briefly if cricket inspired such dubious devotion in all young boys, but before she could frame a tactful question, Peter excused himself and went to see what was keeping Nell.

The day nursery had soft rugs, soft chairs, and a hard horsehair sofa. A map of the world had been painted on one wall, and the others held framed pencil drawings of Penford Hall, the ruined castle, and the harbor. Emma suspected that the drawings were the fledgling efforts of a young Grayson.

An enormous black-and-white rocking horse sat near the windows, a butterfly net leaned in one corner, and low shelves ran right around the room. The shelves were filled with books and toys and mysterious, unmarked boxes that might have held puzzles or models or brigades of toy soldiers. The large table at the center of the room had been set for supper, and Crowley stood over a long row of chafing dishes, waiting to serve the meal.

It took Emma several minutes to realize that the toys had been arranged in alphabetical order, a few minutes longer to figure out that the fifth place at the table had been set for Bertie. She looked from the wooden abacus to the stuffed zebra, and back to the encyclopedias piled on the chair to give the small brown teddy needed height, and wondered if all children behaved this way.

Emma raised a hand self-consciously to her hair. Mattie had brushed it until it crackled, then let it fall around her shoulders like a cloud. Nanny Cole had sent up the sapphire pendant that now hung around Emma's neck, and the pair of satin pumps that graced her feet. Nanny Cole, Mattie had informed her, as she threaded a thin silver ribbon through Emma's hair, was a stickler for accessories.

Emma's hand dropped to her lap when Derek ambled in, wearing the same faded jeans and wrinkled workshirt he'd worn to Penford Harbor. He hadn't even bothered to comb his hair. At the sight of Emma, he stood stock-still, then spun on his heel and left the room.

Emma looked confusedly at Crowley, who responded with a silent shrug. The glass of lemonade had barely touched Emma's lips when the hall door banged open again and Nanny Cole barreled in, her twin set and tweed skirt still trailing bits of yarn and snippets of thread.

"Up you get," she commanded, and Emma jumped to her feet. "Let's have a look at you." Blushing furiously, Emma turned in a circle while Nanny Cole muttered, "Lady Nell was right. Color suits you." A needle-pricked finger jabbed in the direction of Emma's chair. "Sit," Nanny Cole barked. Raising her head, she bellowed, "Lady Nell! Front and center!"

Peter came out first. His eyes were bright with anticipation and a certain furtiveness, as though he knew a wonderful secret they were all about to share. He came to stand beside Emma, then fixed his gaze upon the open doorway and waited.

The lights dimmed suddenly, a match flared, and Emma heard the hiss of escaping gas. She looked over as Crowley held a match to a gleaming brass gaslight mounted on the wall above the chafing dishes. He replaced the frosted chimney before circumnavigating the room, lighting gaslights as he went. When he'd finished, the day nursery was flooded with a diffuse, golden light that made Emma's new dress shimmer.

On his way back to his post, Crowley paused at Emma's elbow. "Have no fear, Miss Porter," he murmured. "Lady Nell requested that we use the gaslights this evening, but they are merely a temporary arrangement."

"What the bloody hell else would they be?" thundered Nanny Cole, blazingly affronted. "Think we'd pipe *gas* to the *nursery?*" She would have gone on to greater heights of vituperation, but even Nanny Cole fell silent when Nell stepped into the room.

The little girl was wearing silk. Her gown was white and floor-length, high-waisted and puff-shouldered, with long, close-fitting sleeves. Lacy wrist-frills hid her dimpled hands, satin slippers peeped demurely past the seed pearls at her hem, and a diminutive tiara twinkled among her golden curls. Her small chocolate-brown escort wore a black top hat and a dashing black cape lined in red silk. Radiant in the gaslight's gentle glow, Nell regarded them serenely, a tiny, ethereal empress, a fairy queen of charm and dignity, holding court.

Nanny Cole caught herself in the midst of a curtsy, growled, "It'll do," and blustered from the room. Emma, who had risen at Nell's entrance, had to remind herself forcibly not to bend a knee when Nell offered her hand.

"Good evening, Emma." The little girl looked past Emma, and her composure cracked a bit. "Papa!" she exclaimed. *"Mais, que vous êtes beau!"*

"Speak English, if you please, Queen Eleanor." The good-natured remonstrance came over Emma's shoulder, and she turned to see Derek standing there, tall and broad-shouldered and flawlessly attired in white tie and tails, shoes polished, hair combed, and chin freshly shaved.

"That was fast," said Emma, trying not to stare.

"Had Hallard's help. Someone else's, too, I think." Derek looked suspiciously at his daughter. "I don't seem to recall packing this outfit."

Nell's innocent blue eyes widened. "I found it in the storeroom, back with Mum——"

"Why don't we all sit down?" Peter broke in. "Come on, Nell." He took his sister unceremoniously by the wrist and led her to the table.

Derek hesitated for a moment, then drew himself up to his full height, executed an elegant half-bow, and offered his arm to Emma.

Nell proved to be a charming hostess, encouraging her father to tell of past adventures, which ranged from being chased by a disgruntled ewe through a hilly field in Yorkshire to finding himself at the business end of a broadsword wielded by a drunken caretaker who'd discovered him prying up floorboards in a summerhouse in Devon.

"Tell Emma what you did then," Nell coaxed.

"I know how much a broadsword weighs," Derek replied, with a self-effacing shrug. "It's no match for a crowbar."

Derek's anecdotes gradually gave way to another kind of conversation, in which his daughter took the lead. Derek listened avidly as Nell described her new play group, and seemed taken aback when she informed him that Peter had dropped out of the Boy Scouts. Slowly, it dawned on Emma that Nell was bringing her father up to date on happenings at home.

"Yorkshire, Devon—your job seems to involve a lot of travel," Emma observed, wondering how long it had been since Derek had really touched base with his children.

"It does," Derek agreed. "Didn't so much when Nell was little, but it's built up over the years."

"It can't be easy, with a family," Emma commented.

"Wasn't, at first, though having the workshop at home made it a bit easier. Had an au pair from Provence for a while—that's where Nell learnt her French. But now we have a marvelous housekeeper. Lives in. Treats Peter and Nell as though they were her own."

"She doesn't tell us stories," Nell pointed out. "Not like Aunt Dimity."

Emma put her fork down and looked questioningly at

Derek. "That's the second time I've heard Nell mention that name. The duke said something about an Aunt Dimity, too. Who is she?"

"A kind woman we met while I was working on the church in Finch," Derek replied. "The Pyms introduced us to her."

"She lives in London, but she's bosom chums with Ruth and Louise," Nell informed her. "Aunt Dimity sent you here."

Derek smiled indulgently. "Forgive my daughter. She has an overactive imagination, though in this case she may be right. Dimity Westwood does good works through something called the Westwood Trust. Grayson's grandmother was on the board, as Grayson is now."

Emma nodded. "So Grayson spoke to Dimity, and Dimity spoke to the Pyms, and they—" She turned to Nell. "Perhaps you're right, Nell. Aunt Dimity may have had a hand in bringing me to Penford Hall."

"Of course she did," Nell said blithely.

"She tells fantastic stories," Peter put in. "Better than books."

"She looks after people," Nell said. She cast a sly glance at her father as she added, "And bears."

"Now, Nell, we've talked about Bertie before," Derek scolded gently. "It was splendid of Aunt Dimity to give him to you, but you know very well that she made him brand-new, just for you." Turning to Emma, he said, "Nell's convinced that Bertie was around when she was a baby, that he somehow disappeared, and that Aunt Dimity 'returned' him to her. Don't know where she got the notion, but—"

"It's all right, Papa," Nell said forgivingly. "You just forgot, is all. Bertie says it's because you were so sad when Mama died."

Peter choked on a mouthful of lemonade, and Emma

patted his back, feeling a jab of impatience as the now-familiar shadow settled over Derek's features. Surely the children were allowed to mention their own mother in his presence. Who else could they talk to about her? The housekeeper? The affairs of the Harris household were none of Emma's business, but she wasn't about to let Derek spoil the children's evening—or hers—with another wave of self-pity. Leaving Peter to Crowley's ministrations, she took the bull by the horns.

"Well," she said briskly, "I'm sure your father had a lot on his mind when your mother died, Nell, but that was a long time ago. You'd never forget Bertie now"—she kicked Derek under the table—"would you, Derek?"

Grunting, Derek shot her a look of pained surprise, but answered hastily, "No. Certainly not. How could I forget old Bertie?" Bending to rub his shin surreptitiously, he added, "Peter, what on earth are you doing?"

Peter had slipped away from the table. "I'm helping Mr. Crowley," the boy said, flushing.

"There's no need, Master Peter," the old man said. "I quite enjoy stacking crockery."

"Why don't you play with the Meccano set, Peter?" Nell suggested, with a sidelong look at Emma.

"Splendid idea," Derek said. Noting Emma's puzzled expression, he told her, "I believe they're called erector sets in the States. Bits of metal, pulleys, motors. It's quite good fun. Peter built a working drawbridge for a science fair last year. Had to go into the school to explain that engineering is, in fact, a science."

"But the table's full," Peter pointed out. "Where will I set it up?"

"Come on," said Emma, kicking off her shoes, "we'll set it up on the floor."

"On the floor?" Peter said doubtfully.

"Why not?" said Derek, loosening his tie.

The mechanical masterpiece they created that evening would have made Rube Goldberg proud. After a tentative start, Peter hunkered down beside Emma and Derek on the rug, his tongue between his teeth and his tie askew, totally absorbed. The three of them carried on long after Crowley had cleared the table, while Queen Eleanor sat sidesaddle on the rocking horse, holding Bertie in her arms, humming softly to herself, and smiling down on them.

14

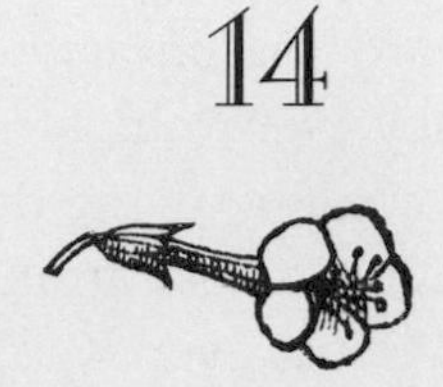

Syd Bishop came back from Plymouth the following day, ostensibly to supervise the installation of a hospital bed and other medical equipment. In fact, it was Crowley who directed the workmen, and Mattie who took charge of Susannah's things, while the paunchy, balding agent sat in the library, a shaken man.

"She don't know me," he'd said, when Kate Cole had guided him into the dining room, where Emma, Derek, Peter, and Nell were just finishing a leisurely lunch. The children had greeted Mr. Bishop politely while Emma and Derek exchanged troubled glances. The man did not look well.

Kate looked even worse. "Susannah has regained consciousness," she told them. Her voice was rough-edged, her eyes were bruised with fatigue, and her dark hair was tangled. "She seems to have lost her memory"—Syd groaned and Kate tightened her hold on his arm—"but it may be only a temporary condition. Dr. Singh hopes she'll be able to travel soon." Kate leveled a meaningful stare at Derek as she added, "I think Mr. Bishop—Syd—could do with a stiff drink."

Derek rose from the table at once. "Peter, Nell—run along to Bantry and stay with him. I'll join you later." The children exited quietly through the French doors, while Derek moved to put a supporting arm around Syd's shoulders. "Buck up, old chap. Susannah must be a great deal better or there wouldn't be all this talk about releasing her from hospital. That's good news, wouldn't you say?" As he spoke, Derek steered Syd out of the room and down the hall toward the library.

Kate waited until they were out of sight, then walked shakily to the nearest chair and sat down, covering her face with her hands. Emma rose from her place to join Crowley, who was hovering over Kate, but Kate waved them both away. "Nothing wrong," she said weakly. "Stupid of me. Just tired."

Crowley folded his arms and looked down his long nose at Kate. "We've been missing our meals, haven't we, Miss Kate. We've been staying up until all hours." He clucked his tongue and stalked from the room in high dudgeon before Kate could say a word.

Emma gestured to the bowl of peaches, the silver coffee service. "Can I get you anything?" she asked.

"Crowley will see to it." Kate brushed a strand of hair back from her forehead and reached for a napkin.

"He's right, you know." Emma pulled a chair closer to Kate's and sat down. "You do look as though you've been burning the candle at both ends."

Kate leaned toward Emma, weaving slightly, punch-drunk with exhaustion. "Television, radio, newspapers, magazines—it takes some candle-burning to keep the lot of them away from the hall."

Emma nodded thoughtfully. "Yes, Bantry told me about the trouble Grayson had a few years ago. I suppose you've made a special study of trespassing laws?"

Kate responded with a short, humorless laugh. "Why bother when we've had so much practical experience?"

Emma looked at her uncertainly. "But Bantry told me you were a lawyer—a solicitor."

"Is that what Bantry told you?" Kate raised a hand to her cheek and chuckled softly. "The old dear must be protecting my reputation." Kate leaned back in her chair and sighed. "If I were as old as Crowley, or a man, it wouldn't pose such a problem, but a young woman sitting at the foot of Grayson's table without benefit of clergy . . . Can't blame Bantry, really. Sometimes I wonder what I'm doing here, too."

"Grayson seems to depend on you," Emma said.

"True," Kate agreed. "Especially now. It's a real mess this time."

"But you don't act as his solicitor?"

Kate sighed. "I'm just the girl from Penford Harbor, Grayson's childhood chum. Good old Kate, that's me." She closed her eyes. "Sorry, Emma. Good old Kate is feeling older than usual today."

"Don't worry—I know just how you feel." Emma raised a hand to straighten her glasses. "But if you're dissatisfied with the . . . the situation, why do you stay?"

Kate's eyes opened and she turned her head to stare at Emma for a moment before replying firmly, "Penford Hall is my home, too."

The two women sat in silence until Crowley returned, bearing a large bowl on a silver tray. The scent of chicken soup wafted across the room, reminding Emma of Herbert Munting and his multilevel henhouse in the village.

"Miss Kate," Crowley declared imperiously, "Madama has prepared this especially for you. You are not to leave the table until you've finished every drop." He placed the bowl before Kate and remained standing over her, as though he intended to keep track of each spoonful. "We wouldn't want your mother to see you like this, now, would we, Miss Kate?"

The wistful expression on Kate's face gave way to one of warm affection. She reached up and punched Crowley lightly on the arm. "Humbug," she said fondly. "Do you know how long it's been since you've threatened to turn me in to Mother?" She faced Emma. "He used to do it all the time when I was a little girl. Had me and Grayson trembling in our wellies till it dawned on us that he'd never really rat us out."

Unmoved, Crowley pointed sternly to the bowl. "The bouillon is cooling rapidly, Miss Kate."

"Will we see you at supper?" Emma asked.

" 'Fraid not. I only came back to make sure Syd got here in one piece. It's all been a bit much for him. Gash will drive me back to Plymouth this evening, and I'll stay there with Grayson to arrange for Susannah's return. Dr. Singh thinks we should be able to bring her back in three or four days."

Crowley opened the hall door. "I beg your pardon most sincerely, Miss Porter, but Miss Kate really must eat, then get some rest."

Kate smiled wryly and picked up her spoon. "If you'll excuse me, Emma, the warder here prohibits talk during mealtimes."

Good old Kate is growing restless, Emma thought as she headed for the library. Still, it was unlikely that she'd ever leave Penford Hall. She seemed to love the place as much as Grayson, and the staff treated her with a special tenderness. To Bantry, Kate was the pride of Penford Harbor, and she was clearly the apple of Crowley's eye.

Slowing her pace, Emma thought back to her conversation with Bantry early that morning. She'd found him in the kitchen garden, watering the vines on the birdcage arbor. When she'd asked if he knew what had happened to the oilcloth, he'd led her to a side room that served as his potting shed. It had been roofed over with tightly joined wooden boards and fitted out with a workbench, shelves, cupboards, a pegboard with hooks, and a standing pipe that supplied water from the hall.

Bantry had pulled the oilcloth from behind a coil of rope in one of the large cupboards. It had been washed and neatly folded, but Emma could see a ragged tear at one corner, where a grommet had been pulled out.

"Gash brought it back with him from Plymouth," Bantry told her, "after he dropped off Kate and His Grace. Have to remember to bring it down to Ted Tregallis for mending."

Emma fingered the frayed edges thoughtfully. "Did you tear it when you uncovered the wheelbarrow the other day?"

"What're you talkin' about, Miss Emma?" Bantry squinted at her, perplexed. "I never uncovered the barrow, and I'd've had a thing or two to say to anyone who did. Don't hold with leavin' things lyin' about for the damp to get at 'em." He put the oilcloth back in the cupboard and brushed his palms together. "Nope. Lads on the chopper must've torn it, when they was loadin' poor Miss Susannah aboard."

Or, thought Emma, turning into the long corridor near the library, someone yanked the oilcloth off of the barrow hard enough to tear it. She slowed her pace once more. Peter had discovered blood on the handle of the grub hoe, hadn't he? Emma came to a full stop as a moving image filled her mind.

In the clear light of morning, a faceless figure ripped the oilcloth from the barrow, seized the hoe, and swung the long handle at Susannah's head. Susannah crumpled soundlessly and tumbled down the stairs. Panicked, the attacker shoved the hoe back into the barrow and fled the garden, leaving Susannah for dead.

Could that person have been Kate? Kate seemed to share Grayson's fanatic loyalty to Penford Hall, and where there was fanaticism, there might be violence. Emma removed her glasses and pinched the bridge of her nose unhappily. She liked Kate. She admired the way Kate had kept her head when dealing with the emergency in the garden, and her temper when faced by Susannah's taunting. Still, Emma conceded reluctantly, Kate had a motive to silence Susannah. If the duke's cousin exposed a cover-up of Lex's murder, Kate Cole would lose everything she held dear.

As she approached the library, Emma felt a prick of anger toward Susannah for stirring things up, but it passed quickly. No one deserved a death sentence for asking uncomfortable questions. Emma reminded herself that she would do better to reserve her anger for the person who'd passed that sentence. Replacing her glasses, she opened the library door. Derek caught sight of her, got up from his chair, and crossed to meet her.

"Derek," she began, but he cut her off.

"Not now," he murmured. "Think you should hear what Syd has to say."

Syd was seated on the couch. His face was ashen and the whiskey glass trembled in his hand. A fire was burning in the hearth and he stared at it without blinking. He didn't seem to notice Emma's arrival or Derek's return. "Poor kid," he mumbled. "Poor kid."

Derek slid into his chair and waited for Emma to take the one beside him. He rested his hands on the arms of the chair, crossed his legs, then asked in a soft, level voice, "You've known Susannah for a very long time, haven't you, Syd?"

It was like watching a hypnotist at work. Syd, the compliant subject, sat motionless, speaking in a flat monotone, as though a tape recorder were unreeling somewhere inside of him. "My grandpa was a tailor, and my old man went a step up, into fashion. That's how I got my start, setting up my old man's London office. Small potatoes, nothing fancy, not like them big shots on Savile Row. Stupid bastards wouldn't take a look at Suzie."

"But you would," said Derek.

"You bet I would. Suzie's ma brought her to me when she was, let's see, now . . . fifteen? Luckiest day in my life. Never seen anything like her. A regular ice princess. There's a lotta guys'd give a kid like that all kinds of crap. Not me. Always looked out for her. Never let her take crap offa nobody."

"You worked very hard to get her started," prompted Derek.

"Not as hard as Suzie. Lotta kids know what they want. Not so many want to work to get it. Always been a hard worker, Suzie has." Syd paused to wet his lips, then went on in his low monotone. "She hadda be, after her old man blew his brains out."

Emma turned, wide-eyed, to Derek, who motioned her to silence, then resumed his gentle interrogation. "When did that happen, Syd?"

"Like I told you, Suzie was just a kid. Her old man got suckered into some cheesy investments and lost his shirt." Syd shrugged. "Who hasn't? There's worse things could happen to a person, am I right? This poor schmuck didn't think so. Checked into a hotel in Ipswich and put a gun in his mouth. Left Suzie's ma in hock up to her fanny. That's how come Suzie started working. That's how come she won't quit."

"Why should she quit, Syd?" Derek's voice suggested

only mild curiosity, but his knuckles were white on the arms of his chair.

"Not so much work anymore. Not top dollar. Not for a while now. It's a short-term deal, am I right? Fashions change, models get old. One day you're it, the next day the phone stops ringing. Happens alla time. Truth is, Suzie's broke."

"But she was so successful," Derek protested.

"She hadda pay off her old man's debts. And support her old lady. And now she's buyin' stuff she can't afford. What else is new? It's hard to swallow, knowin' nobody wants you. Don't know how we're gonna handle the doctor bills."

"I've told you not to worry about that," Derek soothed. "I'm sure that Grayson will see to anything the National Health doesn't cover."

"Damn right he will. He owes it to her."

Derek leaned forward in his chair. "How do you mean, he owes it to her?"

Syd slowly turned to face Derek, like a teacher disappointed by an inattentive pupil. "I told you," he said wearily. "Grayson's father, he's the one gave the bad tip to Suzie's dad. He's the reason Suzie's dad killed himself." He reached out a shaking hand to pat Derek's knee. "Hey, it's history, am I right? Maybe it'll work out for the best. Could be the publicity's all Suzie needs to get back on top." The old man's eyes returned to the fire. "Once they fix her kisser . . ."

Derek went to sit beside Syd. He removed the whiskey glass from the older man's unresisting grasp and placed it on the end table. "Why don't you let Hallard take you upstairs for a nice lie-down?" he suggested. "It'll do you a world of good."

"Yeah. I could use some shut-eye. Gotta be fresh for Suzie." Syd looked down at his rumpled plaid jacket and touched a finger to his gaudy floral tie. "Lookit me. A regular fashion plate."

Emma gazed through her glass of whiskey at the fire. The flames blurred and flickered, but they seemed to give off little heat. Derek stood close to the fire, one arm resting on the mantelpiece, as though he, too, had felt the sudden chill.

"I wonder . . ." Emma murmured. "Grayson knew all along that he'd inherit Penford Hall and that he'd need a fortune to restore it. Do you think he befriended Lex—"

"In order to kill him and take his money?" Derek shook his head. "Doubtful. If Grayson could've predicted Lex's success, he could've made his fortune in the music industry."

"I suppose you're right," Emma conceded. "But he must have known about Lex's drinking habits. And everyone knew how wild he was. Richard once said that Lex would do anything on a dare. So, when opportunity knocked . . ."

". . . Grayson simply arranged for Lex to kill himself." Derek nodded. "Very convenient. Who's Richard?"

"An old friend," Emma said, too carelessly. "He was a big fan of Lex's."

"Poor chap. Tone-deaf?"

Emma suppressed an unseemly snort of laughter and ignored the question. "So what have we come up with? Grayson arranges Lex's death and embezzles his money—electronically. Susannah, looking for a way to avenge her father's suicide, roots out Winslow—your boyhood friend, the banker—and Winslow discovers something funny about Lex's books. Susannah comes to Penford Hall bent on blackmail—"

"To punish the House of Penford for her father's death," Derek put in.

"And she ends up with her head caved in."

"That seems to be the gist," said Derek.

Emma frowned. "But it's been five years since Lex died. Why did Susannah wait so long to make her move?"

"Had to woo a cooperative banker?" Derek suggested. "It'd take some time to sweep old Winslow off his feet." Sighing, he finished the last of his whiskey and set the glass on the mantelpiece. "What a tangled web we've woven, Emma. And not a single strand to show to the police."

"I'm not so sure about that." Emma tapped a finger against the side of her glass. "Susannah wouldn't have come to Penford Hall empty-handed, not with a score like that to settle. I think Winslow told her more than she let on. I'm willing to bet that she came here with some sort of hard evidence to flaunt in Grayson's face."

"A pity she can't tell us where to find it," Derek commented. "What do you make of Susannah's amnesia, by the way? Could she be faking it?"

"Possibly. The smartest thing she can do is pretend she's forgotten everything. She's at their mercy, after all." Emma swirled the whiskey in her glass. "I had an interesting conversation with Kate after you left. She's just as crazy about Penford Hall as Grayson is."

"Unfortunate choice of words," Derek said, "but I see your point. It would make sense for Susannah to approach Grayson through Kate. She does act as his lieutenant."

"I was thinking . . . Maybe Kate scheduled a meeting in the chapel garden to discuss Susannah's demands. And maybe the meeting got out of hand." Emma quickly recounted the scenario she'd envisioned: the confrontation in the garden, the angry exchange of words, the sudden grab for the hoe's long handle, the tearing of the oilcloth, the silent fall, the panicked escape. "Whoever tore the oilcloth from the wheelbarrow knows something about Susannah's accident," Emma concluded. "I'd hoped we might be able to dust the oilcloth for fingerprints or something. But when I checked with Bantry this morning, he'd already cleaned it."

Derek had strolled away from the fire and was standing very near Emma's chair. He looked down at her in silence for what seemed a long time, then nodded, as though confirming something. "You're very good at that, you know."

"At what?" Emma touched a hand to her glasses self-consciously.

"Thinking things through. Imagining what it must have been like. Not my strong point, imagination."

"It's not mine, either," Emma protested. "I just try to think logically."

"Nonsense," Derek chided gently. "You've a very creative mind. A logical one, as well, but what good is logic without intuition?" Shoving his hands into the pockets of his faded jeans, he turned to face the fire. "Why didn't you tell me about the oilcloth last night in the nursery?"

"Oh, I don't know." The firelight made Derek's blue eyes sparkle as brightly as they had the night before. "It just didn't seem to be the right time or place, I guess."

"Suppose not," Derek agreed. "Had a splendid evening, though." He glanced shyly at Emma. "You?"

Emma's energetic nod sent whiskey sloshing onto the Persian carpet. As Derek knelt to wipe it up, Emma shrank back in her chair, crimson with embarrassment.

"Meant to thank you for the swift kick, by the way," Derek said. "I was drifting, wasn't I. Nell's complained of it before, but I thought she was just . . . being Nell. Don't understand what she's getting at half the time. A kick on the shin, though. Hard to ignore." He sat back on his heels, and his gaze was level with Emma's. "Was I really that bad?"

Emma wanted to comfort him, but couldn't. From everything she'd seen and heard, Nell's complaints seemed sadly justified. Carefully placing her whiskey glass on the end table, she said, "You must miss your wife terribly."

Derek looked down at the damp handkerchief in his hands. "Sometimes—when I'm working—I forget."

"Is that why you work so much?" Emma asked, very gently.

Derek raised his eyes, perplexed. "Not at all. That's for the children. I want to give Peter and Nell everything Mary wanted them to have."

She would have wanted them to have more time with their father, Emma thought, but she said nothing. She had no right to tell Derek how to run his life.

"Well, anyway, thanks." Derek's gaze lingered on Emma for a moment, then he rose to his feet, stuffed the handkerchief into his back pocket, and returned to stand before the fire. "Funny, really," he said, folding his arms. "I like Grayson enormously and I don't care a fig for Susannah. Yet all I can think about is protecting her from him. It's because she's helpless, I suppose."

"As helpless as we are," murmured Emma. Clearing her throat, she added quickly, "I mean, there's not much we can do to protect her, is there?"

"Not unless we can talk with her, find out if she has anything we can show to the authorities." Derek turned to stare at the fire. "Kate said she was due back in three or four days? Not sure what we should do. Let me think about it."

"I will, too. In the garden." Emma got to her feet. "Derek," she said hesitantly, "if you're not doing anything else, I could—that is, Bantry and I could use some help out there."

"I know," said Derek, his eyes still on the fire. "Nell told me. Unfortunately, I'm still looking for Grayson's bloody lantern."

15

As it happened, a mild pulmonary infection kept Susannah in the hospital for ten days. During that time, her head injuries improved steadily and her memory began to return, though it was sketchy and incomplete. She recognized Grayson and called him by name, but Kate's existence seemed to have, literally, slipped her mind. Overall, however, she seemed to be well on the way to recovery. Kate called every day with a progress report, which Mattie cheerfully passed along to Emma every morning.

Kate's public-relations campaign and Newland's cordon of watchers seemed to be paying off. Reporters who showed up at the gates were politely informed that His Grace would answer questions or pose for pictures at his hotel in Plymouth. The few who sneaked in over the walls were escorted from the grounds before they'd gotten halfway through the woods.

Still others tried their luck in Penford Harbor, where they were met not by resentful silence but by an avalanche of monologues. The Tregallis brothers regaled them with fishing stories, Herbert Munting lectured them on chickens, and Jonah Pengully grumbled about everything under the sun—except the one thing the reporters wanted him to grumble about. Like the other villagers, Jonah refused to say a word about the duke.

"It was brilliant," Derek enthused when he returned from a foray into the village. "Like watching a football match. Every time Grayson's name came up, Jack tossed the story to James, who booted it to Ted, who slipped right back into some flummery about cod-fishing." The village team won the match hands down, routing the visitors without giving up a point. The newspaper coverage slowed to a back-page trickle.

Nanny Cole continued to supplement Emma's wardrobe with dresses in fine wool, velvet, and hand-printed silk, hand-knitted sweaters in slate blue and dusty rose, two more pairs of trousers, and a third gardening smock. By the end of the ten days, Emma felt as though she'd acquired a private couturière, and Mattie shared her delight, pointing out details of workmanship that Emma never would have noticed. Emma's sole attempt to express her gratitude in person was met with a gruff "Stop being a ninny and get *out* of my workroom." After that, Emma simply made sure that the workroom was graced with fresh flowers every day.

She and Bantry spent long afternoons in the library, making up plant lists and discussing what would go where in the chapel garden. Bantry would use only rough copies of Emma's sketches, insisting that the duke would want to frame the originals, and he agreed with Emma's strong intuition that everything planted in the chapel garden should come from the other gardens of Penford Hall. "The dowager duchess would've wanted it that way," he said approvingly. "And we've plenty of plants to choose from."

It was an understatement, as Emma soon learned. The

garden rooms in the castle ruins were as varied and as well tended as any Emma had ever seen. The rock garden was a swirling pastel watercolor—sky-blue primroses and white candytuft, purple lobelia and rosy-pink soapwort. The candytuft and primroses, Emma thought, would look wonderful edging the flagstone walk and the reflecting pool.

Clouds of early blossoms graced the rose garden, and Bantry told her all about the ones not yet in bloom. Emma chose a fragrant nineteenth-century Bourbon rose—*Madame Isaac Pereire,* Bantry informed her—to frame the green door, and a hybrid tea rose to plant beside the wooden bench.

Emma was enchanted by the knot garden. The close-clipped, interlocking chains of low-growing hedges formed a charming double-knot pattern that enclosed a marvelous selection of herbs. There, she discovered the deep purple-blue lavender she would use on either side of the chapel door, along with red sage, bronze fennel, angelica, and golden balm. She found a treasure trove in the perennial border she'd seen the first time she'd entered the castle ruins. Transplanted clematis and delphiniums would soften the stark granite walls, and irises, peonies, lilies, columbines, and a host of other old-fashioned flowers would restore color, form, and texture to the raised beds.

"I'd like a pair of butterfly bushes to tuck into the corners, where the chapel wall meets the garden wall," Emma explained to Bantry, "and a different climbing rose in the center of each of the long walls. We'll plant tall perennials to fill the space between the roses and the corner ledges—lupines, hollyhocks, that sort of thing—with shorter ones in front. The bottom tier should have trailing plants spilling out onto the lawn. The rosy-pink soapwort would work, or the verbena. And we'll need something special to put on the corner ledges."

"We've some nice orchids in the hothouse," Bantry offered.

"Hothouse?" Emma echoed. She hadn't noticed one in the house plans Derek had shown her.

"His Grace put it in year afore last," Bantry explained. "Miss Kate's partial to orchids."

They spent the next day in Penford Hall's conservatory, a two-story glass-enclosed set of rooms tucked away in the west wing. One section was devoted to orchids, ferns, and waving palms, another to miniature fruit trees and topiary, and a third, Emma noted with some amusement, was the source of Nell's almost constant supply of strawberries. Between the conservatory and the garden rooms, she found everything she'd need.

"Don't mean to sound sour, Miss Emma," Bantry cautioned, "but the chapel garden won't be at its best in August."

"I know that, and you know that, but I'm afraid we'll have a hard time convincing Grayson," said Emma, with a sigh. "He told me not to worry about getting it perfect, but I don't think he understands just how imperfect it'll be."

"Aye." Bantry squinted into the distance. "Be patchy this year, a bit better next. Mebbe the year after that it'll begin to come into its own. A good garden takes time."

Bantry knew what he was talking about. He displayed an awesome knowledge of the plants under his care, and spoke of them with an air of affectionate familiarity. "This 'un's daft," he commented, pointing to an early-blooming scarlet rambler. "Thinks it's June already. Does it every year, like it can't wait to come out and say hello."

Bantry's organizational skills were equally impressive.

He'd trained a small cadre of dedicated undergardeners to help him with the mammoth task of maintenance. One by one, Emma met them, sixteen villagers in all, from shy, eleven-year-old Daphne Minion, whose special love was the knot garden, to placid, eighty-six-year-old Bert Potts, who tended the pleached apple trees that bordered the great lawn.

When Emma complimented Bantry on his talent for managing people, he responded casually that his time at Wisley Gardens had served him well. That was how Emma learned that Bantry had spent ten years at the Royal Horticultural Society's 150-acre centerpiece. He'd shrugged off her breathless questions by saying that, all in all, he preferred Penford Hall, where he didn't have to put up with "them smelly tour buses."

That revelation led to several others. When Emma told Derek of Bantry's illustrious past, he reminded her of a conversation that had taken place in the library the night Emma had arrived. Under pressure from Susannah, he recalled, Kate had acknowledged that she and Nanny Cole had once lived in Bournemouth. Bantry, Kate, and Nanny Cole—three of Penford Hall's mainstays—had apparently been forced to leave the hall for greener pastures at some point in the distant past. Curious, Emma and Derek decided to see if the same held true for the rest of the staff.

Judicious questioning of Mattie revealed that Crowley had been living in a furnished bedsitter in Plymouth when Mattie was born. Hallard, Gash, and Newland, Derek learned, had each spent some years in London. With the sole exception of Madama Rulenska, it appeared that all of the servants had left Penford Hall at some point.

Clearly, Susannah's father hadn't been the only one to suffer from the old duke's reversal of fortune. As they sat together in the library four days after Syd's return, Derek theorized that Penford Hall had been all but deserted, much like the village.

"Grayson's father gave them all the sack," Derek concluded, "and Grayson, when he was able, hired them back. Argues for a high degree of loyalty. A pity."

"We can't really trust anyone," Emma agreed sadly.

"We can, though," said Derek. He leaned forward. "Syd's an outsider, and he'd do anything to protect his Suzie. And it wouldn't seem strange for him to want to stay by her side." Derek sighed. "If only we could figure out a way to snap him out of his funk."

Emma nodded. Visibly aged, Syd had taken meals in his room since his return from Plymouth. According to Crowley, he simply sat and stared out of the window. Emma knew where she went when she was upset, but it was ridiculous to assume that the same thing would work for Syd. Or was it?

"Derek," she said slowly, "this is probably going to sound silly, but . . . what if I took Syd out to work in the garden with me?"

"Green-thumb therapy?" Derek mulled the idea over, then shrugged. "Why not? It'd get his mind off of things, get him moving again. Not at all silly."

"I'll ask him tomorrow morning." Emma looked at the fire, feeling satisfied.

Derek cleared his throat. "About the chapel garden," he began. "Sorry I haven't been out to lend a hand. Blasted lantern search is turning out to be more complicated than I'd expected. Place is honeycombed with tunnels."

"Sounds spooky."

Derek smiled. "Not really. Miss the sun, though. Seem to spend all of my time in the dark lately." He glanced at Emma, then looked down at the toes of his workboots. "Miss our little talks, too."

"Do you?" Emma said, taken by surprise. "So do I. I wish we didn't have to talk about such gruesome things, though."

"Know what you mean. Seems we've skipped over the civilized chitchat and gone straight to . . . well . . . murder, theft, attempted murder, and suicide. You know, I always thought detective work would be fascinating, and it is, but it's also a bit . . ."

"Disturbing?" Emma offered.

"Indeed." He bit his lip, then turned toward her. "Look, why don't we give ourselves an evening off? Just talk about . . . well, anything. I feel as though I hardly know you."

"There's not much to know," said Emma, with a shrug. "I was born and raised in Connecticut, but I've lived in the Boston area all of my adult life. I went to MIT and got a job right out of college. I'm still with the same firm, though I've moved up a few rungs on the corporate ladder. I love my work and, as you've probably noticed by now, I love gardening, too. And that's about it." Emma sighed. Her life sounded strangely barren, even to her own ears. "To tell you the truth, Penford Hall's the most exciting thing that's ever happened to me."

"For me, it was the birth of my children," said Derek. "Don't mean to be a bore, but Peter and Nell truly are the most wonderful son and daughter a man could ask for." He reached down to brush a fleck of dust from his left boot. "Have any? Children, I mean."

"No." Emma touched a finger to her glasses. "I never really wanted any."

"Never wanted children?" Derek murmured doubtfully. "I must say that I can't imagine what life would be like without Peter and Nell. But, of course, with your work and, er, being on your own, I suppose it's very sensible of you not to have any. That is, I mean, if you *are* on your own." He gave a nervous cough and looked toward the fire. "Don't mean to pry. It's just that Nell was wondering and, well, I told her that, naturally, there must be *someone* in your life. This Richard fellow . . . ?"

"Richard got married two months ago," Emma informed him.

"Married?" Derek swung sideways in his chair to face her, incredulous. "To someone *else?*"

Declarations of independence, statistics on divorce, and cogent arguments against outmoded social contracts darted through Emma's mind, but none of them seemed as important at that moment as the marvelous, miraculous fact that she was sitting down and empty-handed. She couldn't cover herself in mud or throw her silverware around the room or spill anything on the priceless carpet but tears, and for some reason she didn't feel at all like crying. Unaccountably tongue-tied, Emma bowed her head to hide her confusion and, with rapidly blurring vision, watched her glasses slide off the end of her nose.

Emma's hand shot out, but Derek's got there first. Arm length and perfect vision were on his side: the glasses landed squarely in his palm. He looked up and his fingers brushed the side of Emma's face as he reached for the left arm of the glasses, which was still hooked behind Emma's ear. As he removed it, Emma felt a tickling sensation and shivered, goosebumps running all up and down her arms.

"Looks like a screw's popped out," said Derek. "I'll have a look round." He got down on his hands and knees to examine the carpet minutely. A moment later, he sat back on his heels and held out his hand, triumphant. "Found it," he said. "I've very good eyes, you know."

"Oh, God," Emma breathed.

Derek's salt-and-pepper curls tumbled forward as he

bent low over Emma's glasses, and his strong hands were as dextrous as a surgeon's as he put the tiny screw back into place and tightened it with his thumbnail.

He's a grieving widower, Emma reminded herself sternly. He's got a son and a daughter and a house near Oxford and he's English and he's completely and totally out of the question.

"Not only tone-deaf but a fool as well," Derek was saying. "Of course, who knows where I might've ended up if I hadn't met Mary? Matter of luck as much as anything. The right person. The right time and place."

Emma stared at him blindly and clenched her hands in her lap to keep them from reaching out to brush the curls back from his forehead. It's Penford Hall, she thought. It's the fire and the rain and the sense of isolation that stirs up this foolish feeling of us-against-the-world. It will pass, she told herself. She knew exactly what the future held in store. She'd planned it years ago.

"There." Derek polished the lenses with his shirttail, then bent forward to slip the glasses into place on Emma's face. He frowned suddenly. "Emma," he said, "are you crying?"

Emma brushed the tear away and got to her feet. "It's nothing. I'm just overtired. I've had a long day and there's a lot to do tomorrow. Think I'll turn in."

Derek said nothing, but Emma could feel his blue eyes on her until she closed the library door behind her.

Pleased by Emma's invitation, Syd was as pliant as a lamb. He leaned on her arm as he shuffled slowly down the stone steps in the chapel garden, where Bantry and the children were already hard at work.

"My old man was a businessman," Syd informed her, "and so was his old man. But both of 'em were farmers at heart, you get me? Country people. My grandpa, he grew tomatoes would make your mouth water. And my pop, he always kept a nice patch of pansies for my kid sister, Betty." Syd looked vaguely around at the half-stripped walls and the withered vegetation. "Whatsamatter here?" he asked. "You got a drought or something?"

Nell moved to Syd's side and placed a trowel in his hand. "Come and help me dig up dandelions, Mr. Bishop. Some of them are perfect beasts."

Syd turned the trowel in his hands, then reached out to pat Nell's head. "Sure, Princess, sure. You show me the dandelions, I'll dig 'em up for you."

Peter looked askance at Syd's freckled pate, left the garden, and returned a short time later with a shapeless, broad-brimmed straw hat that had been hanging on the pegboard in Bantry's potting shed. "Here," he said shyly, offering the hat. "It gets pretty sunny out here sometimes."

"Hey, Petey-boy, thanks a million. That's some chapeau." Syd admired the hat at arm's length, then plopped it on his head. "Need to take care of the old noodle, huh? That's real thoughtful of you. You gonna help us out with these here dandelions?"

Syd spent the rest of the morning pottering contentedly from dandelion to dandelion and chatting with the children, the straw hat pulled low on his forehead, his checked pants acquiring a patina of rich, dark soil. When lunchtime came around, he was reluctant to leave, and though he took a nap that afternoon, he was back in the garden the following morning, with a surer step and a clearer mind. The news of Susannah's extended stay at the hospital didn't seem to faze him, and by the next day, Emma was convinced that her green-thumb therapy was working.

She doubted that it would have been half as effective without the children's help. Peter had taken to gardening with a vengeance, and now spent most of his waking hours near the chapel. Nell's approach was more relaxed but no less productive. Her daisy chains decorated Syd's hat and the handles of the old wheelbarrow, and her posies brightened the shelves in the potting shed and the bedside table in the rose suite.

In the evenings, when the tools were put away and the sun was sinking low on the horizon, Nell entertained them all with stories of the bold Sir Bertram's amazing deeds. Emma found herself unexpectedly caught up in Bertie's battles with the evil Queen Beatrice, and Syd was vastly amused by the misadventures of the lazy buffoon, Higgins.

The only one who wasn't amused was Derek, and that was because he never showed his face in the garden. Nell seemed serenely unconcerned about her father's absence, but, though Peter said little, it was hard to ignore the way his head swung around every time the green door opened, and difficult to miss the disappointment in his eyes when Bantry or Syd Bishop came through it.

Emma told herself that it was just as well. She wasn't sure what was going on between them, but, whatever it was, she wanted to stop it before it got out of hand. It would be unfair to Peter and Nell for her and Derek to start something they couldn't finish. Children needed a future, and that was the one thing Emma couldn't possibly give them.

16

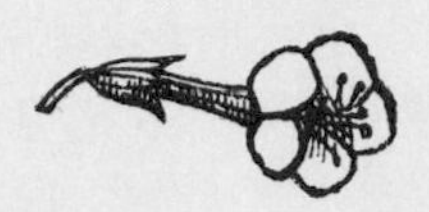

On the eighth evening of the long week following Susannah's accident, Emma dined alone. The candles were lit in the dining room, and Crowley saw her to her chair, but hers was the only place set at the table. Crowley informed her that the children had eaten supper in the nursery with Nanny Cole, and Syd Bishop had taken a light meal on a tray in his room, then gone directly to bed.

"He's not ill, Miss Porter," Crowley assured her, when she expressed mild concern. "Quite the contrary. He informed Hallard that he was retiring early because he intended to be, er, 'up and at 'em' at the break of dawn. Gardening seems to agree with him."

As for Derek, Crowley knew only that Mr. Harris had retired to his room late that afternoon, leaving strict instructions that he was not to be disturbed by the staff.

Emma told herself that she'd worn her newest Nanny Cole creation—a flowery William Morris print in bronze and gold and copper—to suit herself, not to please Derek. Still, she had to admit that, if she'd known that Crowley would be her sole companion in the dining room, she might not have anticipated supper quite so eagerly.

Emma ate quickly, then went up to her room to change into a skirt and blouse and pull on Nanny Cole's heathery angora sweater. She left her room for the library, stopping just long enough to knock on Derek's door, hoping that his instructions to the staff did not apply to her. Receiving no reply, she went on her way. She was usually in bed and asleep by ten o'clock, but she'd been meaning to read up on old Bourbon roses and tonight seemed the perfect opportunity. She peeked into a few other rooms on her way to the main staircase, then wandered into the billiards room, the music room, the drawing room, and various salons on the first floor before settling in the library with one eye on her book and the other on the tall case clock in the corner.

When the clock chimed ten, Emma decided that what she really needed was a breath of fresh air. Armed with a flashlight provided by Crowley, she made straight for the chapel. The moon had not yet risen, and stars blanketed the sky. The castle ruins were a maze of shadows, and she had to step carefully to avoid falling on her face. She wasn't hurrying, she was simply walking briskly, because it was a proven fact that exercise promoted sound sleep and she had every intention of sleeping soundly that night. When she pushed open the chapel's low rounded door, she saw immediately that Derek wasn't inside.

But his son was. Peter was wearing a blue melton jacket over striped pajamas, and warm woolen socks stuffed into brown leather slippers, and he carried a Day-Glo–orange emergency lantern, the kind Emma kept in the trunk of her car at home. He was halfway to the back door by the time Emma's flashlight picked him out, but when she spoke his name, he stopped.

"I'm sorry," said Emma. "I didn't mean to disturb you. I'll go away, if you like."

Peter glanced over his shoulder at her, then looked away again. He shrugged. "I don't mind if you stay."

Emma hesitated. She respected Peter's privacy, but she was curious to know what had lured him to the chapel in the dead of night. He hadn't struck her as the kind of boy who would get up to any mischief, but he was obviously AWOL from the nursery. What had compelled him to risk the wrath of Nanny Cole?

Emma walked slowly up the center aisle. "I'd rather not stay by myself," she said, sitting on the front bench. She was careful to speak softly. She didn't want Peter darting out the back door in the dark.

Peter turned the lantern on and placed it on the shelf below the lady window, then backed slowly to the bench and sat beside Emma, his hands jammed in his jacket pockets, his eyes never leaving the lady's face.

"She's beautiful, isn't she?" he murmured.

"Yes, she is." Even in the darkness, the window retained its power. The lantern picked out glimmerings of color and softened the fire in the lady's eyes. Her face hovered above them, serene as a full moon sailing across a midnight sky.

"Dad says that lots of people think Miss Ashley-Woods is beautiful," said Peter. "But I don't."

Emma kept her voice steady as she asked, "Why not?"

"She's all bones," Peter replied bluntly, "and she has mean eyes. She was bothering Dad all the time before you came. Keeping him from his job."

A job that was, for some reason, very important to the boy. A chill hand seemed to grip Emma's heart. Oh, no, she thought, could it be as simple and as terrible as this?

"Peter," she said, "is this where you were that morning, when Miss Ashley-Woods fell down the stairs?"

Peter's body tensed and for a moment Emma thought

he might bolt. Instead, he gave a forlorn sigh and bowed his head, and the tension left his body as tears began, silently, steadily, falling bright as diamonds on his dark wool jacket.

"Nanny Cole told me to play outside," he said, "but—but I didn't want to. She's supposed to give me lessons and she wouldn't and I was—was angry."

"So you came out here instead?" Emma prompted gently.

"I'm not supposed to," the boy admitted. "Dad—Dad wants me to get fresh air and—and sunshine. But I like it here. The lady needs me." The boy sniffed, then scrubbed at his nose with the sleeve of his jacket.

"Needs you?" Emma asked.

"To tell her that everything will be all right." Peter put a fist to his forehead and uttered a strangled moan. "But I don't know . . . I don't know if it will be anymore. No one will listen to me."

Emma put an arm around the boy's shoulders, then tightened her hold as he turned to bury his face in the soft angora sweater. Awkwardly, tenderly, she smoothed his dark hair. "Did you hear anything while you were in here that morning?" she asked. She hated herself for pressing the point, but she had to hear Peter's reply.

Peter tilted his tear-streaked face up to her. "Not until the shouting started. Then I went out that way"—he pointed to the back door—"and round the outside to the cliff path. I—I didn't want Dad to know I'd been in here. I've never disobeyed him before."

Emma could well believe it. Peter was the most obedient child she'd ever met. "Did anyone see you go out onto the cliff path?" she asked softly.

Peter nodded. "Teddy Tregallis was down in the harbor, on the boat with his dad and his uncles. They all looked up and waved, so I waved back. He's a good chap, Teddy. He's going to be a fisherman when he grows up. He says he likes fishing more than school."

Emma looked down into the boy's luminous eyes and knew he was telling the truth. He wouldn't have admitted to witnesses, otherwise; it would be too easy for her to confirm his whereabouts with the Tregallises. Peter had disobeyed his father's orders and Nanny Cole's instructions, and he'd compounded his wrongdoing by lying about it afterward, but that was the worst of it, and Emma was weak with relief.

"I don't see any reason to tell your father where you were," she said. "I don't think anyone else has to know. Okay?"

The boy gulped and nodded, then lay his head against her, as though the confession had drained his last reserves of energy. Emma thought for a moment that he had fallen asleep, but then he spoke, in a voice so low that she scarcely caught the words.

"Dad says she's perfect and Grayson says her cloak should be gray. But they're both wrong." He sighed. "She should be wearing white."

"That's what the legend says," Emma agreed.

"It's nothing to do with the legend," Peter insisted. "I just know that's how she's supposed to be."

If Emma had had more experience with children, she might have tried to persuade him, for his own good, that his father knew best. But Peter spoke with such conviction that she was willing, for the moment, to try to see the lady as Peter saw her. Closing her eyes, Emma conjured up an image of the cloaked and hooded lady, clad in white.

Slowly, the picture took shape. Streaks of purple, violet, and aquamarine filled the stormy sky, the sea was a swirling mosaic of greens flecked with silvery froth, and the lantern's blaze split the darkness like a bolt of lightning. Now, Emma thought, what would it be like if the cloak and hood were . . .

The image came to her with startling clarity. The billowing black cloak became a pair of celestial wings, and the hood encircling the raven hair was transformed into a glowing nimbus. My god, Emma thought, it's an angel. There was no mistaking it, and she knew beyond all doubt who that dark-haired angel was in Peter's eyes.

"Can you see her, too?" Peter whispered.

Emma could only nod. How could anyone fail to see it? Derek must have known what the window would become once he changed the glass. Had it been too painful for him to face the image of his dead wife, here in this lonely place?

"Dad will listen to you," Peter said.

Emma knew what he was asking, but she had no desire to interfere in Derek's work and no right to intrude on his grief. She wanted to leave the chapel, to forget about the window, but the boy held her there, looking up at her with such hope and trust that she couldn't back away.

Again, she nodded. "I'll try," she promised. "It may not happen right away. It may not happen at all. But I'll try."

"It'll happen," Peter declared, adding more softly, "It has to."

Emma trembled inwardly. "It's getting late," she said. "I think I'll try to get some sleep. How about you?"

Peter stood and together they went back into the hall and up the main staircase to the nursery, where Nell was waiting for them, sitting on the rocking horse, with Bertie in her arms.

"Nanny Cole's snoring like a grampus," Nell informed them.

"You should be asleep, too," Peter scolded. He lifted

Nell down from the rocking horse, buttoned the top button of her white robe, and checked to make sure she had slippers on.

"Bertie wasn't tired," Nell explained. "He wanted to hear a story." She turned to Emma, who was watching discreetly from the doorway. "Will you tell Bertie a story, Emma?"

The request took Emma off guard. "Well, I . . ." She glanced uncertainly at Peter, who was yawning hugely and rubbing his eyes. "Yes, all right, I'll tell you a story, Nell. Peter, you get straight into bed."

"Yes'm. But don't forget to put a glass of water next to Nell's bed. Bertie gets thirsty sometimes." Motioning for Emma to follow, he led the way past a kitchenette, a large bathroom, and a lavatory, stopping when they reached a pair of doors. Peter opened the door on the right, but turned back to shake a finger at his sister. "Only one story," he reminded her, then went inside and closed the door behind him.

Opening the other door, Emma peered into Nell's room, amazed by the trouble the duke had taken to ensure Queen Eleanor's comfort. A bedside lamp cast a soft glow on the child-sized canopied bed, the mirrored dressing table, the skirted chaise longue, and the wardrobe. Everything was white and gold, including the bear-sized rocking chair sitting beside the chaise.

While Nell hung her robe in the wardrobe and crawled into bed, Emma dutifully filled a glass with water in the kitchen. Glass in hand, Emma waited while the little girl fussed over Bertie, making sure that his fuzzy brown head was precisely centered on the pillow and tucking the covers under his chin.

"I hope Peter goes straight to bed," Emma said, moving to place the glass on the bedside table. "He's very tired tonight."

Nell settled back on her own pillow and regarded Emma with that strangely intimidating air of self-possession. "Peter's always tired," Nell said. "I told you that before."

"Did you? I must have forgotten."

"Don't forget," said Nell. She slid one arm out from under the covers and reached over to touch Bertie's ear. "That's why I told you. Somebody should know. Not just me."

"Know what?" said Emma.

"When Papa's away, Peter has to do everything."

Emma smiled. "Now, Nell, you know that isn't true. You have a very nice housekeeper, remember?"

"Mrs. Higgins is a boozer," Nell stated flatly.

Emma nearly laughed. "But in those stories you told us in the garden, Higgins was a clown."

Nell gazed at her levelly. "She's not funny, Emma." Rolling over on her side and curling her knees up to her chest, the child turned her back on Emma. "You can turn out the light now. I'm ready to go to sleep."

Emma was disconcerted. "What about Bertie's story?" she asked.

"Bertie's asleep, Emma. He doesn't need a story."

The frost in Nell's voice told Emma that she'd been rejected as well as dismissed. Unsettled, and sensing that she'd failed some obscure test, Emma stared helplessly at the back of Nell's head, then switched off the bedside lamp and left the nursery.

Back in her own room, she spent an hour on the balcony, trying to figure out what had just happened. Emma might not know the fine points of parenting, but she'd seen Derek go out of his way to dress up for Queen Eleanor, and he'd been equally willing to sprawl across the floor for Peter. A blind person could see that he adored his son and daughter. He'd never leave them alone with a . . . a boozer.

On the other hand, Derek didn't spend much time at home. He hadn't known about Nell's new play group or Peter leaving the Boy Scouts. And why had Peter quit the Scouts, anyway? He loved the outdoors and was always after Bantry to show him how to tie a new knot or identify an unfamiliar insect. It didn't make sense.

Emma turned. From the balcony she could see Derek's crumpled business card, still propped against the clock on the rosewood desk. Since Derek worked out of his home, the phone number on the card would allow her to speak directly to Mrs. Higgins. One telephone call would put her mind at rest about the housekeeper and spare her a potentially embarrassing conversation with Derek. Too bad it was so late.

Emma rubbed her forehead tiredly, remembering that another uncomfortable discussion with Derek was already in the offing. Why in the world had she promised Peter to talk to his father about fixing the window? Emma sighed, then went into the bedroom and turned off the lights. It wasn't fair. After years of doing everything she could to avoid having children of her own, she lay awake now, worried sick about someone else's.

17

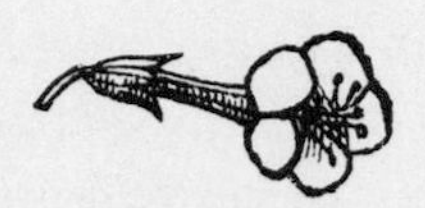

"It's none of my business," Emma muttered, stabbing the pitchfork into the dirt. "Absolutely none." She yanked a mass of bindweed up by the roots and tossed it into the wheelbarrow. They'd finished clearing the south wall and another of the raised beds before lunch, and she was determined to make a start on the lawn before supper. She jabbed the fork back into the earth and leaned on the handle, wiping the sweat from her forehead and wishing she'd remembered to wear her sunhat. It was too hot to work without it. Not a breath of wind stirred in the chapel garden, and the sun beat down relentlessly from a cloudless blue sky.

"Hey, Emma, you tryin' to kill yourself?" Syd Bishop looked over at Peter and Nell, who were sitting like wilted flowers in the shade cast by the chapel's projecting wall. "You kids take a breather. Go ask Gash to squirt you with the hose, or see if Bantry'll let you play in the fountain. Go on. Outta here!"

They'd gotten word that morning. Grayson, Kate, and Dr. Singh would bring Susannah back to Penford Hall the following day. Excitement in the hall had risen to a feverish pitch as the staff threw itself into preparations for receiving their disabled guest and welcoming home their long-absent master.

Bantry was trimming the hedges at the front of the hall and freshening up the tulips in the beds around the fountain at the center of the circular drive. The drive itself looked like an eccentric used-car lot. Gash had emptied the garage and was busily washing Grayson's cars. Why he thought it necessary to wash all of them at once, Emma couldn't say, but the Rolls-Royce, MG, and Jaguar were in line with an ancient but meticulously maintained forest-green Landrover and a badly rusted orange Volkswagen bus. The last, Gash had informed her sadly, belonged to Derek. "Have to do something about it," he'd muttered, surveying the decrepit vehicle with a calculating eye.

Crowley was supervising a phalanx of villagers who were polishing, dusting, scrubbing, or sweeping every inch of the hall. Mattie was fussing endlessly about what linens would look best in Susannah's room, Hallard was pounding furiously at his keyboard, and Newland had his men on alert for last-minute gate-crashers, while Madama and three assistants were preparing a welcome-home supper with more courses than a college catalogue.

Derek hadn't surfaced all day, and Emma was well past being a little peeved.

"Emma, will you quit already? Whaddya tryin' to do, dig your way to China?" Syd removed the pitchfork from Emma's hands with unexpected strength. Raising a gloved hand to shade her eyes, Emma realized that the old man had never looked better. His face had the ruddy glow of good health, and his eyes were clear and alert. Perhaps too alert. Emma quickly averted her angry gaze.

Syd took off his straw hat and plopped it on Emma's head. "Get over there and sit your fanny down before you give yourself a stroke."

Red-faced and winded, Emma stalked over to the wooden bench, folded her arms, and sat. Her hair was sticking to her back, and her face was streaked with mud and sweat. "What are you doing?" she snapped, when Syd came up behind her.

"I'm tuckin' your friggin' wig up in your bonnet. You gotta nice head of hair, Emma, but a cape you don't need on a day like this. Sit still or I'll give you such a clout . . ." Syd twisted Emma's long tail of hair into a French knot and pushed it up into the oversized straw hat. With the hair off the back of her neck, the heat in the garden was almost bearable.

Syd sat down next to her. "You gonna tell me what's eatin' you or do I have to pry it outta you?"

Emma's lips tightened.

Syd leaned back on the bench, stretched his legs out in front of him, and crossed his ankles. He raised his face to the sun. "Okay, so I was a little rocky for a coupla days there. Seein' Suzie all banged up kinda took the wind outta my sails. But I'm okay now. This here chapel garden's like a tonic." He nudged Emma with his elbow. "You think I don't know what you done, bringin' me out here? You think I ain't grateful?"

"I'm not mad at you, Syd," Emma said stiffly.

"I know that, honey. But I gotta return the favor, you understand? Maybe I can help."

Emma took her work gloves off and placed them in her lap, then turned to face Syd. "Do you think Nell is a truthful child?"

Syd's eyes slid toward her. "Sure," he said. "She's a bright kid. She may embroider a little here, a little there, but she knows what's make-believe and what's not."

"Then what would you say if I told you that Nell implied that Derek leaves her and Peter alone for extended periods of time with no one but a drunk to look after them?"

"I'd say you should be discussing this with Derek," said Syd.

"How can I?"

Syd waved a hand in the air. "You go up to him, you say, 'Derek, got a minute?'—"

"No, Syd, that's not what I mean. I mean, in a larger, philosophical sense, what right do I have to interfere? Why should it matter to me what Derek does with his children? It's none of my business."

"Seems to me that, in a larger, philosophical sense, you're already makin' it your business. You get much sleep last night?"

"Not much." Facing forward, Emma ran her hand along the smooth, silvery arm of the wooden bench. Half angry, half embarrassed, she said, "I called there this morning."

"There where?"

Emma sighed. "I called the number on Derek's business card. And a woman answered. She was friendly, in a vague sort of way, but it . . . it did sound as if she'd been drinking. Oh, Syd, I could practically smell the liquor on her breath." Emma drummed her fingers on the arm of the bench. "She introduced herself as Mrs. Higgins."

"You don't say." Syd let out a low whistle, then laced his fingers together and cracked his knuckles. "I'll tell you one thing. If it is true, it ain't Derek's fault."

"How could it not be?" Emma demanded.

" 'Cause he loves those kids. He wouldn't leave 'em hangin' like that. Not on purpose." Syd shrugged. "You ever think maybe he don't know?"

Emma's fingers stopped drumming.

"I mean, the love goes two ways," Syd went on. "Those kids'd do just about anything for him, am I right? That Peter . . ." Syd shook his head. "Never seen a kid wound so tight. Now, there's one who don't tell the truth."

"What do you mean?" Emma asked.

Syd gave her a pitying look. "I raised three sons, Emma. I got five grandsons. You think I don't know when a little boy's telling a fib?" He rubbed the bridge of his nose. "Lies about funny stuff, too. Like, he was tellin' me about a football match at his school, right? And maybe he thinks he can fool me on account of I'm a Yank. But I been in this country twenty years, Emma. I know from football, and not just that the Brits don't call it soccer. And I'm tellin' you, if that kid ever saw a football match in his life, I'll eat that sweaty old hat. Why should he lie about something like that, huh? You tell me."

Nell's words seemed to ring in Emma's ears. *When Papa's away, Peter has to do everything.* Emma realized suddenly that, apart from that evening when they'd built their Rube Goldberg machine, she'd never seen Peter playing at anything. He was the first one in the garden every morning and he was usually the last to leave. Nanny Cole had scolded him for straightening up the nursery, and Bantry had sensed that something was amiss when he'd caught the boy tidying up the potting shed. Emma remembered Peter's vaguely puzzled attitude toward cricket and, with a sinking heart, began to understand why the boy had elected not to attend Harrow. A boarding school would have taken him away from home, where he was needed.

"But that's terrible," she said. "Why can't he just go to Derek and tell him the truth?"

Syd snorted. "You're makin' me lose patience with

you, Emma. You think that kid don't know his father's heart is broke? You think he wants his pop to feel worse?"

Emma was appalled. "You think this has been going on since Derek lost his wife? But Peter was barely five years old and Nell was—"

"Nell was his baby sister, what needed looking after. I'll tell you something, Emma, and it ain't something I tell too many people. I lost my mother, God rest her soul, when I was eight years old. My sister, Betty, was only two. I know what this boy's feeling. What I didn't know was about the drunk. That changes things. You gotta tell Derek about the drunk."

"Can't you tell him?" Emma asked.

"You're the one got the invitation." When Emma looked at him blankly, Syd rolled his eyes. "Emma, what's a person gotta do to get through to you? What do you think, Nell don't know how to keep her mouth shut? You think she tells you about that hooch hound for nothing? You ever heard of a cry for help?" Syd pursed his lips, disgusted. "Oh, I forgot. It ain't none of your business."

Emma flinched.

"So, this is why you been so mad at the poor guy?" Syd asked.

"I am not mad at—" Emma cleared her throat. "I'm not mad at anyone."

"And I'm the queen of Romania." Syd shook his head reproachfully. "What do you think, I'm stupid? You been a pain in the butt ever since that dope did his vanishing act."

"Do you know where he is?" Emma asked, more quickly than she'd intended.

Syd examined his fingernails. "Madama says he's been eatin' in the kitchen at weird hours. Whatsamatta, he didn't tell you?"

Emma swallowed once, then looked down at the ground. "No. Why should he?"

"Because that's what people do when they care about each other," Syd answered simply. He gave Emma a sidelong look. "Am I right?"

Emma's glasses began to slide down her sweaty nose. She pushed them up again and sighed disconsolately. "I wouldn't know."

"You're learnin', though, huh?" Syd squeezed her arm sympathetically. "It ain't easy, bein' in love."

Emma's shoulders slumped. "Who said anything about being in love? And even if I were, that doesn't mean that I would expect Der— whoever I might be in love with to account to me for every minute of his time."

"You like bein' miserable?" Syd asked.

"No, I—"

"Then you gotta lay down some ground rules. Next time you see that dope, you smack him in the kisser and tell him, he ever pulls this kinda stunt on you again, you'll give it to him twice as bad."

"I don't have any right—"

"He gotta right to make you worry?"

"No, but—"

"You gotta be patient with him. But firm. Otherwise those kids're gonna grow up seein' you miserable and never seein' their pop at all."

"Syd . . ." Emma looked up at the sky. It was beginning to cloud over and she hoped for a good rain, to clear the heaviness from the air. "I appreciate your concern, but I must have given you the wrong impression. I have no intention of getting married, ever, much less to someone who already has two children."

"Two kids and a bear," Syd corrected. "You know, Emma, if you'd stop thinkin' so much, you'd save everyone a whole lotta heartburn. Listen to your Uncle Syd.

You turn off that brain of yours and give your heart a chance. It won't steer you wrong. You got my guarantee on that."

Emma looked down at her work-roughened hands, then reached up to brush at a tendril of hair that had escaped from Syd's hat. "I think I'll go in and wash up," she said softly.

Syd reached over and tucked the loose tendril back into place. "Don't be too hard on the guy, Emma. He's out there strugglin', just like the rest of us."

A mountain of thunderclouds had moved in over the sea by the time Emma emerged from her dressing room, freshly bathed and wrapped in her terry-cloth robe. Not a drop of rain was falling, but the sky was an unbroken mass of angry gray clouds, and the temperature had dropped so dramatically that Emma was glad to come in from the balcony. Although it was nearly time for supper, she stretched out on the bed, exhausted. She'd scarcely slept the night before, and she'd been hard at work all day. She was much too tired to sort through her conversation with Syd, or to battle her way through Crowley's cleaning brigade to reach the dining room, and she wasn't really hungry anyway. All she wanted to do was rest her eyes.

Emma awoke with a start. She reached toward the bedside table to grope for her glasses before realizing that she hadn't taken them off. She was still wrapped in her robe. Peering at the jeweled clock on the rosewood desk, she saw that it was nearly midnight. Yawning, she looked around the room sleepily, wondering what had awakened her. Thunder, perhaps? She went to the balcony and saw that the storm had not yet broken, though the wind was blowing hard and lightning flashed far out at sea. Emma shuddered to think what the garden rooms would look like in the morning, then turned as she heard someone knocking at her door.

Wincing guiltily, Emma came in off the balcony. She shouldn't have left her lights on. It was probably Mattie, coming to ask if she needed anything. Summoning an apologetic smile, Emma went to open the door.

The hallway was empty. Emma squinted into the darkness beyond the pool of light falling from her room, but saw no one. Perplexed, she closed the door.

Again she heard a knocking sound. It seemed to be coming from her dressing room. The hairs on her arms prickled as she picked up Crowley's flashlight and hefted it. It was sturdy and she was fairly strong. Creeping quietly to the dressing room, she flung the door wide and leapt back, raising the flashlight above her head.

Nothing. Emma put her head inside the room, then uttered a startled yelp when a loud knock sounded right next to her. It seemed to be coming from her wardrobe. Cautiously, she opened the wardrobe door.

"Derek?" she called softly. "Is that you?"

A muffled voice came through the wardrobe's back panel. "Who else would it be? Glad to know I've got the right address, at least. Think you could let me in?"

"I don't know," said Emma. "You're in back of a wardrobe that must weigh at least a ton."

A muted groan came through the wall.

"Hang on," said Emma. "Let me take a look." She dumped her clothes unceremoniously out of the wardrobe and onto the floor, then flicked on Crowley's flashlight and examined the back panel. "I don't see any hinges, but there's a row of pegs down the center of the panel. Maybe, if I . . ." She climbed into the wardrobe and, crouching, tugged at the top peg. It came away in her hand, and the others followed suit. Stepping back out of the wardrobe, she called, "Try sliding the right side of the panel sideways."

The panel rattled, creaked, and finally began to shift slowly, one half slipping neatly behind the other. Cool, musty air wafted out of the darkness; then Derek emerged, with a flashlight in one hand, dusty smudges on his face, and cobwebs in his hair.

Emma pulled her robe around her and schooled her face into a neutral expression. Derek took one look at her and began to apologize as though his life depended on it.

"Emma, I can't begin to tell you how sorry I am that I didn't let you know what I was up to. I should've come by sooner, and I meant to, but I've been rather on the go these past few days, and I simply lost track of the time, and I know it's a piss-poor excuse, so all I can say is that I hope you'll forgive me and I promise that it won't ever happen again." He paused to take a breath, sneezed three times in a row, wiped his nose on a dusty sleeve, sneezed once more, then peered down at her imploringly and added, "What d'you say?"

Emma was vaguely unsettled by the amount of pleasure Derek's heartfelt apology gave her. "I guess this means that I don't get to smack you in the kisser," she said, half to herself. Then, smiling: "It's okay, Derek. Now, go in the other room and wait there while I put on some clothes."

Emma changed quickly into her gray trousers and Nanny Cole's blue sweater, returned the rest of her clothes to the wardrobe, and joined Derek in the bedroom. He was perched on the arm of one of the overstuffed chairs, peering at a schematic drawing from the old portfolio.

"Told you the place was a honeycomb," he said. "Meant to take my time exploring it, but, circumstances being what they are, I pushed it a bit." He handed her the house plan. "An annotated version."

"Secret passages?" Emma asked, tracing a line of red ink with her finger.

"Most weren't included on the older set of house plans, none at all on the newer ones. Want to see what I've found?"

Emma didn't bother to answer. Instead, she turned off all the lights in her room, switched on her flashlight, and headed for the wardrobe, where she moved aside to let Derek take the lead. Once she'd closed the wardrobe door behind her, she pushed through the hanging dresses and stepped into the gaping hole, then waited while Derek slid the panel back into place. As the darkness enfolded them, Derek said, in a low, excited voice, "You're not going to believe this."

18

The flashlights danced an eerie pas de deux on the smooth stone walls, and the silence was absolute. No moaning wind disturbed the musty air, no lightning pierced the inky darkness. The coming storm might break and shake the rafters, but it would not touch the core of Penford Hall.

The massive building slumbered all around them, and the passage stretched before them endlessly. The floor was dry and level, the ceiling high enough for Emma to walk upright, though Derek crept, half crouching, by her side. They scanned the way ahead, their shoulders touching, the thick stone walls absorbing every sound.

"I imagine the castle had a network of passages just like this one," Derek told her. "Grayson's predecessors probably used it to store their loot."

"But I thought the first duke gave up piracy," Emma objected.

"And what did he get in return? A title and a scrap of land unsuitable for farming. Old habits die hard, Emma, and food must be put on the table. I'll wager the old devil gave up piracy for smuggling and perhaps a spot of wrecking now and then."

In the past, small coastal towns had considered shipwrecks a boon to the local economy. For some, "wrecking" had become a way of life. Emma had read chilling tales of bonfires lit to lure ships to their doom, of sailors left to perish while their vessels were plundered. "The Nether Shoals would make it easy enough," she agreed, with a shudder.

"I'm all for carrying on family traditions," Derek commented dryly, "but there's such a thing as carrying them too far. Ah, here we are." He played the beam of his flashlight on a narrow opening to his right, where a spiral staircase wound away into the darkness. "Runs from the subcellars to the roof," he explained. "This passage and several others feed into it, and at least four rooms open off of it."

"Sounds like a main thoroughfare," said Emma.

"Hasn't been used for a long time, though. Took hours to get the hinges on all the doors oiled up and working properly." He jutted his chin upward. "Our first stop is up there." Emma started forward, but Derek put an arm out to block her way. "Not so fast. We'll have to kill the torches first."

"You want me to turn off my flashlight?" Emma peered uncertainly into the gloom.

"I'm afraid so. It's the only way we'll be able to see if light's leaking around the doors. If it is, we'll have to assume that someone's on the other side and pass them by."

"But what if someone's asleep inside one of those rooms?"

Derek shook his head. "No bedrooms lie off of this staircase. I've checked."

Emma watched unhappily as Derek turned off his flashlight and hooked it on his belt. She understood the need for caution, but she wasn't thrilled by the idea of groping her way up an unfamiliar staircase in utter darkness.

Derek seemed to read her mind. When she hesitated, he reached for her hand. "We'll take it slowly," he promised. "One step at a time." He tightened his grip. "I won't let you fall."

Smiling weakly, Emma thumbed the switch on her flashlight. Derek vanished, the walls seemed to close in around her, and she was acutely conscious of the great weight of stone hanging just above her head. Please, God, she prayed, as her heart began to race, please don't let my palms perspire.

Derek's disembodied voice was reassuring. "Remarkable, isn't it? Like being in a mine. I'm just glad there aren't any rats."

Emma's hands turned to ice. "You're sure about that?" she asked faintly.

"Quite sure." He tugged her gently forward. "Come on, now, slide your foot straight ahead. . . ."

Climbing the stairs wasn't so bad, once Emma got the hang of it, although it would have been easier if she hadn't been straining to hear the rustle of rodent feet. Her imagination populated the darkness with tiny glowing eyes and razor-sharp teeth, and though she tried to ignore the morbid fantasy, she couldn't quite shake the feeling of being watched.

Derek stopped and Emma squinted as his flashlight flared, illuminating a narrow landing and a sturdy wooden door. A heavy iron ring was bolted to the door, and Derek reached for it.

"We'll have to keep our voices down once I open the door," he warned, passing his flashlight to Emma. "This room's buried in the servants' wing." Gripping the iron ring with both hands, Derek planted his foot on the wall, and heaved. As the door swung silently toward them, Emma nearly screamed.

"*Rats,*" she hissed. Her heart began to thud and her knees turned to water and Derek's strong arms were all that kept her from fleeing headlong down the stairs.

"No, no, no," he whispered urgently, his breath warm on her face. *"Computers."*

"Wh-what?" Emma slowly turned her head to peer again into the room. Raising a hand to straighten her glasses, she saw that the red and orange pinpricks punctuating the darkness weren't beady rodent eyes, but the telltale lights of a bank of electronic equipment. Beyond the thunder of her pounding heart, she heard the steady hum of computers at work, a sound she'd heard every day for the past twenty years. Limp with relief, she laid her cheek on Derek's chest and murmured, "Sorry."

"No need for that," Derek soothed, his hand floating lightly through her hair. "Be still a moment, get your bearings."

A strange, halting note in Derek's voice made Emma tremble. Raising her face to his, she saw him wince, and it was only then that she realized she'd jammed both his flashlight and hers directly into his rib cage.

"Oh, God, I'm sorry, Derek," she said, but though she tried to pull away, he only drew her nearer, and the kiss, when it came, was so sweet and so surprising that she forgot about the flashlights altogether.

Derek remembered, fortunately, and when at last they paused to take a breath, he caught both flashlights neatly before they clattered down the stairs. As Emma's senses swam back into focus, she murmured muzzily, "We shouldn't, Derek, we really shouldn't."

"Quite right," he breathed, burying his face in her hair.

"Not here, at any rate. You'll break both our necks. What do you wash your hair in, Emma? Incense?" When Emma made no answer, he wrapped his arms around her and closed his eyes. "I know," he whispered. "Not the right time or place. May never be, for us. I never expected to find you, and I know you weren't looking for me."

"It could never work," said Emma.

Derek took a deep breath, then blew it out in a long sigh of resignation. He straightened, and looked down at Emma. "I know," he said softly. "It's just a dream."

"Just a dream," Emma murmured. She pulled away, touched a finger to her glasses, then turned unsteadily toward the colored lights. "Let's take a look."

The room they entered was unlike any Emma had seen in Penford Hall. Not a single painting hung on the stark white walls, no carpet covered the tiled floor, and although the furnishings were expensive and extremely well made, they weren't priceless antiques. As her flashlight glided over computers, printers, fax machines, photocopiers, and telephones, Emma felt as though she'd stepped into the nerve center of a modern office building.

"Oh my," she breathed, as the beam of her flashlight came to rest on a sleek black computer at the center of the room. She approached it slowly and rested one hand on the monitor, watching in awe as numbers, graphs, and complicated charts scrolled rapidly across the divided screen.

"What is it?" Derek whispered.

"A Series Ten," Emma replied. "I've read about it, but I've never gotten my hands on one before."

"Latest thing?" They stood a little ways apart, and carefully avoided each other's eyes. Emma's voice was too businesslike, Derek's too chipper, and they both spoke much too quickly.

Emma nodded. "It's based on a new, high-performance chip. Five times the speed, more capacity than you can imagine."

"What's it doing?"

"Monitoring ongoing transactions." Emma studied the screens. "Looks financial to me. Money transfers. Deutsche marks, pounds, Swiss francs, yen." She frowned. "Wait a minute. There should be . . ." Shining her light around the room, Emma spotted a wall-mounted rack covered with wires. "I thought so. High-speed data lines. He'd need them to keep current with international markets." She bit her lip, perplexed, then gestured for Derek to return to the spiral staircase. When the door was safely shut, she asked, "Why would Grayson need that kind of setup? It's powerful enough to run a fair-sized corporation."

"Why don't you ask the machine?"

Emma shook her head. "Too risky. It'll report any interruptions in its automatic functions. And I think it's safe to assume that Grayson's done what he could to protect his data. We'd need a password, maybe even a series of passwords, to do anything at all."

Derek nodded thoughtfully. "Does this prove that Grayson could've fiddled Lex's accounts?"

"All it *proves* is that he knows a lot about computers. What it *suggests* is that, if Lex's accounts were kept electronically, Grayson could've made them dance. Oh, damn." Emma rattled her flashlight, which was beginning to fade. "Don't suppose you have an extra set of batteries?"

"Sorry." Derek switched off her flashlight and hung it on his belt. "Take mine. It's not much better, but it'll last long enough to get us where we're going. No need to turn it off. The next stop on our tour is a bedroom, but it is definitely unoccupied."

A dozen steps took them to another long, low corridor that led away from the silent heart of the hall to a second door, identical to the first. Again Derek braced himself to tug on the iron ring, and when the door swung open this time, Emma recoiled from the howl of the wind. It seemed deafening after the stillness of the staircase.

"Good Lord," said Derek. "Hope the Tregallis boys' boat is safely into port. Not a night to be out fishing."

"I hope Bantry's harvested the runner beans," said Emma. "That wind will strip the arbor bare." She peered into the room, but her view was blocked by some kind of heavy fabric. "A tapestry?" she asked. She lifted the edge of the cloth, then ducked under it. Closing the wooden door behind him, Derek ducked under the tapestry after her.

There was nothing stark or modern about this room. It was sumptuous, crammed with furniture that looked as though it had been there for a very long time. The canopied bed was hung with richly embroidered black satin curtains, and a pair of caryatids held up the marble mantelpiece. The painting on the ceiling featured a dozen languid, buxom beauties whose thin gowns left little to the imagination. They reclined on facing couches, waited on by plump cupids who flitted through a pristine blue sky.

A pair of gold brocade chairs faced the hearth, and four dainty green velvet chairs were grouped around a gaming table. A green velvet divan sat before the draped windows between a pair of ornately carved end tables, and there was a low, cushioned bench at the foot of the bed.

A dizzying array of objects crowded every table and shelf: vases, candlesticks, paperweights, porcelain figurines, lacquered boxes, photographs in silver frames. Paintings large and small covered the walls, each featuring a different garden scene. Emma turned eagerly to Derek, then lowered her eyes and tried to sound casual. "Is this Grandmother's room?"

Derek nodded. He crossed to open the drapes, then stood with his back toward Emma, as though mesmerized by the intermittent flashes of lightning. "I've exceeded my brief by coming here," he admitted. "Grayson asked me expressly to leave her room alone."

"Isn't it the most logical place to look for the lantern?" Emma asked.

"Grayson assures me that they've searched it thoroughly. It's clean, as far as the lantern is concerned." He glanced over his shoulder with an unexpected twinkle in his eye.

Emma was unable to suppress her excitement. "Come on, Derek, show me."

"Don't suppose I should take such pleasure in this," he said, crossing from the windows to stand before a lute-strumming marble angel perched upon a marble pedestal, "but it's really quite wonderful. Watch." He grasped the angel's head and tilted it forward, and the wall behind the pedestal swung away into darkness.

Emma was astonished. "How did you even know to try that?"

"I didn't. I was just poking around and bumped into it. Thought I'd broken the blasted thing. Want to take a look inside?"

Emma edged past the decapitated angel into a round room with seamless marble walls rising to a domed ceiling. The curving walls were inset with a series of arched niches, and each niche held a stringed musical instrument. An antique mandolin was nearest to her, its neck intricately inlaid with mother-of-pearl. Beside it was a lute, and next to that . . .

Emma stared, dumbfounded, as the beam of Derek's

flashlight picked out a shiny black electric guitar inlaid with a silver lightning bolt, the trademark of Lex Rex.

"I don't believe it," she breathed, turning to face Derek, who had followed her into the room.

"Didn't think you would," said Derek proudly. "Doesn't really prove that Grayson murdered Lex, though."

An eerie peal of laughter cut through the moaning wind, and Emma gasped as a flash of lightning from the bedroom window limned a familiar figure in the doorway. Derek stiffened, then swung around as a voice sounded behind him.

"Don't be squeamish, dear boy," said the duke, stepping into the room. "Of course I murdered Lex Rex. And I know precisely what I'm going to do with both of you."

19

"You're back early, Grayson." Derek took an unobtrusive backward step that placed him between Emma and the duke. "We didn't expect you until tomorrow."

"Disappointed?" Grayson asked.

"Not at all," Derek assured him. "Merely . . . surprised."

"I can see that," the duke commented dryly. "Had I known of your interest in antique musical instruments, I would have returned sooner."

Emma moved to Derek's side. She appreciated his chivalrous instincts, but it was maddening to stand behind him, unable to see the duke. If something dreadful was about to happen, she wasn't going to let Derek face it alone.

She was content to let him do the talking, though. So far, the two men were acting as though this were nothing more than a chance encounter at a somewhat unusual house party. Derek's sangfroid suggested that it was perfectly normal to be facing a murderous madman in a secret room, lit only by the dimming beam of a dying flashlight and the brief white fire of lightning.

"It's this ghastly weather that brought me home," the duke was saying. "It may clear up overnight, or it may settle in for a week. Since neither Kate nor I could countenance another week in Plymouth, home we came, jiggety-jig."

"Leaving Susannah behind you?" Derek asked.

"Indeed not." The duke turned his head, distracted by a loud thump and a few muttered words that came from the dowager's bedchamber. The keening wind made it impossible for Emma to identify the voices. She gripped Derek's arm involuntarily as the duke turned back to them, smiling.

"As I was saying," he continued, "Dr. Singh gave Susannah the all-clear, so we brought her with us, one big happy family. She's in her room now, with Mattie and Nurse Tharby." Grayson looked at Emma. "Nurse Tharby is Dr. Singh's assistant, though she'll be his equal once she's completed her studies. I believe you met her proud mother at the Bright Lady."

Emma nodded. She recalled Mrs. Tharby very well. She also recalled how loyal the villagers had been when facing the onslaught from the press. They wouldn't welcome anyone who threatened the generous lord of the manor. They might even see to it that Susannah took a sudden and entirely plausible turn for the worse. The same thought must have crossed Derek's mind, for his arm had turned to steel beneath the soft cotton of his blue workshirt.

"Like to see her," he said, with absolute composure. "Susannah, that is. Welcome her back. Let her know she's among friends."

"Not possible, old man." The duke raised his hands, palms out. "Nothing to do with me. Nurse's orders. If she declares that Syd and Mattie are to be Susannah's sole companions this evening, I'm afraid we must bow to her authority."

Derek relaxed a bit. "Syd's up there, is he?"

"Planning to camp there, by the looks of it. I say, Emma, it was awfully clever of you to put him to work in Grandmother's garden. Magical place, that garden. It's done him a world of good."

The duke turned his head again as a wavering glow began to penetrate the darkness in the dowager's bedroom. Fire? Emma thought. She cast an uneasy glance at the marble walls and tried very hard not to imagine what would happen if the duke barred the only exit after setting the well-oiled antique instruments ablaze.

"Please," said the duke, facing them once more, "won't you join me? It's frightfully uncivilized to stand chatting in doorways. And we have so much to talk about." As he turned on his heel and left the room, Derek looked down at Emma and smiled encouragingly. Emma couldn't quite return his smile, preoccupied as she was by thoughts of how thick the walls were in Penford Hall's hidden passages, and how easy it would be to seal someone—or a pair of someones—in an out-of-the-way dead end. She comforted herself with the knowledge that Derek was probably as good at demolition as he was at restoration. With a bit of luck and the blade of his penknife, they'd be able to dig their way out. In a year or so.

Gathering her courage, Emma followed Derek through the doorway.

They reentered the dowager's bedchamber in time to see Crowley rise, red-faced, from the gold-veined marble hearth, where his exertions had produced a brightly burning fire. Emma saw at once that the divan had been moved to one side of the fireplace, a high-backed gold brocade armchair to the other, and the ornate end tables had been pushed together to form a coffee table.

Hallard stood nearby, illuminating Crowley's labors with a gold candelabra filled with flickering white candles. Kate was there, as well, in an oatmeal-colored fisherman's knit pullover and dark-brown trousers, standing with folded arms before the door-concealing tapestry. No one seemed surprised to see them.

As immaculate as ever, Grayson was dressed in fawn cavalry twills, a hacking jacket, an ivory shirt, and a silk tie. He nodded cordially to Crowley as he sank into the gold brocade chair and motioned Emma and Derek toward the divan.

Crowley tugged his waistcoat into place, straightened his black tie and upright collar, then gestured for Hallard to follow him through a pair of white-and-gold doors that led, apparently, to the hallway.

For a moment, the only sounds were the moaning wind, the snapping fire, and the distant rumble of thunder. Then another rumble sounded, just outside the bedroom doors.

"Watch where you're going, you nincompoop!"

"Sorry, Nanny, but your needles nearly caught me in the—"

Emma jumped as the bedroom door banged open and Nanny Cole swept in, magnificent in a red plaid robe and brown corduroy slippers, clutching a yarn-filled basket bristling with half a dozen lethal-looking knitting needles. Chief Constable Trevoy trailed after her, carrying a flashlight and keeping a close watch on the basket.

"You're a ninny, Tom Trevoy, and you always were," Nanny declared. "A poke in the goolies might stiffen your backbone, but I doubt it. Now, stop your whingeing and fetch me a chair!" She paused to glower at Derek and Emma, growling, "Nosey-parkers. Can't bear nosey-parkers." Peering around the shadowy room, she demanded, "Where's that blasted daughter of mine? Comes mincing in without so much as a by-your-leave. Ah! There you are!" She crossed over to Kate, while Chief Constable Trevoy hastened to move the other gold brocade chair close to the fire, then sat meekly on the low bench at the foot of the bed, stroking his red mustache.

"Kate, you look like death," Nanny Cole barked. "Off to bed with you, my girl, quickstep march!"

"I'd very much like Kate to stay," Grayson murmured.

Nanny Cole's lower lip protruded obstinately, but all she said was "Suit yourself. But don't blame me if the chit keels over. I've a good mind to dose the pair of you before the night is through."

The sound of footsteps in the hall announced the arrival of Gash, the chubby mechanic, and Newland, the taciturn gatekeeper. Newland went over to conduct a low-pitched conversation with Kate, then parked himself before the hall doors, rolling his long silver flashlight from hand to hand with the contained energy of an athlete. Emma's heart sank as she realized that, although the gatekeeper was in his mid-sixties, he was in remarkably fine physical condition.

Gash approached the duke. "Power plant's buggered," he reported. "We've got the backup generator for emergency systems and alarms, and we still have the telephone, but the rest'll have to wait till morning."

"I'm sure you've done your best," said the duke.

"Always do, Your Grace." Gash nodded to Derek and Emma, then took a seat beside Chief Constable Trevoy.

A moment later, Newland opened the doors for Crowley and Hallard. Each carried a large silver tray, which they placed on the tables at Emma's knee. Crowley's tray held an enormous silver teapot, nine cups and saucers, a silver creamer and sugar bowl, nine teaspoons, and a stack of small plates. Hallard's was freighted with four three-tiered pastry stands filled to overflowing with dainty, crustless sandwiches.

"About bloody time," grumbled Nanny Cole. "What's Madama sent up?"

Hallard pointed out paper-thin slices of lamb piled on nutty homemade bread, with a side dish of fresh mint sauce; morsels of lobster on toast rounds, topped with a dab of mayonnaise; triangles of white bread filled with translucent wafers of turbot; a round of cheddar cheese, a bunch of glistening grapes, and a bowl of peaches.

A flurry of activity ensued, as tea was poured and sandwiches were distributed. Although Emma had slept through supper, she had little appetite, and the rattle of her teacup on its saucer betrayed her nervousness. Were she and Derek about to be tried and convicted by the duke's kangaroo court? She stared gravely at her teacup, then frowned, vaguely puzzled. What kind of kangaroo court served *tea* to the accused? She raised her eyes to search the faces that surrounded her. How could she feel threatened by these people? They'd shown her nothing but kindness. Newland was an unknown quantity, of course, but apart from him—and Nanny Cole's knitting needles—did she really have anything to fear? Gradually, Emma's nervousness subsided, to be replaced by an intense curiosity. What was the duke up to?

"Where's Bantry?" Emma asked suddenly.

"With the children," Kate replied. She had pulled a chair over to sit slightly behind and to one side of the duke. "We didn't want them to be alone on a night like this."

The duke polished off his sixth sandwich while Emma was still toying with her first. He flicked the crumbs into the fire, put his dish on the tray, then leaned back in his chair to survey the group.

"I think that's all of us," he said. "Crowley, Hallard, do have a seat. You hover with great aplomb, dear chaps, but surely it's inadvisable after such a tiring day." When Crowley and Hallard had settled soundlessly at the gaming table, the duke went on. "Since this is the first chance I've had to see some of you since my return, let me start off by saying what a pleasure it is to find myself once more at home and in your company.

"I can't tell you how deeply I appreciate everything you've done in my absence. Newland's defense of the perimeter was nothing short of brilliant. Tom's orchestration of the villagers sent the invaders packing with all due speed, taking nothing with them but the somewhat dazed impression that Penford Harbor is inhabited exclusively by a bunch of daft wheezers." Gash clapped the chief constable on the shoulder and gave Newland a hearty thumbs-up. "Thanks to the rest of you, I never had a moment's worry about the smooth running of the household. As you can imagine, it made my task in Plymouth that much easier."

"How're we doin'?" Gash inquired.

The duke smiled. "You'll be pleased to know that the tabloids have deemed Penford Hall unworthy of their attention." He paused as a murmur of approval washed through the room. "And we owe that happy development to the untiring efforts of our dear old Kate."

Kate smiled shyly. "I seem to recall that you played a role as well, Grayson."

"Without your support, I'd've wilted," the duke declared. "Sorry, old thing, I'm afraid you must take full credit for a job well done."

"Here, here!" called Crowley, and Kate flushed as a ragged cheer went up.

"Your Grace." Chief Constable Trevoy raised his hand. "About Miss Ashley-Woods—"

"We'll get to that a bit later, if you please, Tom. At the moment we must attend to our honored guests." The duke crossed his legs and tilted his head to one side, regarding Derek quizzically. "I can understand your desire to view my grandmother's collection of instruments privately, Derek, but I must confess that I am somewhat disappointed in you."

"Not half as disappointed as I am in you, Grayson," Derek retorted mildly.

"You agreed to keep away from Grandmother's rooms, did you not?"

"The circumstances have changed."

"Have they?" The duke shook his head. "Your perception has, no doubt, but the circumstances are much the same as they've always been."

"They most certainly are not," Derek countered. "I haven't *always* known you to be a murderer, a thief, and a liar."

"Dear me . . ." The duke raised a hand to fan his face. "Such heated accusations. I've always admired your forthrightness, so I shan't complain now, but honestly, old man, you quite singe my eyebrows with the warmth of your convictions. I presume you will permit me to offer a word in my own defense?" When Derek nodded curtly, the duke leaned forward, his brown eyes flashing, all trace of good humor gone.

"Yes, I murdered Lex Rex, and I had every right to do so."

"Look here, Grayson," Derek began, but the duke would not be interrupted.

"As for being a thief, I deny that categorically. I only took what was mine, and even Milord will agree that hardly qualifies as theft. A liar, though . . ." Grayson sat back in his chair again and examined his fingernails. "There you have me, dear boy, for I am nothing if not a liar, and an unrepentant one at that." He raised his eyes to Derek's. "The very worst sort. But I feel compelled to tell the truth before you and Emma . . . depart. You are an old and trusted friend, Derek, and you, Emma, are my gardening angel. It grieves me to see the suspicion in your eyes. Before this night is through, I intend to put you both out of your misery. My friends . . ." He paused, and Emma stiffened as Derek's arm went around her shoulders. "May I present the late, and most assuredly unlamented, Lex Rex?"

Emma waited, then looked slowly around the room. There was Crowley, sitting quietly, his head tilted attentively toward the duke; Hallard, gazing absently into the middle distance; Nanny Cole, knitting a sweater in cobalt blue; Newland, keeping watch from the doorway; Kate, gazing gravely at Grayson; Tom Trevoy, stroking his mustache; Gash, leaning against the foot of the bed, his hands folded serenely across his round belly. Emma looked up at Derek, saw that his confusion mirrored her own, then turned back to the duke. "Excuse me?" she said.

Derek was more severe. "Don't like charades, Grayson," he said bluntly. "Never have. If you've got something to say for yourself, you'd best come out with it."

The duke sighed. "That's what I thought you'd say. Well, all right, then . . . Pour yourselves another cup of tea, everyone. This may take some time."

20

The rain came then, pounding down without preamble. It swept in from the sea and dashed against the bedroom windows, driven by gusts that would leave the rose bushes in tatters, flood the great lawn, and flatten every one of Madama's vegetables. Emma thought of the freshly turned topsoil in the chapel garden and wondered if it would all be washed away by morning.

Newland, monitoring the storm's progress through the earphone of a shortwave radio, confirmed that gale warnings had been sounded all up and down the coast and that residents had been advised to sit tight.

Chief Constable Trevoy placed a quick call to the village, where Mrs. Tharby cheerfully informed him that all was well, the boats were safe at harbor, and the only casualty so far had been Mr. Minion, the butcher, who'd slipped on a slick cobblestone and sprained his left wrist. Dr. Singh had seen to the injury and Mr. Minion had recovered sufficiently to hoist a few by candlelight at the Bright Lady.

Gash had long ago wired the hall's windows with sensors. If a pane was broken, the beeper in his pocket would sound and its digital readout would give him a rough idea of the window's location. The staff as a whole seemed remarkably nonchalant about the storm.

"We're part of the headland," Gash explained. "Whole bloody rock'd have to blow away afore any harm'd come to Penford Hall."

Hallard added wood to the fire, Crowley refilled cups, and Nanny Cole ate a few more sandwiches, while Derek fidgeted impatiently, and Emma peered worriedly at the driving rain. Very gradually, activity slowed, and a deep stillness fell over the room. Tearing her gaze from the windows, Emma saw that everyone was seated, and that all faces were turned to Grayson.

He was standing near the bedside table, staring down at a photograph in a brown leather frame. Gently, he picked it up, dusted it lightly with his sleeve, and returned with it to his chair, where he sat gazing at it for a few more silent moments before handing it to Emma.

Emma looked down at a portrait of a British army officer. The background was smoky and indistinct, the uniform unrelieved by gleaming brass or bright ribbons. Slender and fine-featured, light-haired and sporting a pencil-thin mustache, the man bore a striking resemblance to the duke, save for the great sadness in his eyes. In his right hand he gripped a riding crop, but his left sleeve was folded back on itself and pinned at the shoulder.

"My father." The duke sat with his face turned toward the fire, and his animated hands lay becalmed on the arms of his chair. "The thirteenth duke of Penford was an unhappy man. I leave it to you to decide if it was due to his unfortunate place in the succession, but I'm rather more inclined to blame it on his unfortunate place in history.

"He lost his own father and all of his uncles in the

Great War. He lost his first wife in a daylight raid on the Plymouth dockyards, his arm in the Ardennes, and his second wife, my mother, shortly after I was born." He glanced at Derek, then lowered his eyes. "To pneumonia. Not even a healthy son and heir could put paid to all of those losses, and he became something of a recluse."

Derek stirred restlessly. "Look, Grayson, I'm very sorry, but—"

"Patience, dear boy," said the duke.

Nanny Cole glared at Derek. "It's your fault we've been dragged out of our beds in the middle of the night, so you just keep still or I'll box your bloody ears."

Chastened, Derek fell silent.

"My father," the duke continued, "left much of my upbringing to my grandmother, who saw to it that I was educated at home by a governess who has since passed on. My grandmother was a wonderful woman in many ways, but she was . . . selectively attentive. If I was neatly dressed and well behaved, she would spend hours with me. When I was bad-tempered—"

"Never had a bad-tempered day in your life," Nanny Cole stated firmly, and the others murmured their agreement.

"Let us say, then, that I was, at times, overly energetic," the duke conceded.

"Bouncing off the walls, more like," muttered Gash.

"At such times," the duke continued doggedly, "which occurred far too often in my grandmother's estimation, I was banished from her presence."

"And dumped in our laps," huffed Nanny Cole.

"Not that we minded," Gash put in.

"Didn't say we *minded,* did I?" retorted Nanny Cole.

"As a result," Grayson went on, "I spent most of my formative years under the watchful eyes of Nanny Cole and the rest of the staff. I adored my grandmother, but these good people . . ." He let his gaze travel slowly around the room. "These good people, I loved."

"Mawkish nonsense," muttered Nanny Cole. "Get a grip, Grayson, or you'll have Kate blubbering."

"Mother," said an obviously exasperated Kate, "will you please allow Grayson to speak?"

"Never been able to stop him, have I?" Nanny Cole scowled at her daughter, but remained silent as Grayson continued.

"My father's decision to withdraw from the world had a catastrophic effect on both the hall and the village. New tax laws encouraged him to dabble in speculation, but he'd neither the skill nor the patience to succeed at that game. He was forced to sell our land in Kent and Somerset, and to dismiss the underservants, all of whom came from Penford Harbor. When they sought employment elsewhere, their houses were left vacant and the village began a slow and painful decline.

"As for the hall . . . Well, I'm sure you've heard the story many times before, Derek. Routine repairs were neglected, and the place began to fall apart. My father closed off room after room, until we were all living cheek by jowl in the central block."

"It were a bad time," Gash murmured, and the others nodded solemnly.

"I'd no idea how bad," Grayson commented. "The staff shielded me from every hardship and made it seem like jolly good fun to be bunched together like that. After my grandmother died, however, Father dismissed the staff and began selling off the contents of Penford Hall."

"Was he allowed to do that?" Emma asked, with a timid glance at Nanny Cole.

"He wasn't, actually," replied the duke. "The hall and

all that it contained were entailed to me and should've been handed down intact. But with Grandmother gone, there was no one to stop him." The duke's gaze roved over the walls, taking in every painting, every priceless ornament, while his hands caressed the rich fabric on the arms of his chair, as though reassuring himself that it was real. "I'm so proud of Grandmother for hiding her emeralds," he said softly.

From the corner of her eye, Emma saw Nanny Cole raise her eyes to Kate, who looked quickly away.

"We think she must have done the same thing with the lantern," Grayson went on, "and for the same reason. Unfortunately, she neglected to inform anyone of the hiding place. By then, you see, there was hardly anyone left to tell." The duke folded his hands and tapped the tips of his thumbs together. "Imagine waking up each day to the loss of a beloved sister or brother, uncle or aunt, and you will begin to comprehend the distress I felt when my father began to dismiss the staff. Soon only Nanny Cole remained, and I refused to believe that Father would send her away. With Grandmother gone, Nanny Cole was the only mother I had."

"I was the only one left to make your blasted bed, you mean," Nanny Cole put in. Her knitting needles had stopped moving and she peered fondly at the duke. A faint pink flush rose in the old woman's cheeks as she sensed that the attention of the room was on her, and she pulled her needles back into action, growling, "You just get on with the story, my lad."

"Where was I? Ah, yes . . ." The duke sighed wearily. "Father then informed me that I was to be sent away to school. That was bad enough, but on the afternoon of the very same day, not a month after my grandmother's death, I saw her harp being loaded into a van and taken away. You must understand that the harp was her prize possession. Its removal forced me to face the awful fact that nothing and no one was safe.

"Father and I had a terrific set-to that evening, at the conclusion of which I ran away. I was a mere boy at the time—Peter's age—and the weather was as rough as it is tonight, so I didn't run very far. I went to the lady chapel, in fact, to have a good, self-pitying weep. Much to my amazement, Aunt Dimity was there when I arrived—"

"Dimity Westwood?" Derek asked.

"There's only one Aunt Dimity," Grayson replied.

"But how did she know—" Emma left the sentence unfinished.

The duke smiled and shook his head. "I have no idea. She'd learned of Grandmother's death, of course—"

"And she may have heard rumors about the sale of the harp," Kate put in.

"Perhaps," said the duke. "But . . ." He shrugged. "Who knows?"

A tingle crept down Emma's back. Dimity Westwood was beginning to sound vaguely supernatural. She returned long-lost teddy bears to bereft little girls, and she just happened to appear out of nowhere to soothe tormented little boys. And the mysterious woman might have had a hand in bringing Emma to Penford Hall, as well. Emma glanced up at Derek's sapphire eyes and broad shoulders, wondering how far Aunt Dimity's powers extended, then shook her head and gave her full attention to the duke.

"Aunt Dimity listened to my woes," he was saying, "then told me, flat out, that I would think of a way to save the hall. I don't remember what happened next, but when I awoke the following morning, I felt as though I'd been reborn. I saw clearly that an enormous task lay ahead of me—but not an impossible one. That made all the difference."

As though galvanized by the memory, the duke pushed himself out of his chair and stood before the fire. Thrusting one hand into a trouser pocket and clutching a tweedy lapel with the other, he struck a professorial pose. "Now," he said, "if one asks an adult how to raise an enormous amount of capital in a relatively brief period of time, the adult will invariably reply . . . ?" He raised an eyebrow and stared expectantly at Emma.

" 'Rob a bank'?" Emma ventured.

"Bravo, Miss Porter." The duke nodded his approval. "If, however, one asks a child the same question, one will receive two dozen different answers, each one more outrageous than the last. I speak as an authority on the matter. I came up with a dozen dozen different schemes over the next few years, but dismissed them all as too time-consuming and/or dangerously illegal.

"Then, one night at school, Pogger Pratt-Evans was listening to some particularly noisome rock music. When I asked him to turn it down, Pogger replied with the immortal words . . ." The duke turned his face to the ceiling and enunciated each word carefully, as though he were reciting Shakespearean verse. " 'Fat lot you know about music. These guys must be good—they've made millions.' "

The duke closed his eyes for a moment, as though savoring the words, then began to pace excitedly before the fire. "I couldn't sleep a wink that night, not with 'they've made millions' ringing in my ears, and by morning I had put together a plan—an outrageous, ridiculous, impossible plan, which I knew in the depths of my twelve-year-old heart would save the hall. In fact, I think it's fair to say that it was at that moment that Lex Rex was born."

Derek frowned. "Are you saying that *you're*—"

"I am not," the duke declared. He came to a halt squarely in front of the fire, his hands in his pockets, his hair a golden halo above his shadowed face, looking as though he'd never quite left his twelve-year-old self behind. "I'm saying only that an idea was born." He spread his arms wide. "It was this distinguished collection of geniuses who nurtured that idea until it became the loathsome creature we know as Lex Rex."

"You mean, you're all—?" Emma touched a hand to her glasses and looked from one wrinkled face to another. "You're *all* Lex Rex?"

"Our star pupil triumphs again," proclaimed the duke. He gave them no time to digest this startling news, turning quickly to ask Kate to go on with the story.

Kate Cole cleared her throat. "As you know, Mother and I had moved to Bournemouth after the old duke gave Mother the—after Mother left Penford Hall."

"Broke her heart to leave," said Nanny Cole, eyeing her daughter with unexpected gentleness. "But we couldn't go back to the village. Bloody place was deserted. No school, no children to play with . . ."

"So we went to Bournemouth, where Mother worked as a seamstress."

"Kate was never happy there," Nanny Cole went on. "Only time she perked up was when she got Grayson's letters. So, when she came to me with his crack-brained scheme, I thought, Bugger it, I'll jolly them along. Anything to get Kate up and punching again." Nanny Cole sighed and looked down at her cobalt-blue yarn. "Hated to see her in such a funk."

"Mother was wonderful," said Kate. "She drew all sorts of costumes and I sent the drawings on to Grayson. We wrote to each other three or four times a week. His plan didn't sound preposterous to me."

Nanny Cole snorted. "None of Grayson's plans ever sounded preposterous to you, my girl." She glanced at Crowley with a devilish grin. "Remember the two of 'em tunneling under the arbor, looking for pirate gold?"

"I do indeed, Nanny," Crowley replied. "Quite a time we had, pulling them out. I believe it was Miss Kate who christened Lex Rex. Isn't that right, Nanny?"

"Very true," Nanny Cole replied. "Lex from Alexander —one of Grayson's other names—and Rex . . . Well, she wanted her duke to have a promotion, didn't she?"

"I thought it sounded well together," Kate explained, coloring. "At any rate," she hurried on, "it seemed to me that the most important part of the plan was that it be carried out in secret."

The duke nodded eagerly. "Quite right. If I didn't want to spend the rest of my life as Lex Rex—and I most certainly did not—we would require the help of people whose loyalty and discretion would be absolute."

Kate smiled. "Grayson had kept in touch with everyone, not just the staff but the remaining villagers, as well, those who'd refused to abandon Penford Harbor. We selected a core group and, with Mother's help, began to visit them, one by one, to sound them out."

"The response was quite astonishing," said the duke. "Within the year, we had the entire staff working together to breathe life into Lex Rex. I knew that I wanted to do something with pop music, but I wasn't sure what. Hallard's the one who figured that out."

"Mmmm?" Hallard peered absently at the duke.

"I was just telling Derek and Emma that you invented Lex Rex," said the duke.

"Yes, yes." Hallard blinked owlishly. "Just created a character, really."

"Hallard," the duke informed Emma, "is also known as Hal Arden."

"The writer?" Emma gaped at the bespectacled old man. "Spy novels?"

"My publisher prefers to call them espionage thrillers, but never mind," said Hallard. "Don't hold much with labels."

"But I've read everything you've ever written!" Emma exclaimed.

"He'll autograph a complete set for you, won't you, old man?" The duke beamed at Hallard. "Our writer-in-residence was instrumental in putting together Lex's biography."

"Just listened to His Grace and Miss Kate, really," said Hallard. "Bit of a poser, really, making a character who was literally three-dimensional. But I liked the challenge."

"And rose to it," declared the duke. "Hallard was the one who discovered that ownership of England's great estates falls into five basic categories: surviving families, few and far between; foreigners who wish they were English; corporations, which use the houses as retreats for harried executives; the National Trust, which turns them into museums—"

"And pop stars," Hallard concluded. "Interesting subject, really, and His Grace made the research that much easier. It was like having an agent in place, really, with him spying on kids like Pogger and telling me what they fancied." Hallard leaned forward, rubbing his palms together as he warmed to his subject. "Lex Rex couldn't be a pretty-face pop phenomenon, y'see, because we couldn't have people concentrating on His Grace's face. We didn't want a band with too much staying power, either. A medium-sized hit twice a year for five years would do us nicely. I figured that, if *Time* magazine called Lex the next Beatles within the first two years of our run, we'd done the job."

"Their predictions inevitably fade," explained the duke. He smiled slyly and scratched the end of his nose. "Hallard wrote the lyrics for Lex's songs, as well. 'Kiss My Tongue' was, in my opinion, one of his noblest efforts."

"I don't know," Kate teased. "I've always been fond of the ecological motif of 'Slug Soup.' And let's not forget 'Chafe Me, Baby,' and—"

"That'll be quite enough out of the pair of you," Nanny Cole scolded. "Hallard may have written tripe, but *you*, Grayson, wrote the putrid music."

"I did," Grayson admitted sheepishly.

"But you're a talented musician," Emma exclaimed. "How could you bring yourself to—"

"Create such cacophony? I was following Hallard's script. Everything about Lex had to be off-putting, to keep people at bay. And there Nanny Cole came into her own."

Nanny Cole eyed him suspiciously, then turned to Derek and Emma. "I designed Lex's costumes and makeup," she said. "I created his bloody-awful image. Had to turn Grayson into a raving lunatic. Not as much of a stretch as he'd like to think."

"Nanny's costumes were brilliant," Grayson said. "She has the soul of a poet and it embarrasses her terribly. Hence the bluff exterior."

"I'll buff your posterior if you don't stop," Nanny Cole growled, and Derek flinched as she grabbed him by the wrist. "Keep still," she ordered as she held the sleeve of the nearly finished sweater up to Derek's arm. "Good Lord," she muttered, dropping the arm. "Built like a bloody great ape."

Grayson snorted. "Nanny shaved my head and painted it red for the cover of the first album. I promise you, not even Grandmother would've recognized me once Nanny had finished with her paint pots. I scarcely recognized myself."

"Surely you made some personal appearances," Derek said, rubbing his wrist.

"Very few," said Kate. "Lex refused to attend ceremonies of any kind and he was never seen in public without his makeup. It was perfectly in keeping with the character we'd established."

"The press posed some danger," Grayson went on, "but Hallard solved that as well. Whenever they showed up, Lex would scratch himself rudely and spout all those words one mustn't say on the telly, at decibel levels impossible for microphones to miss. And we had Newland here, to look after security."

Newland nodded but, unlike the rest of the staff, made no effort to explain his role. An uneasy silence enveloped the room, and everyone turned to Kate gratefully when she broke it.

"And then there were the videos," she said.

"A godsend." Grayson clapped Derek on the shoulder. "Remember the chaps I ran around with in Oxford?"

Derek nodded.

"One of them is a well-known rock singer now. I won't mention his name, as he's made an assiduous effort to deny his bourgeois past, but he's the one who put me on to rock videos. That's how we were able to get in at the right time."

Kate's eyes were dancing. "Lex Rex became the first pop star to take full advantage of the video boom. And we filmed them right here, in Gash's studio."

Gash twiddled his thumbs. "Jury-rigged from start to finish. Had no idea what I was doing, but that didn't bother His Grace. Had no capital, neither, so I had to make do. Cleared out one of the subcellars, soundproofed it as best I could. Bought secondhand stage lights and cheap video equipment and off we went."

Emma rolled her eyes, recalling the praise Richard had heaped on Lex Rex's "rough-edged authenticity." She wondered what he would say if she told him that the qualities he most admired were due solely to inexperience, ineptitude, and a tight budget.

The duke flopped into his chair and crossed his legs. "As it turned out, we had eight years in which to plan the whole thing, down to the smallest detail. I was twenty years old when my father died."

"Grayson came down from university to follow in his father's reclusive footsteps and disappear from public view," Kate went on.

"When I reappeared, I did so as Lex Rex," said the duke. "After eight years of intensive study, I was able to give rock-music fans exactly what they wanted. Then, of course, I gave them more of the same."

"Look at any best-seller list," Hallard murmured thoughtfully, "and you'll know where that idea came from."

"But . . ." Emma scratched her head. "But what about the Series Ten?"

"The what?" said Hallard.

"Hallard simply uses the computers," the duke put in. "We leave the rest to Crowley."

"Crowley?" Derek and Emma chorused.

From his place near the gaming table, Crowley smiled his polite, distant smile, tugged at his stiff cuffs, and folded his hands in his lap. "After leaving the old duke's employ," he began, "I moved to Plymouth, to be near my only daughter." He looked down at the floor for a moment, then shook his head. "What the others have failed to tell you is that it is not a simple matter for a person of mature years to find employment. Nanny Cole had her flair with the needle; Gash, his mechanical skills; Hallard, his God-given gift with words; and Newland . . ." He squinted at the tight-lipped security man. "Well, I'm not at all sure what Newland got up to, but I do know that his talents are in demand in many places.

"But what did I have to offer?" Crowley sighed. "Thirty years of loyal service counts for very little in the modern world, it seems. You can imagine my relief when I eventually won a post at a bank, entering check numbers on a computer. It was a very low-level position and tedious to the extreme. Sheer boredom led me to read up on computers and to explore my little machine's capabilities."

"Crowley was to the keyboard born," the duke declared. "He took to programming like a duck to water, and he's a dab hand at code-cracking, too. He's had the best trackers after him, and they've yet to find a single broken blade of grass. Only one came within shouting distance, but he backed off."

"Tut, tut," Crowley murmured, accepting the tribute with a self-effacing wave of the hand.

"He salted records with facts about Lex's alleged background," said Kate, "and he managed every pound of Lex's income."

"He managed to make it disappear," the duke put in. "Crowley tied Lex's money-trail in so many knots that it would have taken a magician to unravel it. He made it appear as though Lex had frittered away his fortune on playthings." The duke clucked his tongue. "Just another self-indulgent pop star."

Emma pictured Crowley's storklike figure hunched over the keyboard of a computer late at night, after the bank had closed, sailing freely through the electronic networks, and she was filled with awe. It wasn't every day that she got to meet a natural-born hacker who'd discovered computers at such an advanced age.

Derek rubbed his jaw. "I don't know, Grayson. This doesn't sound like you. I find it difficult to believe that you could be quite so cynical."

"Of course I was cynical, dear chap," the duke acknowledged easily. "But you must admit that it was a healthy sort of cynicism. Lex Rex did not wish to be loved—he wished only to be paid. It kept his ego in check, kept his mind focused—it kept him from drink, drugs, and all the other slings and arrows that had slain so many before him. He never promoted such things, either. My alter ego's only sins were poor taste and a severely limited vocabulary—"

"Which you enjoyed to the hilt," Nanny Cole reminded him.

"Well . . . yes," the duke admitted, with a shame-faced grin. "It was rather . . . liberating." He tugged on an earlobe, then settled back in his chair, businesslike once more. "At the end of the second year, we'd earned enough to replace the roof and begin restoring the hall's interior. In four more years, we'd amassed a fortune, which Crowley invested with good results. Computers were not the only thing he studied at the bank."

Derek nodded. "Then you decided that it was time for Lex's abrupt departure from the world of rock music."

"Poor old Lex," the duke agreed, with mock sadness. "He never was much of a sailor, was he, Tom?"

"No, indeed, Your Grace." The chief constable chuckled. "It were the Tregallis boys that fixed that up. Born fishermen, they are, and want nothin' more'n to carry on as their father had done. The Tharbys at the Bright Lady felt the same way, and so did old Jonah Pengully and my mother. So we worked it all out with Hallard and watched the weather maps, waitin' for a storm. When it looked as if a likely one was brewin', His Grace hightailed it for France—"

"I was traveling a great deal by then," the duke added, "recovering my family's scattered treasures."

"Me and the boys went aboard His Grace's yacht," the chief constable continued, "and had a fine old time, smashing it to bits. Ted and Jack steered it onto the shoals, and James picked them up in a dinghy."

"Only expert sailors could've managed that trick," Derek commented. He looked thoughtfully at the fire, then frowned. "But why go to all that trouble? Wouldn't it have been safer to stage his death somewhere else, to make it a bit less spectacular?"

Kate shook her head. "Lex's death would've attracted attention no matter where it took place," she said flatly. "This way, we could control the situation and make the best use of the resources we had at hand."

"Taciturn Cornish villagers make very credible eyewitnesses, really," Hallard explained. "Lots of practice at it, I suppose, with all the smuggling that used to go on."

"But what about the press?" Derek asked.

"A temporary nuisance," Grayson said dismissively.

"Still," Derek persisted, "you were taking an awfully big risk, weren't you? How many people were involved? Fourteen? Fifteen? And now you'll have to add me and Emma to the list. I've no doubt that Newland knows his stuff, but how can you be sure there'll be no leaks?"

"We can't," the duke replied simply. "Look, Derek, I may very well be the dunderhead Nanny considers me to be, but Hallard isn't."

Hallard was cleaning his glasses with his handkerchief. "Just have a devious mind, really. I knew the truth would come out eventually. It's human nature to want to share a secret." He carefully replaced his glasses, then folded his handkerchief and returned it to his pocket. "So I prepared a story line for every situation we're likely to face."

The duke smiled indulgently at Hallard. "It's no use grilling him on what those story lines may be. He's got them hidden away on Crowley's blasted Series Ten, with instructions on how to get at them, should we ever need to. But he hates discussing his work. Won't even let me read his book flaps."

"Pesky things always give the plot away," Hallard put in.

"All we know for certain," said the duke, "is that Hallard's come up with a number of likely and unlikely scenarios for us to follow. Based on his past performance, I have every confidence that, whatever happens, the outcome will be satisfactory for all concerned."

Emma sipped tea that had long since grown cold, then put her cup and saucer on the tray. "There's one more question I'd like to ask, if I may," she said. "The answer may seem obvious to you, but . . . Well, it sounds so complicated, and it took so long to plan. I'm just wondering why you were all so willing to help out."

Uncertain looks were exchanged, throats were cleared, fingernails were examined, and feet were shuffled. Finally, Gash proposed an answer.

"It was fun," he said. "Whether Lex Rex panned out or not, we had a good time working on him. When you get down to it, fixing flats in the local garage can be pretty bloody boring."

Now Crowley spoke up. "Self-interest played a role, as well. There was always the outside chance that His Grace's scheme would succeed, that we would achieve our individual goals. All I wanted was to return to my place at Penford Hall. Newland wanted a quiet patch of woods to prowl, Gash dreamt of a first-rate garage, and Hallard wanted privacy and time to write."

"It's the same in the village," said the chief constable. "As I said before—"

"Balls!" roared Nanny Cole, rattling her knitting needles. "Sod that nonsense, Tom Trevoy, and the same goes for you, Ephraim Crowley. Fun and self-interest—what a load of rubbish." She sniffed derisively. "You know as well as I do why we listened to His Grace, and why we went ahead when common sense told us we hadn't a chance in hell of succeeding. It was *him.*" She looked proudly at the duke. "He's a proper little wizard, is our Grayson, and always has been. He can charm water from a rock. He can twist a stiff-necked old biddy like me around his little finger."

"Now, Nanny . . ." Grayson murmured.

"Don't you 'Now, Nanny' me, you cheeky blighter. They all know what I'm talking about. They know how you make folks believe that everything's possible, that dreams were *meant* to come true. If you'd told us we could fly to the moon, we'd've tried to build a bloody rocket." She glared fiercely around the room. "And I dare any of you to deny it."

No one took up the challenge. Derek ran a hand through his curls, then shook his head, bemused. "Fascinating," he murmured. "Truly fascinating. And, in all that time, no one ever suspected the truth?"

The duke didn't answer at first. A faint smile played about his lips as he rose and stood staring silently into the fire. Finally, he spoke. "In all those years, only one person saw through my ruse, and that was because I wanted her to. When the *Great God of Thunder* album went platinum, the fourteenth duke of Penford received a request for a rather hefty donation to a certain children's fund in the City. I can recall the accompanying note word for word. It said: 'Perhaps you can see your way clear to making other children's dreams come true.' It was signed by Aunt Dimity."

21

Outside the warm cocoon of the dowager's bedchamber the storm raged on. Thunder cracked and rolled, lightning slashed the roiling sky, and driving rain battered the windows and walls, the roofs and towers, the balconies, turrets, and terraces of Penford Hall.

Crowley and Hallard had cleared away the tea things, replacing them with a decanter of port and nine delicately etched wineglasses. The decanter was passed from hand to hand, the aromatic wine glinting ruby-red in the firelight.

What an amazing story, Emma thought. It was the most amazing— No. The most amazing story was that she had been permitted to sit there and listen to such an amazing story. Sipping the sweet wine, she contemplated the still figure of the duke. She knew that she was in the presence of a remarkable man, a man who inspired such devotion that those who knew him best had given years of their lives to ensure that his dream would come true.

Nanny Cole's offhand comment about building a rocket to the moon was more apt than the old woman probably realized. The world of rock music must have been as alien to these elderly people as the red dust of Mars, yet they had mapped the terrain and exploited it as fearlessly as any team of space explorers.

While clearing away the tea trays, Crowley had described Lex Rex as a limited partnership in which all members of the core group, staff and villager alike, held equal shares. Thanks to Crowley's impeccable management, each person in that room was independently wealthy. All of them could have left the hall behind to build their own castles, but they stayed on, because Penford Hall was their home, and the world beyond its walls offered nothing they didn't already have.

"Grayson," Derek said gruffly, "owe you an apology, old man. Shouldn't have doubted you. Sorry I did."

"Me, too," Emma added. "I should have trusted the Pym sisters. They told me you couldn't be guilty of any serious wrongdoing, and they were right."

"Were they?" the duke mused. He turned his glass slowly in his hands. "I'm not so sure. One person, at least, appears to have suffered greatly as a result of my scheming. We mustn't forget about Susannah."

"What do you mean?" Derek said sharply.

"Can't you guess?" the duke asked in return.

Derek's eyes narrowed and he glanced down at Emma, who nodded for him to go on. Looking back to the duke, Derek said, "Susannah told me she had reason to believe you'd had a hand in Lex's death." He hesitated. "Do you know about her father?"

"Syd told me, on the way to the hospital," Grayson answered. "Until that moment, I had no idea that such a tragedy had occurred. When I think of her poor mother coming here, asking for help, and being turned away . . ." Grayson bowed his head. "No wonder Susannah felt unable to approach me directly. But we'll discuss this matter later. Please, continue."

Derek explained the way in which Susannah's accident had triggered doubts in his own mind about the circumstances surrounding Lex's death. He described the reasons he'd enlisted Emma's aid, and the gradual evolution of their suspicions. "But none of it matters now, does it?" he asked. "If you were prepared to deal with the consequences of exposure, then none of you would've had a motive to harm Susannah. Her fall must have been an unhappy accident."

"Unhappy, to be sure," said the duke gravely, "but not, I fear, an accident. Tom?"

The red-haired chief constable nodded grimly. "Knew there was some funny business going on the minute I heard about her shoes. Kate told me they was all clean and shiny, like she'd just polished 'em up that morning."

Emma could picture Susannah's high-heeled shoe poking out from beneath the oilcloth; the broken heel had gleamed in the morning sun, but it hadn't registered until now. "It had rained the night before," she said slowly. "If she'd walked to the chapel garden in those shoes, they would have been muddy."

"And they wasn't even wet," the chief constable declared. "But I didn't hear about it until two days later. The evidence was gone by then, and the crime scene was contaminated, as they say, so I thought I'd just ask around, quiet-like, before reportin' to my superiors. Asked Newland to give me a hand." He stared down into his wineglass. "Between us, we've been able to account for everyone in the hall and the village. We've come up with a lead, but . . ." His voice trailed off and he looked to the duke for support.

The duke cleared his throat, then ran a finger around the inside of his shirt collar. He favored Derek with a troubled, almost apologetic smile, then hunched forward and said, in a confidential murmur, "You see, old man, we know that Susannah was pestering you a great deal. As you observed earlier, it's difficult to keep secrets in a place like this."

Derek blinked in surprise. "Grayson, if you're accusing me—"

"I'm not. Madama has confirmed that you were breakfasting with Bantry in the kitchen." The duke wet his lips. "Fact is, old man, I'm accusing your son."

"Peter?" Derek stared at the duke in astonishment.

The duke sighed regretfully. "Wanted to discuss this with you privately, but . . . The truth of the matter is that Peter was seen going into the garden early that morning."

"By whom?" Derek demanded.

"Bantry. He didn't think anything of it until Tom and Newland had struck everyone else off the list. It was only then that he recalled Peter's repeated expressions of concern about Susannah interfering with your work. Viewed in that light, the boy's presence in the garden on that particular morning suggested the possibility . . ." The duke averted his gaze. "I'm sure you understand what I'm getting at."

"Yes," Derek murmured, setting his wineglass on the tray. "Yes, I quite see."

"No," Emma broke in. "You don't see at all. None of you do." She reached for Derek's hand and hoped that Peter would forgive her. "Peter did go into the garden that morning, but he didn't spend any time there. He was in the chapel until the shouting started; then he slipped out through the back door and went around the outside to the cliff path. You can check with the Tregallis brothers. They saw him go out there." She pulled Derek around to face her. "He didn't want to get into trouble for hanging around the chapel. That's why he told you he was—"

"Shouting?" Newland spoke from the doorway, then came to stand over Emma. "Did you say that the boy heard shouting?"

"Well . . . yes," Emma replied, unnerved by the man's hawkish gaze. "That's what he told me."

"First I've heard of any shouting," Newland growled. He surveyed the other faces in the room. "Any of you lot forget to tell me about shouting?"

As murmurs of denial sounded all around her, Emma tried to recall whether she or Nell had cried out upon finding Susannah. She was sure they hadn't. She clearly remembered being impressed by Nell's calmness and amazed by her own, but, before she could open her mouth to reply, she felt a tremor pass through Derek's body.

"My God," he murmured, half to himself. "If none of you were shouting, then Peter must have heard someone else." His head snapped up. "I breakfasted alone that morning. Bantry only stopped by for a cup of coffee." He grabbed Emma's arm and pulled her to her feet. "Come on. We've got to get up to the nursery."

As they darted into the darkened hallway, Emma's mind raced. She refused to believe that Bantry would harm Peter, but he might have lashed out at Susannah. She remembered that first afternoon in the garden, when he'd spoken so harshly against anything that threatened to disrupt the peace of Penford Hall. He'd known where the grub hoe was and he had the strength to wield it. He'd cleaned the oilcloth, as well, and stowed it safely in his cupboard. And now it looked as though he'd tried to cast suspicion on Peter, the one person who might identify his voice and place him in the garden with Susannah at the crucial time.

Footsteps pounded behind them and flashlights glinted maniacally from the rippled panes of leaded glass that lined the long, arcaded corridor. The main staircase loomed ahead and Derek leapt for it, nearly colliding with Bantry, who was hastening downstairs.

Derek seized the old man's shoulders, shouting, "Where's my son? What have you done with my boy?" until Newland got to him and wrestled him away.

Bantry took a faltering step backward, then sat abruptly on the stairs, squinting dazedly as half a dozen flashlights focused on his nut-brown face. When he had elbowed his way to Bantry's side, the duke bent down to ask calmly if Master Peter were still in the nursery.

The old man shook his head. "No, Your Grace," he said earnestly. "I were just comin' down to tell you. The boy's gone. Don't know how he slipped by me, but he's not in his bed nor anywhere else up there." He gripped Grayson's arm urgently and jutted his grizzled chin toward the windows. "He's taken his jacket and a torch, Your Grace. Lady Nell thinks he's out there in that storm."

Without a second thought, Emma headed down the stairs.

"Where are you going?" Derek cried.

"To the chapel," she replied, over her shoulder. "Don't you see? He's gone to check the window."

Derek shook off Newland's hold and plunged down the stairs after Emma, while Grayson hung back, issuing rapid orders to his troops. The last thing Emma heard before reaching the entrance hall and turning for the dining room was Nanny Cole calling out to Kate to phone for Dr. Singh.

"Should've brought the flashlight," Derek muttered as they groped their way through the darkened dining room.

"I don't think it'd be much use out there," Emma said. The wind buffeted the French doors, and rain gusted in sheets against the panes. "I won't be much use, either," she added, raising a hand to her glasses. "I won't be able to see a thing."

"We'll be even, then," Derek said wryly. He reached for the door handles and, when Emma nodded, he flung the doors wide.

Emma gasped as the cold rain hit her, and she was soaked to the skin before reaching the terrace steps. Tucking her chin to her chest, she fought her way across the lawn, blinded by the driving downpour and slipping on the sodden grass until they reached the relative sanctuary of the ruins, where the wind's roar became a moaning chorus as it swirled and eddied through empty hearths and gaping doorways.

Trailing fingers along the rain-slicked walls, Emma sprinted down the grassy corridor until she reached the banquet room, where the constant strobe of lightning showed a scene of utter chaos. Stakes and leaves and flattened stalks littered the graveled path, and vines streamed from the arbor's dome like pennants in the wind. Derek tried to rush ahead, tripped, and sprawled, but Emma hauled him to his feet, and together they staggered forward to the far end of the room and the corridor beyond.

They left the green door banging on its hinges as they stumbled down the chapel garden's stairs. Waterfalls spilled from the raised beds' low retaining walls, and the flagstone path was a mire of clinging mud. Emma longed to reach the stillness of the chapel, to slam the door on the storm and catch her breath, but although Derek strained against it, the chapel door refused to budge. Teeth chattering, Emma darted forward to add her weight to Derek's, and the door slowly gave way, moving inward inch by inch, until the gap was wide enough for them to slip inside.

Emma paused to wipe her glasses, then gazed about in stark confusion. Peter's orange emergency lantern lay on its side on the granite shelf, pointing toward the back door. The back door had been left wide open, and the force of the wind that ripped through the doorway had shoved the benches askew and held the front door shut against them. The old wheelbarrow had been wedged into the gaping doorway, and a rope stretched tautly from its wooden handles into the seething darkness.

"What the—" Derek turned to Emma, but she was already tugging on the rounded door, held fast once more by the roaring wind.

"Don't touch the barrow until we've had a look outside!" she shouted. "We don't know what that rope is holding!"

Derek seized a pitchfork and used it to lever the front door open. It banged shut again behind them as they raced up the stairs and out of the chapel garden. Together they ran along the garden wall, but when they swerved into the rocky meadow, the wind slammed into Emma and drove her to her knees.

"Go!" she screamed when Derek stopped to pull her up, and he barreled ahead, while she groped blindly for the wall on hands and knees, searingly aware of the long fall that lay only a few yards away.

The knuckles of her flailing left hand scraped rough stone and she struggled to her feet. Hugging the stone wall, she stumbled forward until she reached the corner, rounded it, and saw the faint pool of light outside the chapel's rear wall, where the rope stretched, glistening, over the edge of the cliff and straight down into the devouring darkness. Derek was almost there, the rope was almost in his hand, when Peter's lantern faded and winked out.

"No!" Derek's anguished cry rang out above the roaring wind, and Emma froze, paralyzed by fear. Then,

through her rain-blurred glasses, Emma saw the air begin to shimmer.

The glow was all around them. It came from nowhere and from everywhere and grew brighter by the minute, until the rain glittered bright as diamonds, bright as Peter's tears, streaking downward like a million falling stars. Emma saw her bloodied knuckles, saw the blades of stunted grass, saw each rock and leaf and puddle as clearly as though it were midday.

Derek saw the rope. He lunged for it, and Emma leapt to help him as he dug his heels into the rocky ground, hauling fiercely, hand over hand, his muscles straining against his rain-drenched shirt. The rope bit into Emma's palms and fell in coils behind her, but she looked only at the point where it slithered slowly over the cliff's edge.

All at once, a hand came into view, white-knuckled, clinging to the rope. Then Peter's face appeared, and as his shoulders rose into the light, Emma saw that he was tied fast to the limp and pallid form of Mattie.

Derek eased them onto solid ground, then flicked his penknife open and cut the rope. As the light began to fade, he hugged his son, kicked the wheelbarrow aside, and shoved the boy toward Emma, who swept him into the safety of the chapel, where she held him at arm's length, scarcely believing that he was alive and in one piece.

Peter wobbled slightly on his feet, blinked dazedly, then stiffened. His mouth fell open and he tried to raise his arm to point, but his eyes rolled back in his head and he tumbled, fainting, into Emma's arms. Emma glanced over her shoulder as Derek stumbled in, carrying Mattie, and in the last fluorescence of the fading light, she thought she saw the lady in the window, clad in white.

22

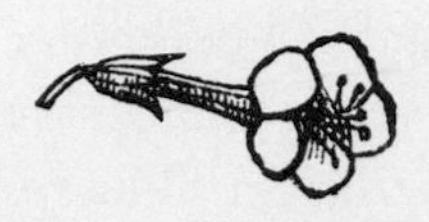

The moment Derek closed the back door, Grayson, Gash, and Newland came barreling into the chapel. They'd been struggling with the front door for some time, their efforts hampered by flapping slickers and the blankets they were carrying.

"Dear old Kate," Grayson said, draping a blanket across Emma's shoulders. "Jolly brilliant of her to think of the flares, what?"

Shivering, Emma pulled the blanket tightly around her. She'd tried to get a clearer look at the window, but the lights, and everyone's attention, were focused on Mattie, who lay on the rear bench, unconscious. "Grayson—" Emma murmured.

"Hush." Grayson squeezed her shoulder and turned to watch Newland, who was crouching beside Mattie, checking her pulse. "Not a word, my dear, not until we've got you all back in the hall." Newland looked up and Grayson nodded. "Right, then. Everyone ready? Off we go."

Derek cradled Peter in his arms, Gash and Newland carried a blanket-wrapped Mattie between them, and Grayson put an unexpectedly strong arm around Emma's waist as they left the chapel to face the storm once more. Emma felt lightheaded, and she moved through the mud and the pelting rain on legs that had turned to rubber. The castle ruins closed around her, then fell away, and the light in the dining-room windows hovered like a dream on a distant horizon.

Kate and Hallard were there, bearing ornate candelabras, since the electricity was still off, and they led the motley parade to the library, where Dr. Singh was waiting. Chilled to the bone, Emma told Grayson to go ahead with the others, then made her solitary way up the darkened staircase and through the silent corridors to her room, oddly comforted by her ability to find her way without a light to guide her.

The rose suite was warm and dry and quiet. Emma let the rain-soaked blanket slide from her shoulders, dried her glasses on the quilted coverlet, then knelt on the hearth and fumbled with numb fingers to start a fire. She gave up, finally, pulled the coverlet from the bed, and huddled beneath it, too exhausted to move. She wasn't sure how much time had passed before she was aroused from her stupor by the sound of a voice from the hallway.

"Emma, honey. It's me, Syd. You think maybe you could get the door?"

Syd Bishop's candles were balanced on a round tray. "Room service," he announced, placing the tray on the low table between the pair of overstuffed armchairs. "Hot coffee, and a bowl of chicken soup. I'd go straight to hell if I was to say it's as good as my grandma's, God rest her soul, but I'm tellin' ya, Madama musta stole her recipe." He filled a cup with steaming coffee and handed it to Emma, wincing when he saw her bloodied knuckles. "Ouch. Caught yourself pretty good there, huh? And what are you doin', sittin' here all this time in wet clothes? C'mon. Let's get you changed before you catch pneumonia."

Syd's years behind the scenes at fashion shows had not been wasted. He knew how women's clothing worked and was disarmingly matter-of-fact about nudity. He stripped off Emma's dripping clothes and tucked her into her blue robe, wrapped a towel around her head, and sat her in an armchair without spilling a drop of her coffee or bringing the faintest blush to her cheek.

The coffee had revived her and the scent of chicken soup proved irresistible. While Syd bent to start a fire, Emma emptied the bowl, then sat back, wishing there was more. Her hand was sore and her knees were beginning to ache, and she knew she'd be stiff later on, but at that moment, with a bowl of warm soup inside her and a second cup of coffee to sip, a soft chair to sink into and a fire beginning to crackle at her feet, she felt as though she'd washed ashore in paradise.

"Is Peter all right?" she asked, as Syd settled into the other chair.

"Petey-boy? He's gonna be just fine after he gets a little shut-eye. I'm tellin' you, Emma, I'm so proud of that kid, I could bust." He turned to pour a cup of coffee for himself. "He saved Mattie's life, you know."

"No, Syd," said Emma. "I don't know. What was she doing out there?"

"Tryin' to off herself." Syd nodded, picked up his cup and saucer, leaned back in his chair. "Crowley found a note."

"Oh, no," Emma whispered.

"Yeah, I know. Terrible thing. Terrible. Such a young girl. She's gonna be okay, though. Busted her arm and banged herself up pretty good, but the doc, he says she'll be fine."

"But *why?*"

"Didn't know how to explain things to Crowley. Didn't want her old grandpa to be ashamed of her." Syd paused to drink from his cup, then looked toward Emma. "She's the one what clobbered Suzie."

"Mattie?"

"That's what the note was about. There was pages and pages of it and, I'm tellin' ya, it was a real eye-opener." Syd put his cup on the tray, folded his hands across his stomach, and sighed. "Mattie had her heart set on goin' into the industry," he began. "She was crazy about Suzie, real thrilled about meetin' a pro. So, when Suzie told her to come to the chapel garden that morning, and to keep everything hush-hush so Nanny Cole's nose wouldn't be put outta joint . . ."

. . . *I couldn't say no, Granddad.* Mattie paused to listen for a moment, then smiled. It was much too late for anyone to be knocking on her door. It was only the wind that had disturbed her, rising to a keening wail outside the window of her room. Such a nice room. She'd cleaned it from top to bottom after supper, and put her things neatly on the dresser, where Granddad could find them and send them home to Mum afterward. Now all that remained was the note. Mattie chewed thoughtfully on the end of her pen, then bent to her task once more.

I put all my sketches together and packed my blue bag with the dress Nanny helped me make—the crêpe de chine, with all the tucks. Nanny says it's my best one yet, but I wanted a professional opinion, so I just had to show it to Ashers. And then I thought about accessories. You know how strict Nanny is about them, but I didn't think my dress needed too much fuss and feathers, as Nanny calls it. The right pair of shoes would be enough. Mattie raised her pen from the paper and looked toward the windows again. The wind was blowing harder than ever, and that was good. It would make everything easier.

* * *

"She snuck the shoes outta Suzie's room," Syd explained, shaking his head. "Poor kid thought it'd be real impressive to show her dress with Suzie's shoes."

I put the shoes in the bag with the dress, Mattie wrote, *and told Nanny I was going down to help Madama. Then I told Madama I was going up to help Nanny. Then I came out to the garden, where Ashers was waiting. I know you don't like Ashers, but she was wonderful, at first. She said I had a real eye for detail and she told me she could put me in touch with all the right people. Can you imagine? I thought I'd died and gone to heaven.* Mattie reread the last sentence, then scratched it out.

I was very happy, she wrote instead, *until Ashers started asking those questions. You know, the ones she was asking Mr. Harris, about that grotty band that stole His Grace's boat. I told her I didn't know anything about it, but she said that you did, and told me to ask you.*

I couldn't do that. I tried to be nice about it, but Ashers kept after me, just the same way she kept after Mr. Harris. She got really mean, Granddad. She started shouting at me. She called you a thief. She said she'd have you put in prison if I didn't help her. Mattie's hand began to tremble and she reached for her cup of cocoa to steady her nerves. This was the hard part.

"Things kinda got outta hand," Syd went on. "One minute Suzie's standin' at the top of the stairs, laughin' at the kid, and, the next thing Mattie knows, she's got the grub hoe in her hands and Suzie's out cold on the ground."

I didn't mean to hurt her. Mattie underlined the words. *I just wanted her to stop saying all those awful things about you. And then she was lying there, not moving, and I knew*

I'd done a dreadful thing. Not just dreadful for me, but for everyone.

You never talk about it, Granddad, and neither does Nanny Cole, but Mrs. Tharby at the Bright Lady told me how bad it was after that rock singer drowned, and I knew this would be even worse. I didn't mind going to jail, but His Grace might have to close up the hall if the newspaper people started coming round again, and I couldn't let that happen. You've been so happy here.

So I tried to make it look like an accident. You can probably guess how. I broke one of Ashers's high-heeled shoes, and took off the flats she was wearing. I put the high heels on Ashers and hid her flats in my bag. I put the flats back in her room the next day. Mattie put down her pen, and reread what she'd written, then turned to stare at her reflection in the window. It had begun to rain.

"All the time Suzie was in Plymouth, it was grindin' away at Mattie," Syd said. "And when they brought Suzie back to the hall, she kinda cracked. Said it'd all come out once Suzie got her memory back, so she might as well save everyone the trouble of a trial. And she hadda tell her grandpa the truth, so he could tell the police so nobody else would get blamed for it. Also so he'd know how sorry she was for what she done and not be too mad at her for . . . for not sayin' goodbye." Syd sighed again and shook his head, adding softly, "Kids."

That one word summed up Emma's complex feelings. She should have known something was bothering Mattie the moment the poor child fainted in the entrance hall. "Do you think they'd let me see her?" Emma asked.

"Nah," said Syd. "She's out cold, and so's Crowley. Nurse Tharby thought he was havin' a cardiac when he came staggering into Suzie's room with all them scribbly pages. Poor guy." Syd leaned over and punched Emma in the shoulder. "But I'm tellin' you what I told him. You got nothin' to blame yourself for. Mattie put on a helluva good act and it ain't your fault you couldn't see through it."

"Thanks, Syd, but . . ." Emma set her coffee cup on the tray and turned to face Syd. "I should have paid attention, at least. I treated Mattie as though she were invisible."

"That's 'cause she was makin' herself invisible. You gotta believe that, Emma. Hey, look, things worked out okay, didn't they? Thanks to you and Derek and Peteyboy, Mattie's got a long life ahead of her, plenty of time to get over all of this garbage. Things could be worse, am I right?"

Emma smiled wanly. "When you're right, you're right, Syd." She leaned toward him. "Do you know the rest of it? How Peter ended up saving her?"

"Not for sure, but I can make a good guess. Let's see, now." Syd squinted into the middle distance. "Mattie's gonna toss herself off the cliffs, right? But maybe she changes her mind at the last minute. And then she slips—you know better 'n me how slick it is out there—and she goes over accidental-like. And she ends up on one of them little ledges, holdin' on to one of them tough old bushes."

Emma nodded. "Then Peter goes out to the chapel to check on the window. . . ."

"And he hears somethin' funny out back," Syd went on. "And when he figgers out what's wrong, he goes and grabs some rope from Bantry's shed—"

Emma interrupted. "Why didn't he come back to the hall for help?"

Syd shrugged. "Hey, Mattie's out there hangin' in the breeze. Maybe he figgered he didn't have time to spare.

So Petey drops the rope to Mattie, but she can't use it on account of her busted flipper. So he goes down to help her—"

"And then *he* can't get back up," Emma broke in. "So he ties himself to Mattie, and stays to ride out the storm with her." She slumped back in her chair, one hand on her heart. "My God . . ."

"Yeah." Syd's voice was filled with satisfaction. "You ask me, Petey-boy deserves a medal." He let the silence linger for a moment, then gave Emma a sly, sidelong look. "You didn't do so bad yourself. You and Derek, you made a pretty good team, huh?"

Emma looked at the fire, embarrassed. "Yes, well, that was . . . automatic. The only thing I could think about was that, if anything happened to Peter, I'd . . . I'd . . ." Emma shook her head and looked at her hands. "He's such a good kid."

"Nell ain't so bad, neither, once you get used to her."

"Afterward," Emma went on, slowly raising her gaze to the fire again, "when I had Peter safe with me in the chapel, just for a split second, I thought I saw . . ." Emma held back. She could tell the truth to Syd without mentioning the window. It might be better to say nothing of that until she'd seen it in the clear light of day.

"I saw something that made me realize how unfair I've been to Derek," she continued. "I can't begin to understand what he went through after his wife died. I'm sure he's done his best to look after Peter and Nell since then, and I know that, once I've told him about the problem with Mrs. Higgins, he'll straighten it out right away."

"That's real big of you, Emma," Syd commented dryly.

Emma glanced at Syd's impassive face, then looked quickly back to the fire. "I realized something else, too," she said, in a voice so low that Syd had to lean forward to hear it. "Derek's already lost his wife, and tonight he nearly lost his son. I . . . I don't want him to lose anyone else."

"Interesting," Syd murmured, nodding judiciously. "Excuse me, but is it old-fashioned of me to want to hear a little mention of love in there somewhere?"

"Well, of course I love him, Syd." Emma toyed with the belt on her robe. "I fell in love with him the minute I laid eyes on him. Isn't it ridiculous? And I just know he's going to ask me to marry him," she added worriedly. "That's the kind of man he is."

"I should hope so," Syd stated firmly. He wrinkled his nose suddenly. "Is that the problem? What've you got against marriage?"

"I'm not sure anymore," Emma said, with a helpless shrug. "I mean, it's not as though I've tried it. Maybe it just frightens me because everyone says it's so unhappy."

"Of course it's unhappy!" Syd shouted. Lunging to the edge of his chair, he turned to Emma, exasperated. "And it's boring and crazy and funny and sad and everything else you can think of, and then some. 'Cause that's what marriage is. It's life times two, the most complicated equation there is. You can spend a whole lifetime workin' on that one, Emma." Syd eased himself back into his chair and refolded his hands across his stomach. He stared silently at the fire for a moment, then leaned toward Emma and said quietly, still looking at the fire, "You know, Emma, those people who think you gotta be happy all the time"—he dismissed them with a wave of his hand—"they're kids. They shouldn't be messin' with marriage, which is for grown-ups. But you, Emma. You ain't no kid."

A slow smile returned to Emma's lips. "No, Syd, I'm not." She ducked her head sheepishly. "But what if he doesn't ask me?"

"Oh, I got a feeling he'll be reminded."

Emma turned to Syd, alarmed. "Syd, you *wouldn't*—"

"Not me," said Syd. "I won't say a word." He reached over to fill his coffee cup again. "Y'know, Emma, honey, when I left the library, Derek and Grayson were having a little drink. They didn't look like they was goin' anywhere."

"Really?" Emma pulled the towel from her head and ran her fingers through her damp hair. "After everything he's been through tonight, he should be in bed." She stood up. "I think I'll go downstairs and . . . and make sure Grayson doesn't keep him up too late."

"Yeah, that duke, he's a real chatterbox," said Syd, putting the pot down. "You sure you ain't too tired?"

"Isn't it amazing? I thought I'd be exhausted, but I feel wide awake. It must be the coffee."

"Must be." Syd sipped from his cup, but refrained from further comment.

Emma left the room without a candle, but again she found her way easily in the dark. She had no idea what time it was, but she suspected that most of the hall's inhabitants were in bed and asleep. She met no one on her way down the stairs and saw no lights until she opened the library door.

The library was flooded with light. Dozens of candles, in candlestick holders of every conceivable size and shape, stood flickering from every available surface. Grayson and Kate were seated side by side on the couch, and Derek faced them from his accustomed chair near the fire. His curls were almost dry, and he'd changed into fresh jeans and a cobalt-blue cableknit sweater. Grayson had changed, too, into another well-cut tweed jacket, another immaculate shirt and silk tie.

Derek looked up as the door opened, and Kate and Grayson turned to look as well, and Emma suddenly remembered that she was wearing nothing but her robe and slippers. But it didn't matter. Nothing mattered but the glorious fact that Derek was still awake.

"Emma?" Derek rose from his chair. "Shouldn't you be in bed?"

"I was about to ask you the same thing." Emma crossed over to stand before him, unable to decide whether the sweater or Derek's eyes were a deeper blue. "How's Peter?"

"Sound asleep," Derek assured her. "He was a bit delirious, but Dr. Singh says there's no sign of any head injury, so we think it must be due to shock."

"Delirious?" Emma asked.

"Babbling about the window changing color," said Derek. "Not surprising, really. D'you know you were right? The young fool went out in that godawful storm just to make sure his precious window was intact."

"Fool?" Emma echoed, a hint of heat in her voice.

"I say, Derek, old man," murmured the duke.

"One moment, Grayson." Derek looked down at Emma, perplexed. "Yes. Fool. What would you call a ten-year-old boy who risks his life to look at a bloody window?"

Emma's foot began to tap. This wasn't the conversation she'd had in mind. "I'd call him a very worried little boy," she replied evenly.

"Worried?" Derek laughed. "I'd say he's verging on delusional. Let's face it, Emma. Those were hurricane-force winds out there, and Peter's not exactly a tower of strength."

"And I suppose you are?" Emma folded her arms.

"Er, Emma?" Kate's soft voice held a touch of concern.

"In a minute, Kate." Emma adjusted her glasses, then squared her shoulders. "Are you aware of the fact that that puny son of yours saved Mattie's life tonight?"

"He's lucky he didn't get her killed," Derek retorted.

"Lucky?" Emma's voice cracked. "How about courageous and heroic and brave? How about magnificent? Frankly, I think Peter's luck ran out when he got you for a father."

"What do you mean by that?" Derek sputtered.

"I mean that, if you can look at what he did tonight and see nothing but foolishness and luck, then you don't deserve your son. For your information, the window *has* changed."

"*What?*" chorused Grayson and Kate.

"Now *you're* sounding delusional," scoffed Derek.

"If anyone's delusional, it's *you,*" Emma shot back. The discussion was spinning out of control, but she couldn't turn back now. "You're the one who thinks that everything at home is fine and dandy."

"I don't see how my home situation—"

"Do you have any idea what Peter's gone through while you've been feeling sorry for yourself? When's the last time he brought a friend home from school?" Emma demanded. "Why did he drop out of the Boy Scouts?"

Derek stepped back, self-righteous and thoroughly confused. "Peter's very conscientious about his studies. Why, Mrs. Higgins says—"

"Mrs. Higgins?" Emma squeaked. "Have you smelled Mrs. Higgins's breath lately? I imagine the only work she does is propping her feet on the coffee table when Peter's vacuuming the carpet."

"Hoovering the carpet? What on earth are you talking about? You can't possibly know what Peter does when he's at home."

"Give me Mrs. Higgins's job description and I'll tell you exactly what he does. You ask Nell. Better yet, pay Mrs. Higgins a surprise visit, or just give her a call. I did, and it was very enlightening."

Derek was aghast. "You've been spying on me?"

"I've been paying attention to your children, which is a hell of a lot more than I can say for you."

Derek drew himself up and looked down at Emma from a great height. "For someone who never wanted children of her own, you seem to be taking an inordinate amount of interest in mine."

"Someone has to!" Emma snapped. "And if I were around, someone would. But there's no danger of that. I wouldn't marry you if you were the last man on earth." Emma fell back a step, remembering a moment too late that she hadn't yet been asked.

Derek's recall was unfortunately precise. "Who said anything about getting married? One kiss and you've already got us racing up the aisle? You *must* be desperate."

"A woman would have to be desperate to even consider marrying you!" Emma roared.

"Emma, Derek, please." Grayson's voice was calm and conciliatory as he came to stand between them. "You've both been through a dreadful experience. I'm sure that everything will look quite different after a good night's rest. Kate, old thing, why don't you take Emma upstairs and—" He stopped short as Emma turned the full force of her wrath in his direction.

"If you call Kate 'old thing' one more time, I'm . . . I'm going to smack you in the kisser. Why don't you put that poor woman out of her misery?"

"*Emma,*" Kate muttered urgently, reaching over to touch Emma's arm.

"You stay out of this," Emma barked, pulling her arm out of reach. Glaring at Grayson, she went on, "Can't you see that she's in love with you? And she *wants* to get married, though I can't for the life of me understand why. So let's get down to business. Grayson, are you going to marry Kate or not?"

Grayson touched his tie nervously and lowered his eyes. "Forgive me, Kate. I'd hoped to make this announcement at a more suitable time and place, but since Emma's being so . . . so refreshingly direct—"

"Just answer the question," Emma commanded.

"Yes, Grayson," added Kate, rising to stand behind Emma, "just answer the question."

"Of course I intend to marry you, Kate," Grayson said, with as much dignity as he could muster. "I've intended to marry you all along. But I couldn't."

"Why not?" Kate and Emma said together.

"It wouldn't have been proper," Grayson replied, as though the answer were self-evident. "I didn't have Grandmother's ring."

While Kate sank back onto the couch, open-mouthed, Emma gaped at the duke, too stunned for words. Next she did something she'd never done before and would probably never do again. She seized the duke by the knot of his silk tie and jerked him toward her, thundering, "Do you think Kate cares about *jewelry?*" Then she pushed the duke aside and stalked toward the door. "*Men!*" she roared, before gathering up the skirts of her blue robe and marching from the room, slamming the door behind her for good measure.

23

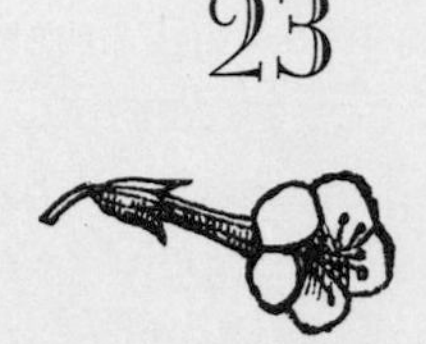

When Emma awoke, it was late afternoon, the sun was streaming through the balcony door, and Nell was sitting cross-legged on the end of her bed. She was watching Emma's face intently, and when Emma's eyes opened, she clambered across the bed to sit companionably near Emma's pillows.

"Your bath is ready," she said.

Emma blinked sleepily, not quite sure whether she was awake or only dreaming. The friendly little girl in the rumpled blue jeans and kelly-green sweater, who was toying with the laces on her scuffed sneakers and whose curls were as tousled as Derek's, bore little resemblance to the picture-perfect and coolly self-possessed Lady Nell she'd come to know. Emma's eyes widened as the dream child leaned over to pat her shoulder with a very real hand.

"Don't worry, Emma," Nell said consolingly. "Everyone won't be mad at you forever."

Emma's only response was a prolonged and pathetic groan.

"That was a good scold you gave Papa last night."

Nell's voice was filled with admiration and an unaccustomed earnestness. "I never heard anyone scold him like that before."

Emma peeked over the edge of the bedclothes, horrified. "You weren't there, were you?"

" 'Course I was," said Nell. "Up in the gallery."

"You should've been in the nursery," Emma reminded her.

"Bertie wanted to know what was going on. You can see everything from the gallery. I watched Dr. Singh fix Mattie's arm. He's a good doctor." She pointed to Emma's bruised knuckles. "You should let him fix your hand."

I should donate my body to science, Emma thought miserably. A twinge shot through both shoulders as she reached for her glasses, and there was a distinct tenderness where her knees met the bedclothes through her flannel nightgown. Her palms were sore and her knuckles throbbed, but those aches and pains were minor compared with the pangs of conscience that assailed her. How could she have let herself go like that? Why had she said all those dreadful things? Kate would probably strangle her, the duke would banish her, and Derek would never speak to her again. She put her glasses on and lay back on her pillows, wondering what on earth had come over her.

Whatever it was, it seemed to be affecting Nell, as well. The ethereal princess who'd carried herself with such dignity and grace was now bouncing on the bed and looking as though she were bursting with news. More extraordinary still, her bear was nowhere in sight.

"Where's Bertie?" Emma asked.

"Keeping Peter company," Nell replied. "Dr. Singh says he's supposed to stay in bed all day. Do you want to have your bath now?"

"I don't know, Nell." Emma sighed. "I may just stay in bed for the next few weeks."

Nell giggled. "That's what Bantry said when he saw the garden."

Emma braced herself for more unpleasant news. "How bad is it?"

"It's a bloody mess," Nell replied cheerfully. "But Bantry said he'd still rather be out there than in the bloody hall with a bunch of bloody lunatics. Oh, Emma, it's been *such* an exciting morning."

"I'll bet it has," Emma said weakly. She looked toward the balcony door, then propped herself on her elbows, knowing that she had to get up. She couldn't leave Bantry to clean up the garden rooms by himself. "You can tell me all about it while I'm having my bath."

Emma watched in amazement as Queen Eleanor scrambled to the floor and scampered toward the bathroom, shoelaces flying, tossing a stream of gleeful, breathless chatter over her shoulder.

Groaning, Emma swung her legs over the side of the bed and hobbled toward the bathroom, feeling as old as the Pym sisters but not half as spry. Nell was waiting for her in the dressing room, and when she opened the bathroom door, billows of steam emerged, redolent with the heavy scent of camelias.

"Use a little bath oil?" Emma asked, wiping the steam from her glasses.

Nell nodded proudly. "Smells pretty, doesn't it?"

As the clouds of steam dissipated, Emma saw a stupendous mountain range of bubbles covering the tub. One majestic peak had made its way over the lip of the mahogany surround and was cascading slowly to the floor. Emma put a towel on the sudsy puddle, then reached into the tub to feel the water. It was still blessedly hot.

With a fine sense of decorum, Nell had remained in the dressing room, leaving Emma to face the laborious task of pulling her nightgown over her head, wrapping her hair in a towel, and easing herself gingerly through the bubbles and into the water. The heat was so deliciously soothing that Emma could almost imagine getting dressed and facing the consequences of her intemperate behavior. But not just yet. Not until she had a better idea of just what she was about to face. Settling back against the terry-cloth pillow, she called to Nell.

Nell entered the bathroom carrying Emma's blue bathrobe in both arms. She heaped the robe on the marble bench across from the tub, then climbed up to sit beside it, her sneakers dangling well above the floor. "Do you feel better now?"

"I'm beginning to," Emma replied. "Thank you, Nell. A long soak in a hot bath is just what I needed."

"Grayson, too. But just his head. That's what Kate told him, anyway."

Emma thought that one through, then blanched. "You mean, Kate told Grayson to go soak his head?"

"Uh-huh. At breakfast. She said he needed to get his pri-pritor—"

"Priorities?" Emma suggested.

Nell nodded. "She said he had to get those straight. And then Nanny Cole tried to talk and Kate told her to shut up."

"She *didn't,*" Emma gasped.

"She *did.* I heard her. Nanny Cole looked very surprised. And then Kate threw her napkin on the floor and stomped out of the dining room."

Emma closed her eyes and slid slowly down the back of the tub until the water was lapping her lower lip.

"And then Papa said what did Grayson expect and

Grayson said why didn't Papa ring up Mrs. Higgins and Papa said why didn't he mind his own business"—Nell took a quick breath before racing on—"and Grayson said children were everybody's business and Papa said he was a fine one to talk and why didn't he get some of his own and then *Syd* told them both to pipe down and stop acting like a pair of palookas."

"Oh, God . . ." Emma moaned, covering her face with her hands.

"It was *wonderful.*" Nell kicked her legs back and forth, wriggling with delight. " 'Specially Kate. She shouts almost as good as you do."

"Now, Nell, there's nothing good about shouting," Emma protested feebly. "It's never good to lose your temper. I feel terrible about shouting at your father. I said all sorts of things I shouldn't have said."

Nell nodded sympathetically. "Papa says I do that all the time."

"Well, sometimes you can hurt people by doing that. I'm sure I hurt your father." Emma wiped bubbles from her chin. "I'm going to have to apologize to him."

"You can't," said Nell. "He's gone."

"Gone?" Emma asked. "Gone where?"

"I don't know. He stomped out of the dining room, just like Kate. But he didn't throw his napkin."

"That's good," Emma said hopefully.

"He threw his *whole plate!*" Nell's peal of laughter rang with such unabashed joy that Emma couldn't help smiling, though she was ashamed of herself for doing so. "That's when Bantry stomped out to the bloody ruins and Nanny stomped up to her bloody workroom and Grayson stomped off to the bloody library. Syd and I helped Hallard clean up Papa's eggs," she added virtuously.

Emma sobered as the mention of Syd Bishop reminded her of Susannah, and of Mattie. Pushing herself up and moving the bubbles aside so that she could see Nell more clearly, she asked, "Did anyone mention how Mattie's doing?"

Nell's swinging legs slowed, then stopped. "Mattie's sleeping," she said briefly. "Dr. Singh gave her some pills. Crowley's sitting on a chair next to her bed. He's been there all day. And Syd's . . ." Nell scratched her nose. "Syd's with Susannah, but she's awake. I heard them talking. Syd said . . ." Frowning, Nell scratched her nose again, then fell silent.

Wordlessly, Emma reached for a towel and wrapped it around her as she rose from the tub. Stepping quickly to the bench, she pulled on her blue robe, then sat beside Nell, looking down on her tousled curls. Nell's head was bowed and her hands twisted restlessly in her lap, as though seeking the kind of comfort only Bertie could provide.

In her own way Nell was as tough and brave as Peter, Emma conceded, but she wasn't Lady Nell or Queen Eleanor or a wise old woman in disguise. She was just a little girl who'd been working hard to make sense of the world on her own, and who'd learned enough to realize that she couldn't do it anymore. Nell had come to Emma, finally, to help her make sense of the world.

"What did Syd say?" Emma asked, putting her arm around Nell's shoulders.

Nell's troubled eyes scanned the sink, the mirror, the ceiling, and the towel rack, finally coming to rest on Emma's knees. "Syd said that Mattie . . . hit Susannah." She began to rock, very slightly, back and forth. "Was Syd telling the truth?"

"Yes," said Emma. "Syd was telling the truth."

"Oh." The rocking stopped for a moment, then resumed. "Was Mattie angry?"

Emma rocked with the child. "Mattie was afraid and

confused. She didn't mean to hurt Susannah. And she's sorry that she did."

"Is she very sorry?" Nell asked.

"She's very, *very* sorry," Emma confirmed.

The little girl stopped rocking, snuggled up to Emma for a moment, then sat back and released a rushing sigh. "Poor Mattie," she said. "Poor Susannah."

Yes, Emma thought, poor Mattie, and poor Susannah. The best they could hope for was that Syd would be able to convince Susannah that Mattie had suffered enough already.

Nell had clambered off the bench and was kneeling at the side of the tub, carefully molding a mound of suds into a rounded dome. Emma went to kneel beside her.

"I know about the window," Nell said suddenly.

Emma kept her eyes on the little girl's busy hands, feeling preternaturally alert to Nell's every word. "What do you know about the window?" she asked.

"I know that it's changed," Nell replied. "I went to see it today, for Peter. It's white, like an angel. Peter says it's Mummy."

Emma watched as Nell teased her dome of bubbles into a taller, narrower shape that bore a faint resemblance to the silhouette of the lady in the window. "Do you believe what Peter says?"

Nell stared at the glistening, quivering pillar of fragrant bubbles. "I don't remember Mummy," she said softly, "but I think angels are in heaven." She blew on the sudsy sculpture, and bubbles swirled into the air. "Could she be in two places, do you think?"

Emma shrugged. "I don't see why not. What do you think?"

"I think Mummy can be wherever she wants to be," Nell concluded firmly, as though the subject had been settled to her satisfaction. She rested her chin on her hands and said slyly, "I know something else about the window, Emma."

Emma was so relieved to see a mischievous glimmer return to Nell's eyes that she was willing to play along. Leaning her own chin on her hands, she asked brightly, "What's that, Nell?"

"I know what made it change."

"Do you?" Emma asked, trying to sound enormously intrigued.

"Uh-huh." Nell nodded vigorously. "It was the light."

Emma sat back on her heels and stared at the child, disconcerted. "The light?"

"The really bright light that lit up the rain last night. That's what made the window change."

Emma frowned slightly. "Are you talking about the flares Kate shot off?"

Nell snickered. "Kate said Grayson was a twit and she didn't know anything about any ratty old flares. It's not flares, Emma."

Emma's heart began to beat double-time. "But you saw what made the light? You saw where the light came from?"

"You can see everything from the gallery," Nell reminded her.

"Can you show me where the light came from?" Emma asked.

" 'Course I can."

Emma nodded. It was ridiculous to let herself get so excited. Nell had probably been working on a story all morning and was about to try it out. Except that all of Nell's stories so far had been true. Emma pulled the towel from her head and let her hair fall loose. Ignoring mild protests from her back and shoulders—the hot bath really had worked wonders—Emma scooped Nell up from the floor and carried her across the bedroom and out onto the balcony.

"Okay, now, Nell," said Emma, swinging the child onto her hip, "show me where the light came from."

Nell slowly raised a dimpled finger until she was pointing directly at the elaborate wrought-iron finial on the top of the birdcage arbor. Emma's jaw dropped.

"Emma?" Nell asked, fluffing Emma's hair.

"What is it, sweetheart?" Emma asked distractedly.

"What's a palooka?"

Emma looked at the child's face, only inches from her own, then planted a kiss on Nell's cheek and put her on the ground. "I'll explain while I get dressed," she promised, taking the little girl's outstretched hand and leading her back into the bedroom.

24

Grayson was trudging stolidly up the main staircase when Nell and Emma came hurrying down it. He stood to one side, eyeing Emma warily until he caught sight of her left hand, which Nell had insisted on bandaging from wrist to fingertip with what seemed like several yards of white gauze and an equal amount of medical tape acquired, according to Nell, from the stores of the ever-helpful Nurse Tharby.

"Good Lord, Emma," Grayson exclaimed. "I'd no idea you'd injured yourself."

"Just a scratch," Emma said. She flexed her hand to prove it, then tucked it out of sight in the front pocket of her violet-patterned gardening smock. Looking down at the toes of her wellington boots, she began, awkwardly, "Er, Grayson—"

"I'll meet you in the banquet hall," Nell said abruptly. She looked from Emma's face to Grayson's, then turned and ran back up the stairs.

When Nell's footsteps had faded into the distance, Emma tried again. "Grayson—about last night. I can't tell you how sorry I am. My behavior was inexcusable and I apologize."

"Oh, I don't know. . . ." Grayson leaned back against the banister and sighed. "Had it coming, I suppose."

"That may be true," Emma said, "but it shouldn't have come from me."

The duke smiled wryly. "I've gotten plenty of it from Kate since then. Kate and everyone else. Even Crowley, preoccupied as he is, found time to sniff disapprovingly in my direction when I stopped by to look in on Mattie. But, then, Kate always was his great favorite."

"How's Mattie doing?" Emma asked.

Grayson's smile faded and his brown eyes clouded over. "Time will tell," he replied gravely. "Dr. Singh believes that she'll recover from her physical injuries readily enough, but as for the rest . . ." Grayson sank down onto the stairs, as though too burdened by misery to consider finding a more comfortable spot. "It's my fault, of course. I can't help thinking that, had I been more welcoming to Susannah—"

"Hold on a minute, Grayson." The birdcage arbor would have to wait. Emma looked down at the duke's slumping shoulders and remembered the way he'd showered the staff with praise for creating Lex Rex, shrugging off his own contributions. The duke's generous nature seemed reserved for others; he kept all the blame for himself.

"Before you start the mea culpas, may I remind you of a few things?" Emma sat beside Grayson on the steps, rested her hands on the padded knees of her gardening trousers, and regarded the duke with sympathetic eyes. "I don't mean to speak ill of the . . . ill, but Susannah did show up here without an invitation. She used a very tenuous family connection to move herself and her manager into your home for an unspecified amount of time. While she was here, she hounded Derek and insulted your staff. She was rude, overbearing, and malicious, and her sole purpose in coming here was to ruin you because of something your father did. I'm not saying that Susannah deserved to be hit in the head with a grub hoe, but . . ." Emma put her hand on the duke's shoulder. "Under the circumstances, I'd say that you were more than gracious to your cousin."

Grayson rested his chin on his fist. "Perhaps you're right," he said reluctantly. "Still, I can't help feeling that, if I hadn't placed so much importance on preserving Penford Hall, Mattie might not have gone to such drastic lengths to protect it."

"Mattie wasn't thinking about the hall," Emma said. "She was trying to protect her grandfather. Besides, if she'd gone to Crowley in the first place instead of going off half-cocked, none of this would have happened."

"True," the duke admitted grudgingly. "Crowley would've given her whatever story Hallard's concocted about Lex Rex's death, and Susannah would've had to lump it. She might even have been persuaded to go away."

"But Mattie took matters into her own hands, and that's not your fault."

The duke squinted at Emma suspiciously. "If I didn't know you better, my dear, I'd say that you were doing your level best to cheer me up."

"I wish I could," Emma admitted. "If Susannah decides to press charges—"

Grayson bowed his head. "Susannah must do as she sees fit, of course, but I hope she'll be lenient. Syd's been in with her since—" He broke off, looking up in consternation as an uproar sounded from the second floor.

"Unhand me, you lout!" thundered Nanny Cole. "I can find my way to Susannah's room without any help from you."

"Sure you can, Mrs. Cole." Syd's voice drifted down to them, pitched to a placating murmur. "But you know how it is—a gentleman always wants to lend a hand to a fine lady such as yourself."

"A *gentleman* wouldn't be seen dead in those bloody awful trousers," Nanny Cole responded tartly.

"Funny you should mention my ensemble . . . Excuse me a minute, will you, Mrs. Cole?" Syd's face appeared over the railing of the second-floor landing. "Emma, sweetheart, how's it goin'? Nell said I'd find you here. Hey, Duke! You still willin' to foot the bills?"

"Absolutely," the duke replied.

"Catch you later." Syd winked before disappearing from view. A moment later, his conversation with Nanny Cole resumed. "Like I was saying, Mrs. Cole, I got a little proposition for you. Strictly business, you understand."

"What the bloody hell else would it be, you appalling tick?" Nanny Cole grumbled, and then a door closed, cutting off the rest of her words.

The duke continued to stare upward for a moment, a thoughtful expression on his face. "Well, well, well," he murmured. "I do believe that Syd's hit upon a possible solution. Susannah's always placed great importance on her career."

"Nanny Cole and Susannah?" Emma turned the idea over in her mind.

"Mmm . . ." Grayson tapped a finger against his lips. "An exclusive new line of women's clothing? A boutique, perhaps?"

"It might work," Emma said doubtfully, "as long as Syd's around to keep the peace."

"There is that," Grayson conceded. He ran a hand

through his silky blond hair, then leaned back on his elbows. "Ah, well. We must simply put our faith in Syd and hope for the best." He eyed the upstairs landing speculatively. "Wonder if he'd consent to act as my go-between. Kate's locked herself in the south tower and won't have anything to do with me. Hasn't happened since we were children."

"You're not children anymore," Emma reminded him. She got to her feet and pulled the duke up with her. Brushing her hands lightly across the shoulders of his tweed jacket, and straightening his tie, she went on, "I've heard that you can charm water from a rock, Grayson. So I want you to go up to the south tower and persuade Kate to come with you to the banquet hall in the castle ruins."

"You want us to come to the kitchen garden?" the duke asked.

"In fifteen minutes." Emma started down the stairs, but turned back to ask, "Do you know where Gash is?"

"Finishing his repairs on the power plant. Hallard will call him for you, though. He's in the library, sorting out the candles." The duke bit his lower lip, bemused. "You're being very mysterious, Emma."

"Fifteen minutes," Emma repeated. "Good luck."

"I'll need it," Grayson muttered, turning to fly up the stairs.

Though Gash had reported that Mr. Harris had driven off in his battered orange van early that morning, Hallard was unable to inform Emma of Derek's immediate whereabouts. Stifling her disappointment, Emma gave instructions to Hallard to pass along to Gash, then invited the bespectacled footman to join her in the banquet hall. "Bring your laptop," she added. "You may be able to use this in your next thriller."

The weather had been the last thing on Emma's mind

when she'd carried Nell out onto the balcony, so she was faintly shocked when she stepped onto the terrace. The sky was a flawless arc of blue, the air was sweet, and a gentle breeze ruffled the grass on the great lawn. Had it not been for the apple trees, now stripped of leaf and blossom and trailing broken branches, she would have been hard-pressed to prove that a raging storm had indeed passed this way. But the apple trees were only a hint of what she would find within the castle ruins.

The storm had ravaged the garden rooms. As Emma surveyed the wreckage, she tried to remind herself that no one had died, but gratitude wasn't easy. The perennial border was a tattered, ragged mess, the rock garden was more rock than garden, and there was not a single bud or blossom left on any of the rose bushes. By the time she reached the banquet hall, Emma was almost numb.

Bantry crouched ankle-deep in mud, plucking green tomatoes from a tangle of battered plants. He'd cleared most of the debris from the graveled path, pulled the broken vines from the towering arbor, and filled the wheelbarrow with salvaged vegetables. When he caught sight of Emma standing dazedly in the doorway, he held out a tomato, calling cheerfully, "Looks like we're in for a spate of Madama's chutney!"

Emma raised a hand to her mouth and shook her head forlornly.

"What've you done to your hand, Miss Emma?" Bantry asked, his brow furrowing.

"Nothing really. Nell was practicing her nursing skills." Emma waggled her gauze-wrapped fingers to reassure him, then folded her arms. The kitchen garden looked as though it had been trampled by a herd of cattle, but there were a few green sprouts here and there.

"Don't you fret, Miss Emma." Bantry tossed the tomato into the wheelbarrow, put his hands on his hips, and surveyed the scene without flinching. "It's a right old mess and no mistake, but we'll sort it out soon enough. That's the way it is with gardens. Never the same two days in a row."

The old man's optimism began to revive Emma, and Hallard's arrival reminded her that she'd come here with a mission. Raising her eyes to the top of the arbor, she asked Bantry if he knew how the finial was attached to the dome.

Bantry squinted upward, scratching his head. "Well, now, Miss Emma, I were just up there this mornin', cuttin' back the runner beans. Seems to me there's a big old bolt holdin' that fancy bit in place."

Gash walked in while Bantry was speaking, and when Emma had relieved him of the toolbox and oilcan she'd asked him to bring, she sent him to help Bantry fetch a ladder from the potting shed. She tucked the oilcan into the pocket of her smock and squatted down to rummage through the toolbox for a hammer and a long-handled monkey wrench. She was slipping the tools into her pocket when she heard Peter call out.

The boy seemed to have grown two inches overnight. He was tearing along the grassy corridor, bright-eyed, undaunted by last night's ordeal. Nell trotted in his wake, carrying Bertie and regarding her big brother with such pride that Emma bit back a reminder about Dr. Singh's orders and flung her arms wide.

Peter ran to her. "Did you see her, Emma?" he asked, breathless with excitement. "Did you see the window?"

"I saw it last night," Emma assured him. "I'm so happy for you, Peter. And you should be very proud of yourself."

Peter dug the toe of his boot into the gravel, blushing

shyly. He hesitated, then looked up at Emma, as though seeking reassurance. "Everything'll be all right now, won't it?"

"Yes," Emma declared, going down on her padded knees to envelop him in a bear hug. "Everything will be fine."

The boy hugged her back, wriggled out of her arms, and went squelching through the mud, calling for Bantry, while Nell remained high and dry on the gravel path, staring thoughtfully at the arbor.

"Don't worry, Emma," she said finally. "Bertie says that, if Grandmother could do it, so can you."

Emma looked at her, perplexed. "How did Bertie know—" She broke off as she caught sight of the next trio of arrivals.

Kate Cole had been lured down from the south tower, but Emma suspected that Syd rather than Grayson had persuaded her to unlock the door. The redoubtable business manager had placed himself between an icy Kate and an increasingly frustrated Grayson.

"Please tell His Royal Highness that I'm here at Emma's request and that I have no intention of remaining in his company for one minute longer than is absolutely necessary."

"Kate says—" Syd began.

"Confound it, Kate," the duke grumbled. "I've said I was sorry. I don't know what more—"

"*Sorry!*" Kate snapped. "Please inform Lord High-and-Mighty that he doesn't know the meaning of the word."

"Kate says—"

"Blast, blast, blast," Grayson muttered.

Gash, Bantry, and Peter had returned with the ladder, and Emma directed them to lean it against the arbor. A car door slammed in the distance, and she wondered fleetingly if Newland had gotten word that something odd was going on and driven up from the gatehouse to investigate. Then she focused her attention on making sure the ladder was planted securely on the graveled path. The top rung reached only to the bottom of the dome, but the decorative metalwork would provide plenty of hand- and footholds. As she helped the men maneuver the ladder into place, the three-way conversation continued behind them.

". . . and you can inform His Gracelessness that I wouldn't touch that ring to save my life."

"Kate wants me to tell you—"

"It wasn't just the ring," Grayson expostulated. "Don't you understand, Kate? I couldn't ask you to marry me until the hall was put to rights. How could I ask you to share my life when I had so little to offer?"

"Please tell—"

"Enough already!" Syd held up his hand to silence Kate, then turned to the duke. "You're a swell guy, Duke, but if I was thirty years younger, I'd poke you in the nose. What do you mean, you had nothing to offer? You think this beautiful lady gives a good goddamn about a ring or a fancy-schmantzy house? You hadda heart to give her, you doofus! You had hopes and dreams, am I right?"

"That's all very pretty, Syd, and I appreciate your concern, but one can't live on—" The duke stopped short. His gaze wavered for a second, then seemed to focus on thin air. "Good Lord," he said, half to himself. "Whatever would Aunt Dimity say if she heard me spouting such nonsense?" He blinked dazedly, and his hand drifted to the knot in his tie. "You're quite right, Syd. I've been so wrapped up in details that I seem to have forgotten the point of it all. I, of all people, should have known that one *can* live on dreams. Oh, Kate . . . I am so dreadfully sorry." He bowed his head, and Syd edged out of the way as Kate slowly unfolded her arms and put a tentative hand on Grayson's shoulder.

"Emma!" Syd hollered, coming to stand with the others at the foot of the ladder. "You tryin' to break your neck?"

Emma had reached the top rung and was stepping onto the narrow wrought-iron ledge at the base of the dome. "I'm fine, Syd," she called down. "Don't worry."

"What, me worry?" Syd replied.

"Have a care, now, Miss Emma," Bantry said. "Them boots of yours is pretty slick, remember."

"Do be careful, Miss Emma," Hallard urged.

"I would've gone up for you, Miss Emma," Gash added.

The mutterings of concern increased until Nell stunned everyone to silence by shouting: "Pipe down, you palookas!"

Emma smiled gratefully at the little girl, and continued her climb. The view from the top of the arbor's dome was spectacular. Sitting with her feet braced in the twining wrought iron, Emma could see the chapel, the beacon, and the sprawling mass of Penford Hall. She saw that old Bert Potts had come up from the village to repair the damage done to his beloved apple trees. And she saw, much to her surprise, an exquisitely coiffed and elegantly robed Susannah sitting in a wheelchair on the terrace, with Nurse Tharby looking on while Nanny Cole waved sheets of sketching paper and spoke emphatically. Emma grinned, then bent to examine the foot-high, dome-shaped finial.

Odd pieces of pewter-colored tin and four slender panes of glass had been cleverly hidden inside the finial, attached to the wrought iron by thin strands of dark wire that had been virtually invisible from the ground. Elated, Emma fitted the wrench to the black bolt and tightened its grip. It took a few taps with the hammer to loosen the bolt, but the oil helped, and soon Emma was able to reach in and unscrew the bolt by hand.

After tossing the tools, the oilcan, and the bolt down to Gash, Emma pulled the finial into her lap, and looked up in triumph, but nearly lost her balance as she saw Derek step out onto the terrace. He glanced in her direction, froze, then ducked his head and turned to go back into the hall.

"*Wait!*" Emma yelled. She pointed to the finial in her lap. *"I've found the lantern!"*

Derek swung around, open-mouthed, and ran down the steps. Inside the banquet hall, pandemonium erupted. The air rang with cries of amazed delight as Bantry scrambled up the ladder to take the heavy finial from Emma and pass it carefully to Gash, who carried it to the ground and placed it on the top step of the birdcage arbor, shouting for Hallard to bring his toolbox. Peter hopped from one foot to another, explaining the significance of Emma's discovery to a bewildered Syd, and Kate left Grayson's side to help hold the ladder as Bantry and Emma descended. A cheer went up as Emma's feet touched the ground, and many hands reached out to shake hers. Emma quickly pointed out that it was Nell who had first located the source of the miraculous light, and Nell was equally quick to give full credit to Bertie.

"I fell asleep," she explained, "but Bertie woke me up when he saw—Papa!" Nell cried, spying her father standing in the doorway. As she ran to greet him, Peter broke off his conversation with Syd and bounded down the gravel path to throw his arms around his father's waist. Derek looked down at his children, swallowed hard, then knelt and pulled them to him, hugging them so fiercely that Nell was forced to caution him against squashing Bertie. Emma watched Derek's gray head bend urgently over the dark one and the light; then she turned away, unwilling to intrude.

The excited babble of voices had faded. There was a clatter and a clank as Gash pushed the pieces of the dismantled finial aside, and the others fell back a step as he lifted the reassembled tin lantern by its wire handle and placed it squarely on the top step of the arbor.

"That about does it," he said, wiping his hands on a bit of rag. He tossed his tools into the toolbox and closed the lid, got to his feet, and stepped away from the lantern. Wordlessly, he turned to face the duke.

Grayson stood where Kate had left him, a few yards away on the graveled path. He seemed fragile and terribly alone, unaware of the eager faces that had turned in his direction or of the quiet shuffling of feet as they moved aside to open a path between him and the lantern. The fine lines around his brown eyes had deepened, and his face had grown so pale it seemed almost translucent. Smoothing a lock of blond hair back from his forehead, he drew himself up, then stepped slowly forward, moving as if in a dream. Kate walked beside him, and together they sank onto the step beside the lantern.

"Kate," Grayson whispered, in a voice filled with wonder. "It's all come true. All of it." The duke raised a trembling hand to his forehead and closed his eyes.

"Of course it has," Kate murmured. "A brave lad saved a life last night and the lady held her lantern high to help him. Of course she did. We always knew she would. It's in the blood, my love. Like you, the lady lets us see a world lit by the light of dreams. Come, now. Up on your feet. We've the Fête to prepare for, and a wedding to plan, and— Lady Nell? What are you doing?"

Nell and Peter had joined the group clustered at the base of the birdcage arbor, and Nell had crept forward until she was within arm's reach of the lantern. The duke's eyes opened and he watched, transfixed, as Queen Eleanor favored him with a regal nod.

"Sir Bertram says it's time to bring the lantern to the lady," she informed him gently, and lifted the tin lantern by its wire handle. She turned a dignified shoulder on the group and picked her way daintily up the path, heading for the chapel.

A bemused look crept over Grayson's face as he got to his feet and offered his hand to Kate. Arm in arm they led the others in a silent procession, with Peter proudly taking up the rear. When they had all disappeared from view, Emma turned to Derek.

He was still waiting at the edge of the banquet hall, like an outcast. His eyes were red-rimmed with fatigue, his chin rough with stubble. His hands were thrust deep into the pockets of the jeans he'd worn the night before, and the same blue sweater was flecked with lint and rumpled, as though it had been slept in.

"I've been home," he said. "Had a chat with Mrs. Higgins. Had a look round her room. What used to be her room." He paused to rub his tired eyes. "I've spoken with the children. We'll talk again, of course, but they . . . they seem remarkably willing to let bygones be bygones." His weary sigh seemed to come from somewhere near his soul. "You're quite right, Emma. I don't deserve them."

"Derek . . ." Emma walked slowly toward him. "I shouldn't have spoken like that to you. I meant to tell you about Mrs. Higgins, but not that way."

"Perhaps it was the only way," said Derek. "Don't think I'd've listened to anyone else."

"But I had no right to say it to you. Do you hear me? No right at all. Before you and Peter and Nell came into my life, I had no idea what it would be like to lose someone I loved. I didn't shed a tear when Richard left, but I swear, Derek, if I lost you I . . . I don't know what I'd do."

"It couldn't be worse than what I've done," said Derek.

"What have you done?" Emma demanded. She stood before him, now, peering up into his guilt-shadowed eyes. "You worked hard, you hired an apparently responsible caretaker, and you raised two children to be strong and clever enough to fool you. Two children who were willing to do whatever it took to give their father time to heal. I think you should be proud of those kids and proud of yourself for raising them. And I think—" Emma's voice broke and she looked down at the muddy toes of her wellington boots. "I think you must be pretty sick and tired of hearing what I think."

Derek pulled his hands from his pockets and reached for Emma's. "I wouldn't say that," he murmured. "Quite the contrary. In fact—" Derek looked down in horror. "Emma, darling, what have you done to your hand? My God, is it broken? Has Dr. Singh seen it? Are you in any pain? Oh, my dear—"

"It's nothing, Derek." Emma unceremoniously ripped the bandage from her hand and tossed it into the mud at the side of the path. "See? Just a few scrapes and bruises where I hit the wall. Nell's the one who wrapped it up like that. She insisted on making sure that it was well protected."

Derek subjected Emma's hand to a close examination before tucking it into the crook of his elbow. "Left hand, eh? I think I know exactly how Nell feels." He closed his hand gently over Emma's bruised knuckles and began strolling toward the chapel. "You know, Emma, there's something I've been meaning to discuss with you."

Emma stepped carefully around and over the few straggling bits of debris that still littered the path. "What's that, Derek?"

"Shall we move to Boston or shall you move to Oxford?"

A sudden dip in the gravel threatened, but Emma sidestepped it neatly. "Well . . ." she said thoughtfully, "I'd like to have the wedding here—"

"You wouldn't mind a wedding, then?" Derek stopped and turned to face her.

Emma looked up into his blue eyes. "Syd tells me you're not the kind of man to offer anything but marriage."

"But is it what *you* want?" Derek insisted.

"After the wedding," Emma repeated firmly, walking on, "I thought we might all move to a third place."

Derek caught up with her, his eyes shining. "A novel solution. Have a particular spot in mind?"

"As a matter of fact, I do." Emma leaned in to Derek as he swung his arm up and put it snugly around her shoulders. "I've never been there, but I did promise to visit. . . ."

Epilogue

"Derek, you darling man," drawled Susannah, "if you don't disarm that son of yours before the show begins, I'm really going to become quite cross."

"Quite right," Nanny Cole chimed in. "Boy's become a menace to society. Jonah's fault, of course. Don't know what he was thinking, handing out water pistols to all the little beasts on the day of the Fête. I've a good mind to boycott his bloody shop."

Having delivered their demands, the oddly matched delegation strode away across the great lawn, Susannah floating as gracefully as ever and Nanny Cole marching with her familiar bulldog gait. Derek watched them go, then popped another strawberry into Emma's mouth.

"I know exactly what old Jonah was thinking," he murmured lazily.

Emma hid her smile behind the broad brim of her sunhat and hoped that her fiancé would keep his voice down. She wanted no more confrontations with Nanny Cole. She'd been up at dawn to put the finishing touches on the chapel garden, and now, in the long afternoon of this lovely high-summer day, she felt positively sybaritic. The ribbon on her sunhat matched the pale-blue frock Mattie had hemmed the night before, and the sapphire on her finger was as blue as Derek's eyes. She reclined against a pile of soft cushions on a cashmere blanket in the shade of a beach umbrella, with her fingers twined in Derek's salt-and-pepper curls, a dish of strawberries close at hand and a half-empty bottle of Dom Pérignon settling into a silver bucket filled with rapidly melting ice.

Derek lay on his back, with his head in Emma's lap, concealing with consummate skill any urgency he might feel about ridding society of the menace his son had become. "He hit Mrs. Shuttleworth square in the shoulder as she was doling out the punch," he commented, selecting a strawberry for himself. "Splendid shot."

Emma was fairly certain that Derek shouldn't be taking quite so much pleasure in Peter's assault on the rector's wife, but she let it pass. Peter had spent the summer discovering the joys of mischief, and if she'd been his age, with a water pistol in hand and a ruined castle to defend, she'd have matched him shot for shot.

"Emma, my dear!" Grayson came bounding across the lawn to fling himself down on the blanket, slightly out of breath and looking very boyish in his white flannels and open-necked white linen shirt. He reached for the bottle of champagne and held it to his forehead. "Just ran the gauntlet in the ruins. I say, Derek, did you know that Peter scored a direct hit on Newland? He'll be having a go at Nanny Cole next."

"He's already had a go at the rector's wife," Derek said complacently.

"You'd be well advised to take him in hand before the show starts," Grayson warned. "Mrs. Shuttleworth may be saintlike in her patience with young hooligans, but Nanny Cole is rather more inclined to box their ears."

Grayson set the champagne bottle back in the bucket, then turned to Emma. "My dear, the chapel garden has everyone agog. As for myself— Derek, do be a good chap and close your eyes. I am about to express my gratitude to your bride-to-be in a most unseemly fashion." Leaning over, he kissed Emma tenderly on the cheek, and remained there for a moment, his face close to hers. "You'll think I've gone completely round the bend, but I could almost see Grandmother sitting there beside the reflecting pool, surrounded by the roses. I really am most awfully grateful." He gazed at her a moment longer, then sat back and wrapped his arms around his knees. "Oh dear," he murmured. "Nanny's going after Debbie."

Emma had already spotted Nanny Cole scolding a red-faced and exceptionally pretty Debbie Tregallis, wife of Ted, the fisherman.

"What the hell are you doing out here?" Nanny Cole demanded. "You and that dratted son of yours should be in the dining room, getting changed."

"I'm sorry, Nanny Cole," Mrs. Tregallis said meekly, "but I can't find Teddy anywhere."

"Shall I tell Debbie that her bloodthirsty little son is happily slaying all comers in the rock garden?" Grayson said from the corner of his mouth. "Ah. Not necessary. Nanny Cole has enlisted another eager volunteer to appear with Debbie in the fashion show. Poor Billy."

Nanny Cole had collared Billy Minion and hauled him over for a quick inspection. She fished a red water pistol from the pocket of his shorts, held him at arm's length, then thrust him toward Mrs. Tregallis, with an abrupt "This one'll do."

The mutinous slouch in Billy's shoulders did not bode well for the fashion show, but Mrs. Tregallis hustled the boy off to the dining room, whispering urgently in his ear.

Emma thought it highly probable that she was threatening to turn him back over to Nanny Cole if he put a foot wrong.

Grayson tossed a strawberry up into the air and caught it in his mouth. "I think—" He paused to wipe the juice from his lips with the back of his hand. "I think the Fête's going rather well, don't you?"

"It's going splendidly. The good people of Penford Harbor have every reason to be happy with their duke," Derek assured him. Emma agreed. A day that had begun with the rector's benediction, and continued with jugglers, magicians, and frenzied preparations for the fashion show on the terrace, would conclude that evening with a piano concert under the stars. Grayson had locked himself in the music room for days on end to practice a piece he'd composed for the occasion. Emma had listened at the door, entranced by the music's evocative beauty, and she'd threatened to wring Derek's neck when he'd suggested that they request a chorus of "Kiss My Tongue."

While Grayson had labored at his piano, the villagers had been hard at work, too, transforming the grounds of Penford Hall into something midway between a county fair and a traveling circus, in which they would be both performers and audience. The green-and-white-striped marquee stretching the length of the eastern wall sheltered trestle tables laden with food, and the air was filled with a hubbub of contented voices, the tinkle of music from the diminutive carousel, and the occasional squawk of a bystander caught in the crossfire within the castle walls.

A determined Daphne Minion had mounted a fierce defense of her knot garden, but Bantry had long ago abandoned the rest of the garden rooms and found solace at the Tharbys' table, hoisting pints with Gash and Newland and hooting with laughter at Chief Constable Tom Trevoy's repeated attempts to master the trampoline.

Nearer the hall, a black-gowned Madama, wooden spoon in hand, silently supervised the endless stream of dishes passing between the kitchens and the striped marquee, while Ernestine Potts handed bowls of cinnamon ice cream to James and Jack Tregallis, and Mr. Carroway cut another wedge of carrot cake for Ted, father of the errant Teddy.

At the far end of the tent, Dr. Singh, Nurse Tharby, and the rector were participating in a wine-tasting presided over by Crowley, who glanced up from his sommelier's cup and his array of dusty bottles long enough to smile at Mattie as she bustled over to Susannah, a bundle of pale-peach chiffon folded over an arm that had long since healed.

"There's something else you should be proud of," said Emma, nudging the duke.

"Nothing to do with me," said the duke. "The knock on the head brought Susannah to her senses, not I. My cousin made amends with Mattie all on her own."

"But you were there, weren't you?" Derek pressed.

"Merely as an observer," said the duke. "I was as surprised as anyone when she confessed to Mattie that her amnesia had been an act, and absolutely floored when she admitted that perhaps she'd pushed the girl into taking a swing at her. Actually begged Mattie's pardon." The duke gazed at his cousin with admiration. "Good of her to take Mattie under her wing."

Emma smiled. As usual, Grayson refused to give himself the credit he deserved, but she knew that his efforts to heal Susannah's wounds had included many small gestures and at least one magnificent one. He'd set aside a suite of rooms for Susannah's exclusive use, so that she might always consider Penford Hall her home. The duke would have given over his own rooms or his grandmother's without demur, but in the end Susannah had surprised them all by selecting a much humbler suite, because of its proximity to Nanny Cole's workroom.

Their partnership had flourished beyond anyone's wildest expectations. Susannah recognized Nanny Cole's genius with the needle, and Nanny respected Susannah's hard-won business acumen. The two abrasive women understood each other very well, and both were committed to teaching Mattie all they knew.

"Oh, how simply scrumptious, Mattie!" Susannah held the peach chiffon out to the light. "You're quite right. We must get Mrs. Tharby out of the mauve at once. Well done."

Grayson's eyebrows rose. "Mrs. Tharby, in chiffon?"

"The mind boggles," Derek murmured.

"Oh, I don't know. . . ." Emma pictured the matronly barmaid dressed in a classic Nanny Cole creation, and found it pleasing. Syd kept saying that Nanny Cole's designs would revolutionize women's fashion, and although Emma suspected hyperbole, she hoped he would be proved right. "That's what I love about those clothes. They're meant for real women, not—"

"Flat-chested chits?" Derek suggested.

"With no discernible hips," Grayson added. He watched as Kate came out onto the terrace, radiant in green linen, a rich, dark shade that complimented the square-cut emerald she now wore on her left hand. "Don't know about you, old man, but I'm rather keen on hips."

"Couldn't agree with you more," said Derek, nestling his head deeper into Emma's lap. "And if someone in the family must be flat-chested, I'd just as soon it were me."

Grayson leapt to his feet to escort Kate back to the blanket, stopping on the way to have a word with Bert Potts and Jonah Pengully, who were seated on campstools facing the entrance to the castle ruins, enjoying the element of havoc Jonah's water pistols had added to the festivities. Jonah's largesse had given him immunity, but anyone else entering the ruins did so at his own risk.

It was a risk people were willing to take. Throughout the day, in ones and twos and small family groups, the villagers had passed through the ruins on their way to admire Emma's handiwork and to pay their respects to the village lass. The lantern had not brightened on the day of the Fête, but no one complained. They'd seen the light split the darkness high above the village on that stormy night in May, and heard of Peter's brave deed. Each felt honored to have witnessed the unfolding of a new chapter in the legend.

The storm had been a setback for Emma's work on the chapel garden. Bantry's contacts in the horticultural community had ensured a supply of shrubs, cuttings, and seedlings from other gardens, but he and his crew had had their hands full replanting the garden rooms, and Syd had been preoccupied with Susannah, so Emma had been left to soldier on alone.

Freed from the lantern search, Derek had helped as much as he could, shoveling the wet soil back into the raised beds and rolling the freshly sodded lawn, but Emma had planted every seed and cutting with her own hands. It had been backbreaking work, and the results were far from perfect. The verbena didn't trail all the way to the ground, and the roses didn't cover the walls. The candytuft was patchy at the edge of the flagstone path, and it would be another year at least before the lavender hedges came into their own. Emma had to admit that her moment of greatest satisfaction had occurred that very morning, when she'd gone out at dawn to plant a cutting that had come from a most unexpected source.

Emma raised her eyes to look toward Nell's table, but her attention was diverted by still another unexpected sight. "I don't believe it," she murmured. Looking down at Derek's sleeping face, she added, "If you want to see Madama talking, you'd better wake up fast."

"Hmmm?" Derek murmured drowsily. Emma watched his blue eyes open and slowly focus. He smiled up at her, turned his head, and squinted at the marquee. "Sorry, love. Don't quite get the joke."

Emma looked again and saw that Madama was alone once more, slicing a loaf of bread in silence. "But she was there a minute ago, Derek, a white-haired woman, with a huge handbag. Madama was talking to her a mile a minute." Emma shrugged. "Go back to sleep. It's not important. The only reason I mentioned it was because it's the first time I've ever seen Madama talk. Do you know, I'm not even sure what language she speaks?"

"Nor is Grayson," Derek observed. "Madama came over as a war refugee, but Grayson's father was never able to ascertain her country of origin. Grayson claims that she must be from Mount Olympus, since she cooks meals fit for the gods." Derek propped himself up on one elbow, displaying more energy than he'd shown for the last half-hour. "Did you say that the woman was carrying a handbag?"

Emma nodded. "A big one. A sort of carpetbag, I think."

"Fascinating. Sounds almost like . . . No." Frowning, Derek shook his head, then stretched out again. "Hardly likely. She rarely leaves London."

A familiar peal of laughter drew Emma's gaze back to the table where Nell sat, resplendent in white georgette, playing hostess to the three guests who had arrived the night before.

"Dearest Nell, that was really . . ."

". . . most amusing, but is Bertie quite sure that the vicar wanted . . ."

". . . a strawberry in his punch?"

"I'm sorry, Vicar," said Nell, contritely. "Bertie's been a terrible palooka lately. I'll get you a fresh glass."

Derek propped himself up on his elbows again, chuckling. "The vicar's going to regret driving the Pyms here after your children are through with him."

"*My* children?" Emma exclaimed.

"I accept no responsibility for their abominable behavior," Derek declared. "Before they met you, they were perfect angels."

Emma caught sight of Peter speaking earnestly with Mrs. Shuttleworth and watched as Nell carried the vicar's brimming glass of punch through the throng without spilling a drop. "They still are, aren't they?"

"Spoken with the sickening conviction of a besotted stepmother-to-be. I rest my case." Pulling himself into a sitting position, Derek reached for his flute of champagne and raised it to Emma in a silent toast, then leaned back against the cushions. "You seemed quite pleased by the thingummy the Pyms brought with them. Couldn't believe you were out there this morning, sticking it into the ground."

"Thingummy?" Emma rolled her eyes. "Derek, that's not a thingummy. It's a tree peony. And it's not just any tree peony, but a cutting from the Pyms' own tree peony, which they grew from a cutting the dowager gave them years ago."

"I see," said Derek, watching Emma's face carefully.

"Ruth says it has amber blossoms," Emma went on. "The flowers can get to be a foot in diameter, and the whole plant can grow as high as seven feet tall. It's going to look wonderful against the north wall."

"Sounds impressive," Derek commented.

"It will be, but it's not just that, Derek." Emma looked eagerly into his blue eyes. "I wanted so badly to have all the plants in the chapel garden come from Penford Hall. I didn't think it would be possible, not after the storm wiped out the garden rooms and I had to use the plants Bantry's friends sent. But the Pyms made it possible, at least in a small way. I've finally planted something in the chapel garden that really belongs there. I can't tell you how good that makes me feel."

Derek set his glass aside and reached for Emma's hand. "I do understand what you mean, love, and I'm very happy for you. Worried, too, of course."

Emma knew what was coming. The Pyms had brought Derek a copy of the Cotswold *Standard,* the nearest thing Finch had to a local newspaper, commenting in stereo that, since they'd received the delightful wedding invitation, they'd thought that Derek might be contemplating making a few other changes in his life. The advertisement describing the fourteenth-century manor house ("with outbuildings and courtyard") had been circled in violet ink. It was a stone's throw away from Finch and had apparently been on the market for some time. Derek had been fretting about it all day.

"I'm sure it'll be fine," Emma said, anticipating the change of subject.

"Doubt it," said Derek. "At that price, it's probably the local white elephant. Are you sure you understand what that means?"

"I think so," Emma replied serenely.

"I'm not talking about unpleasant wallpaper in the breakfast nook, Emma. It's likely to be in very poor repair indeed. I've seen this sort of place before. No indoor plumbing, no roof to speak of . . ." He glanced at her slyly. "I shouldn't be at all surprised if it has rats."

"We'll get a cat," said Emma. "Maybe two. I like cats."

"Yes, but, Emma, my dearest dear, it'll take me at least

a year or two to make the place habitable. Until then you'll be camping out."

"Sounds perfect. Until Peter's finished making up for lost time, it might be better to live in a place that's already a mess."

"But what about Nell? Can't see her and Bertie huddling around a campstove."

Emma removed her sunhat and shook her hair down her back. "Nell will build castles wherever she lives," she said. "I think she'll enjoy helping you build a real one. And the Pyms will be on hand to pamper her."

Derek's eyes crossed suddenly and he flinched as a jet of water passed within inches of his nose. He scrambled to his feet with a roar and the marauders scattered, squealing with delight, save for one scamp, for whom Peter had expressed great admiration, who let rip a parting shot that hit Derek full in the face. Swiping a hand across his dripping chin, Derek flopped sullenly on the blanket and muttered that perhaps the manor house was worth looking into after all.

"A spot of rough living'll do the boy a world of good," he declared. He dried his face with the napkin Emma offered, then cast it aside and grew serious once more. "But what about you, Emma? If I'm spending all my time working on the house, I won't be bringing home many pay slips."

Emma picked up the discarded napkin and dabbed a few remaining droplets from Derek's forehead. "Not a problem," she said firmly. "I love my work and I, too, am very good at what I do. I'm sure I'll be able to find a job in London that I can commute to. I may even set up my own consulting business. I have no qualms about supporting the family until you've finished with the house."

Derek sighed. "Won't leave you much time for a garden," he said ruefully. "The Pyms' tree peony may be the last thing you plant for quite a while."

"I'll have the rest of my life for a garden," said Emma. "And you'll have some time at home with Peter and Nell. It'll give you a chance to get to know each other again."

"If I survive," Derek muttered. He sighed deeply. "You're a stubborn woman, Emma Porter."

"Wait until you see my plans for my home office," said Emma.

"I'll build you the office of your dreams," Derek murmured, and, twining his hand through Emma's hair, he leaned over to nuzzle her neck.

"Now, there's a sight that does an old heart good."

Derek swung around and Emma blinked at the glowing face and startling figure of Syd Bishop. It was the first glimpse she'd had of him all day, and she scarcely recognized him. He wore a relaxed, cream-colored three-piece suit, a shirt the color of weak tea, a silk tie in a deeper brown shot through with streaks of bronze, and, to top it off, a white Panama hat, tilted at a dignified angle above a beaming face. The duke and Kate slowly walked up on either side of him, their faces slack with astonishment.

Syd's smile faltered and he raised his hands with a questioning shrug. Pinching the lapel of his jacket, he asked, "What about it? Mrs. Cole's decided that I need a new look." He lifted his hat and held it rakishly above his head. "So, what do you think? Is it me or is it me?"

Five hundred years of breeding came to their rescue. "My dear fellow," the duke said gracefully, "if Nanny Cole says it's you, who are we to argue?"

Syd replaced his hat and glanced with pleasure at the subdued gold cufflinks on his sleeves. "I gotta admit, it makes me feel kinda young again." His eyes met Emma's as he added, "Not as young as some I could mention."

"Yes, Derek," remonstrated the duke. "What the devil do you think you're up to, disporting yourself so wantonly in front of the children?"

"The children are already used to it, Grayson," Kate informed him.

"We've gotten their permission," Emma added with mock solemnity.

"As a matter of fact," Derek said airily, "I was trying to dissuade my intended from embarking on a very risky venture."

"Anything I can do to help?" Grayson offered.

Derek eyed him warily. "Thanks, old man, but you're the last person I'd come to for help on this particular matter."

"Still worrying about the manor house?" Kate asked, sitting down beside Derek. "I don't know why it bothers you so. Emma's perfectly capable of paying the butcher's bills while you toil away in the drains."

"Spoken like a true duchess," Grayson declared.

Syd clapped him on the shoulder. "This's gotta be a big weight off your back, Duke. Petey tells me you don't got to worry about the Fête for another hundred years."

"I rather doubt that I shall be the one doing the worrying by then, but I take your point." Grayson smiled shyly. "It is a bit of a relief. Funny thing, though. I've spent my whole life preparing for this day, and now that it's here, all I can think about is the wedding."

"You keep thinkin' about the wedding, Duke," Syd advised. "Keep lookin' ahead. You gotta make sure there's a little duke to pass the whole shebang on to, am I right?" Emma tried not to smile as Syd pulled a pocket watch from his cream-colored waistcoat. "Listen, kids, I'd love to hang around, but the show's gonna roll in five minutes and Mrs. Cole'll blow a gasket if I'm not there on time. You comin', Kate?"

Kate sprang to her feet and took Syd's proffered arm. "I wouldn't miss it for the world. Have you seen Debbie Tregallis?" she asked as they turned to walk away. "Doesn't she look beautiful in blue?"

Syd paused to look over his shoulder at Emma. "Not half so beautiful as some I could mention. Catch you later, sweetheart."

"Catch you later, Syd." Blushing, Emma looked out over the lawn. People were streaming out of the castle ruins and away from the shelter of the marquee to cluster at the foot of the terrace steps. Grayson stood with his hands in his pockets, surveying the scene, and nodding warmly to the Pyms, who returned his nod, smiling their identical smiles.

"Terribly good of Ruth and Louise to join the fun," he commented. "Terribly good of everyone to pitch in the way they have."

"Well, I've been useless to you, Grayson," said Derek. "Didn't fix the window or find the lantern."

"Ah, but you found something much more important," Grayson pointed out, "and your children took care of the rest. It's quite fitting. Penford Hall has always owed a great deal to its children."

"Will you be sorry when the Fête is over?" Emma asked.

"I will, as a matter of fact. It's been such a splendid day." Grayson stiffened suddenly. "Good Lord," he said, "is that Teddy Tregallis? Oy! Teddy! Over here, old man!"

Emma looked over to see a tow-headed boy around Peter's age standing in the entrance to the castle ruins, his water pistol hanging limply from one hand as he looked back over his shoulder, grinning broadly. At the duke's shout, he came running, but the smile never left his face.

When the boy had scrambled to a halt at Grayson's side, Grayson put an arm around him and squatted down conspiratorially. "I say, Teddy, old man, it's no good making a target of yourself. Martyrdom's all well and good, in its place, but if you're determined not to be dragooned into service by Nanny Cole, then you mustn't stand around in plain view. Take it from one who knows."

"Yes, sir," said Teddy. "I mean, no, sir."

"Never mind," said the duke, mussing the boy's hair. "They'd probably reject you anyway, in your current damaged state. How'd you bung up the knee?"

The boy bent forward slightly to stare at the neatly taped square of white gauze that covered his kneecap. "Fell down in the ruins, sir, tryin' to hide out in the chapel." The boy looked over his shoulder. "A lady in the chapel fixed it for me. She was awfully nice, sir. Told me about the lady and the lantern."

Grayson's hand slid from the boy's head to touch his own knee as he, too, looked toward the castle entrance. "Did she?" he asked.

"Yes, sir," said Teddy. "Never heard it told like that afore. Said it 'minded her of you and Miss Kate, sir, you bein' the duke's son and Miss Kate the village lass."

"Is that so?" Grayson and the small boy slowly faced one another. "And how did the story make you feel?"

"Can't hardly say, sir."

"A bit dizzy?" the duke suggested. "But in a nice sort of way?"

The boy nodded. "That's it, sir."

The duke blinked rapidly, then pointed down at the cashmere blanket. "You stay here until the coast is clear," he said. He waited until Teddy had seated himself cross-legged on the blanket, then stood, staring once more at the castle entrance.

"You're being very mysterious, Grayson," Emma chided.

Derek's eyes narrowed as Grayson began to walk away. "What's up, old man?"

The duke paused. "Emma, Derek, dearest friends, if you'll excuse me, I—I believe there's someone waiting for me in the chapel." Looking every bit as dazed as Teddy Tregallis, the duke performed a courteous half-bow, then turned and broke into a run.

Nell's Strawberry Tarts

Preheat oven to 375° F. *Makes 8 tarts*

Pastry shells
8 3½-inch tart tins, greased
3½-inch fluted pastry cutter
¾ cup flour
pinch of salt
¼ cup superfine sugar
4 tablespoons butter
2 egg yolks

Filling
1 medium egg
2 tablespoons sugar
2 tablespoons flour
⅔ cup cold milk
⅔ cup heavy cream
1 pound strawberries
4 tablespoons seedless strawberry jelly
¼ cup water
1 tablespoon shredded coconut

Pastry Shells

Sift flour and salt onto work surface. Make a well in the center; add sugar, butter, and egg yolks; work them together until all the flour is worked in. Add a few drops of water if necessary to bind the mixture. Knead until smooth, then wrap in foil and refrigerate for one hour.

Roll out on lightly floured surface. Use pastry cutter to cut out eight circles. Arrange these in the pastry tins. Bake for 20 minutes at 375°, until pale gold. Turn out to cool.

Filling

Cream egg and sugar, add flour, and stir to a paste with a few drops of the cold milk. Warm the rest of the milk, then slowly stir it into the egg mixture. Slowly heat mixture until it boils, then cook it for a few more minutes. Remove from heat; allow to cool. Whip the cream until stiff, then beat it into the cooled mixture. Spoon a generous portion of cream mixture into each of the pastry shells.

In the center of each tart, plant a whole hulled strawberry, point upward. Hull and halve the rest of the strawberries and arrange the halves around the whole strawberry to cover the rest of the filling. Heat the jelly with the water and use it to paint the strawberries, then sprinkle with coconut.